UNRAVELING
OF THE SOUL

Part Three of The Berylian Key
Book Three in the Pantracia Chronicles

Written by Amanda Muratoff & Kayla Hansen

www.Pantracia.com

D1253047

Cover design by Andrei Bat.

ISBN: 978-1-7337011-4-3

Third Edition: February 2022

With the first trilogy complete, we'd like to acknowledge that in the crazy span of a year, we managed to publish three novels without killing each other.

Here's to friendship while writing and wine while editing.

The Pantracia Chronicles:

Visit www.Pantracia.com to discover more.

Chapter 1

Spring, 2611 R.T. (recorded time)

Kin's muscles convulsed, his body howling. He clung to the image of Amarie, holding her face in his mind. Her bottomless ocean-blue eyes. The wave in her dark-auburn hair as it fell against her cheeks. He held onto her like a drowning man clutching driftwood.

A crackle echoed through the stagnant air. Power sizzled as it raked at Kin's exposed back. A ragged cry vibrated his hands, spread on the cold stone floor. The pitch of his voice sounded foreign as it reflected within the small circular atrium.

Dark vines lapped at the blood flowing down his back. The darkness slipped away, drawing cold trails across his skin before they slithered into the shadows crowding the side of the room.

Despite the state of abandonment, the surrounding structure remained intact. Frescos peeled from the plaster framing the cracked stained-glass windows. Nature worked to reclaim the stone with sprawling ivy. It'd been a temple dedicated to the worship of gods Kin no longer placed faith in.

Gasping for breath, he lifted his chin to look at the churning grey clouds. The dark iron skeleton of a glassless dome fractured the sky it'd showcased. His suffering ceased, but thunder from the storm elicited a flinch.

The clouds broke, and rain dribbled down, but Kin couldn't find the strength to move. Struggling for another shaky breath, he fought to control his voice with each icy stab the water evoked amid his wounds. The rain should have brought relief.

His knees ached against the ruined marble floor. Dark stains of muddy blood encircled him, cleansed from the floor by the rain. He didn't know how much of it was his. Fresh streams of crimson seeped through the cracks, joining the rainwater.

The assault of shadows halted, and Kin's body yearned to curl on itself. The agony faded to chilly numbness. Relief fogged his senses, head sagging towards the ground. His hair clung to his cheeks, rain merging with tears. The coppery taste of blood tainted his tongue, but he resisted spitting it out. It meant he was still alive.

Clenching his fists so his nails bit into his palms, he forced himself to remember why he suffered. To fight the haze, he thought of Amarie again. Her mouth against his. Moving in tandem with a fiery need. If Kin forgot Amarie, it'd only be a matter of time before he gave in to Uriel's demands.

Then it would be her bleeding on the floor of this forsaken temple.

Red-tinted water splashed beneath fine leather boots as Uriel emerged from the darkness hugging the concave walls.

Kin recoiled but could barely shuffle to the side. His eyes darted up to his master.

The creature housed within the attire of a noble was something far more sinister than just a man. "Have we learned our lesson, Kinronsilis?" Uriel knelt, water dripping from his chestnut hair down his forehead and through his finely trimmed beard. Wild blue eyes, infected with flakes of obsidian and gold, bored into Kin. The Art kept him young, considering nothing had changed in the ten years Kin had served as a Shade.

Blinking away the droplets, Kin glanced at the shadow behind his master, trying to find words.

The shadow writhed with a pulsing heartbeat. The darkness consuming the room flickered, tendrils prowling like predators at the edge of a campfire's light.

It slunk towards Kin's fingertips, and he rocked back to his knees despite the protests of his back. He cringed as the ruptured skin on his back flexed. He gritted his teeth against a cry of pain. Finally, overwhelmed by the taste, he spat the blood from his swollen mouth while trying to recall what he was supposed to say, rather than what he wanted to.

"Yes, Master." Kin's lips formed the words, somehow without a scowl. "I've learned my lesson. I earned your displeasure." His eyelids drooped as he looked up.

White teeth flashed in the pallid grey daylight shrouded by the storm.

No words could express Kin's regret for his selfish pursuit of power. For becoming a Shade. He'd sworn himself to the man, the creature, of his own will. And now the same Art he'd craved drew his blood and tore his skin.

When the call to return to his master came, he'd delayed, burying Amarie's father with her brother's help. Kalpheus deserved a proper burial, and Deylan would've struggled to accomplish it on his own. The peace it might one day provide Amarie was worth the price he now paid.

Uriel didn't know the depth of his servant's betrayal.

With Kin's blatant disregard for obeying the terms of his service, death should have been a certainty. He'd expected and prepared for it.

Why am I still alive?

The gale passed, Uriel turning his eyes to the sky as hints of twilight broke through and the rain stopped.

Unwilling to keep eye contact with the darkness, Kin averted his gaze to the silver engraved buttons of Uriel's fitted teal tunic.

His master stood, stepping behind Kin.

Fear swelled. The last remnants of rain trickled across his bare torso, his lungs heaving for breath. His back lurched as Uriel's fingers dug into his shoulder. It wrenched his spine straight, and a hiss escaped his lips. The Art within him stirred, but not at his bidding. The corruption in his soul vibrated with hunger, demanding to feed on Kin's life essence. It boomed through him like the alarm bell of the Great Library of Capul, shaking every muscle and turning his vision white.

He landed on his hands again, gasping. Hunched forward on the stone floor, he shook his head to clear the ringing from his ears. The wet marble chilled his palms. As he rolled his shoulders, he expected pain, but it didn't come. Tightness pulled at his skin, like something solid covered it. He reached over his shoulder to touch what should've been mangled flesh and found the smooth surface of jagged scars.

"Those will serve as a reminder." Uriel crossed in front of Kin. "For lying to me. I wouldn't advise testing my mercy again."

The pit of Kin's stomach knotted with dread instead of relief for the end of his punishment. The infection of Uriel's power intensified, testing the bonds he'd forged against it.

The master rolled his wrist, commanding the serpentine shadows at his feet. They wove on each other, coalescing, before flattening into a seat. Translucent shadow proved solid as Uriel sat on it. Wisps curled up, forming armrests.

Uriel's fingers flattened, his large gold signet ring clicking against the surface. "Recount your sins to me."

A test.

Kin had crafted the lies and hoped they'd hold up now.

"I became distracted from my task, Master." Kin bowed his head, hunching over his knees. "And lied to foolishly indulge further in my distraction."

"You participated in the death of a fellow Shade," Uriel hissed.

Kin winced. He loathed the mere suggestion he should have protected Ormon. He'd admitted his involvement, the one truth to his master, to hide the rest.

Ormon represented the worst traits in a human soul. He'd sought a Berylian Key shard, unaware of the secret he nearly uncovered. Convincing Ormon to abandon his task proved impossible. He carried his own wickedness even before Uriel's power infected him and sought vile thrills beyond those required by his task. He'd tried to assault Amarie.

Kin didn't regret the part he played in Ormon's death. His only regret was Amarie had fired the crossbow bolt that ended the Shade's life instead of him.

"I perceived Ormon as a threat and reacted without thinking. I felt frustration in his failure to accept my claim of the shard carried by the girl."

"Now, Kin." Uriel tutted his tongue before Kin could continue. "We both know your claim over that girl went beyond completing your task. What was her name again? Alana told me." He twiddled his fingers, pausing. "Amarie."

Kin's shoulders slouched. It sounded wrong from Uriel's lips. Names brought a sense of knowing, an invisible power over an individual. And the creature he called master had a name too, one he no longer feared saying.

"Amarie is dead." Kin's throat tightened as he imagined it. "I became too attached. Trist located her and killed her." Uriel had happily supplied the information earlier, forcing Kin to act as if he hadn't been there. It wasn't hard to imagine Amarie's broken body, lifeless in his arms. The tears he shed were real, the wounds still deep.

The power she held, the Berylian Key, prevented her permanent death. Housed within her instead of the crystal shards Uriel sought. Without a female descendant to transfer to, the Key's energy would continue to restart Amarie's heart. If Uriel ever found her, there would be no release from the suffering. Uriel's search for the power of the Berylian Key made it impossible for Kin to be near the woman he loved. He'd be a threat as long as he remained a Shade.

"Her death is for the best." The master hummed. "Despite my displeasure with Trist's hasty actions, at least your distraction has been eliminated."

At the mention of her name, Kin pictured Trist's life fading from her eyes, and the warmth of her blood on his fingertips. He'd guessed at Uriel's anger with the older Shade, who'd been demoted just before her death. Uriel withheld any curiosity about the significance of Amarie's power, which he'd surely witnessed while channeling Trist before she murdered Amarie.

"I have a new task for you, Kinronsilis." Uriel drummed a new rhythm with his fingernails.

Bile rose in Kin's throat. A time existed when he'd relished the thought of a new task. A further opportunity to prove himself to his master so he might be granted an addition to the tattoo, displaying his rank among the Shades.

As if the master heard Kin's thoughts, searing pain erupted on the inside of his right forearm. He clawed at the skin, urging himself to keep from scratching it off. Black ink sprouted from his pores, stretching to form two additional shapes. He wondered if his master knew that by granting the promotion it made Kin the most powerful of his servants.

Flexing his fingers, his arm tightened under the new mark. The familiar triangle near the bottom returned, having been taken as punishment for his delay. Kin stared at the newer mark granted for his delivery of a Berylian Key shard. The dotted outline appeared next to the returned triangle, which slashed across the vein in his wrist. Even though the small circular shape represented power he never held before, it hardly seemed worth what he'd given for it.

He'd cruelly pushed Amarie away after her return from death and the Inbetween, breaking both their hearts in the process. The thought of the master's obsidian eyes overtaking Trist's made his stomach writhe. Amarie would never be safe with him. All the master needed to do was glimpse through Kin, and he'd learn the truth of Amarie and the Berylian Key.

Kin's body ached as he stood, a distant throbbing rather than the sharp agony of lashings. Rolling his shoulders, he tested their range of motion beneath the scar tissue. He steeled his expression towards his master.

Uriel's lips formed a smug smile. His fingers curled to look more like claws as they tapped on the black armrest of his shadow throne. He waited, and Kin wondered if the moment would go on forever.

Defiance would only get him so far. Remaining a Shade, even in appearance only, gained him more ground. It was where he could do the most good, to repent for his past ten years.

Since I'm apparently too valuable to kill.

Balling his fist, he placed the tattooed part of his arm against his chest in obedience, bowing his head. "I will serve, Master. I'm ready for my next task."

"Good." Uriel lifted a hand and gestured someone forward.

Kin didn't bother to look at the newcomer as footsteps splashed on the stone. A lingering scent drifted through the air. Roses. Still pungent, but laced with the acrid scent of death.

"Alana." Uriel looked beyond Kin to the auer who stepped beside him.

Her dark features blended with the darkness of the chamber, and Kin wondered how long she'd hidden within the shadows. Alana's raven hair twisted up behind her head with long curls dangling free over her temples. Glimmering unnaturally, her emerald eyes darted in Kin's direction. Her Aueric pinpoint pupils swelled to a more human size in the dim light. She approached with a subtle bow of her head, not elaborating the gesture as she would in any other situation. Alana was a rejanai, banished alongside her brother and older sister. Her disdain for her people and their traditional ways of life festered far worse than Talon's. The punishment for the crimes committed should've been hers alone to bear.

"Master," Alana whispered.

Kin glowered in her direction.

"I'd like you to do me a favor. Our Kinronsilis would do well with extra guidance for a time. He will complete the matter you've been diligently researching."

Alana shuffled an inch forward, a frown crossing her features.

Kin took what pleasure he could in her apparent unhappiness.

Despite Alana's natural talent for the Art, she played the part of a dutiful servant to Uriel. Even directed at her, the request of a favor was ridiculous. Alana would obey regardless, even if she didn't contain the bond Uriel shared with his Shades.

"Which research do you refer to, Master?" Alana's posture grew rigid. "I'm surely capable of completing it on my own should you wish it done."

Uriel's eyes narrowed, and she recoiled with a lowered gaze. "Of that I have no doubt." The master relaxed into his chair with a sigh. "But it's a matter of convenience. Kin must complete a minor task before I grant him the greater, more pressing matter. The capture of Lasseth Frey seems perfectly suited. It gives him the opportunity to prove his loyalty, while eliminating the annoyance of a wayward Shade."

Being sent to retrieve a Shade who'd strayed from service was common. Kin had considered defecting, but traitors were always found and punished with death. Kin didn't recognize the name, though, which was unusual. He made it a point to remember every Shade brought into the fold over the past ten years, in case the task to pursue them came later.

Alana stammered. "Master, forgive my arrogance, but—"

The shadow comprising the Master's chair lashed out like a viper, faster than her Aureic reflexes. The tentacle of darkness struck the side of her face with a resounding thwack.

She gasped, her head jerking to the side. Lifting her hand to the wound, it came away with a smear of maroon blood.

"Don't dare question and there'll be nothing to forgive," the master snapped as the tendril rolled on itself and vanished.

Alana locked her jaw, wiping the blood on her black breeches. The thin slash ran the length of her jaw, red and angry.

"I've spoken, and the task remains the same." Uriel turned to Kin. "You're to accompany Alana and recover Lasseth Frey and bring him before me. As always, I expect decisive action and no remorse." The throne beneath Uriel melted as he stood, as if ice in the hot sun, and dribbled to the ground. The shadows wriggled like worms into the darkness. "Do you understand the task before you, Kinronsilis Lazorus?"

Kin flexed his jaw at the surname he'd been destined to have before his parents had adopted him.

Uriel's laugh reverberated against the wet stone. "What is it?" He stepped forward, daring Kin to meet his gaze. "It's appropriate to use the name of your birth family now that you know the truth. You should enjoy the lofty title Lazorus grants you over the common Parnell. You've already proven yourself as one to chase power, your highness."

Kin's chest clenched. He hadn't expected his master to be so forthcoming about his knowledge of his bloodline.

It's because he knew all along...

"You orchestrated it all," he hissed before he could control his response. It earned him a surprised glance from Alana. "You stole me from my real parents and stashed me away to use when the timing suits you."

"You make it sound so crude." Uriel clicked his tongue. "I saved your life."

"And you certainly benefited from your benevolence. Then your bitch brought me to you when I'd ripened enough to accept service as a Shade. You always intended for me to become your slave. Then what? Use me as a pawn to steal the throne of Feyor?" Kin's nails bit into his palm.

"We both benefit." Uriel reached towards Kin with a charming smile, as if to give him a friendly pat.

Kin watched the hand suspiciously as it closed on his bare shoulder. Pain pulsed through his muscles, as if the wounds on his back reopened a hundred times over, eliciting a gasp.

"Kinronsilis," Uriel chided as Kin's knees buckled. "You must remember your place, especially if I'm to help you achieve all you desire. Doesn't every man dream of becoming a king?"

Chapter 2

Talon paced the small room he'd been secured in after his arrest. The dormitory housing for those visiting the Council of Elders occupied the city block behind the extravagant Sanctum of Law. When they'd escorted him in, he had paid little attention to what the building looked like, but it was constructed in the same way the auer built all their structures. Art-twisted roots formed the walls, while leaves and branches wove to create the ceiling. Preserving life remained paramount in the construction of the lavish holding chambers. The Aueric connection to the fabric of Pantracia enabled them to uphold their ideals and still achieve decadent designs.

A spelled door of greenery covered the only exit, warded against other users of the Art from manipulating it. With patience, he might have been able to work his way around the wards, but he wouldn't make it far. Perhaps his cooperation would lead to some leniency.

His boots shuffled across the lush moss carpet, stomach rolling with nerves. Despite his vague hunger, he ignored the water pitcher and bowl of fruit on the table. He chewed on his thumbnail, instead of his usual habit of the side of his already tender tongue.

The council's sentences, when found guilty of a crime, were merciless and finite. But while awaiting tribunal, prisoners were shown far more care in Eralas than in other parts of Pantracia. The traditional provisions would still be observed, even if Talon and Amarie hadn't gone peacefully.

Amarie's chosen tactics to follow him into Quel'Nian left much to be desired.

I might not even see her again.

Talon's upcoming fate reeked of predictability, but he hoped they would spare her.

He'd built their makeshift home deep within the woods of the auer inhabited island. The danger of being on the island for a rejanai should have encouraged even greater caution. He'd become distracted and hadn't noticed the approach of the battalion.

With the power of the Berylian Key, Amarie needed training to learn how to channel the energy. Her fear of learning the delicate control stemmed from the power overwhelming her in the past, overloading other Art users in the vicinity. He'd witnessed her end the life of an attacking grygurr shaman with nothing more than a touch of her hand. Burning out from the inside would be a terrible death.

He couldn't have predicted Amarie's foolish endeavor to get arrested with him. Hopefully, the council would deem her apparent theft of an auer dagger a light crime, and she would merely face banishment. However, even that ruling would put her at risk again. Eralas should have remained an option for refuge because it was the only place in Pantracia inaccessible to Shades.

Talon's Art buzzed as power rustled the grown doorway, signaling a visitor. He spun, facing the commander who'd arrested them.

Wearing the typical armor of the auer military, she stood in delicate silver plating fitted to her form. The material between the joints, a pearly translucent mesh, didn't look any heavier than linen, but auer craftsmanship made it sturdier than steel. The pale plating stood out against the commander's dark skin. Her stone-grey hair twisted into a tight weave at the back of her head, and nestled among the braids rested a silver circlet. It curved into a triple-wreathed downward point on her forehead, declaring her rank.

Narrowing her hard-set ruby eyes, she tapped the chakram at her hip in a subtle threat. "Talon Di'Terian." Her voice sounded as stiff as her stance. "My name is Commander Lovakesh. I'm to serve as your exponent before the Council of Elders. Unless you have another to accompany you?" She placed her hands behind her back, straightening. The dagger confiscated from Amarie wasn't in her belt anymore, likely passed off as evidence. While it was possible Amarie had stolen the blade during her previous visit to Eralas, doubt lingered in Talon's mind.

The doorway behind Lovakesh remained open, as if testing him.

Talon didn't even glance at it, shaking his head. "I gratefully accept your offer, Commander."

"I don't make it of my own will. It's a required custom for all accused to be granted escort and counsel, even for a rejanai. I merely fulfill what is demanded of me."

"Of course." Talon ran a hand through his hair, loose at his shoulders. "I didn't assume otherwise." He doubted any would willingly take her spot. His eldest sister, Kalstacia, sacrificed her status in the Menders' guild to lessen the sentences on her younger siblings, becoming a rejanai herself. Their parents stayed behind, his mother remorseful. His father was too furious to say goodbye before his children were carted away to the docks of Ny'Thalos, and Talon would never see him again.

Their parents' fate didn't mirror the mercy granted their children. Alana informed her siblings of rumors she'd caught from their homeland. Already banished, Alana and Talon couldn't be tried for additional crimes discovered by the council, so the punishment of death fell to their parents. All fault laid with Alana, and her lack of remorse infuriated Kalstacia, who abandoned them to mourn alone. Talon foolishly remained at Alana's side, persuaded by the bond of blood between them.

Memories of the suffering he'd caused kept Talon somber. Visiting Eralas again made him wonder how he strayed so far. He cursed the day his curiosity dared him to follow Alana into the forest for practice in working the natural energies of the land. After struggling with the foundations, some had whispered he was an odrak, an auer incapable of the Art. While rare, Talon feared the stigma and pity that'd inevitably follow. The nature of the required auer studies proved to be his problem. Preserving energies while manipulating the Art was all the auer taught. The practice of destructive Art, which consumed to repurpose the energy, was forbidden in Eralas. Practicing the simpler, forceful Art remained his only true crime, despite taking the blame for others to lessen Alana's punishment.

Silence hovered while Commander Lovakesh eyed him, staunchly still as he paced towards the back wall. "You're worried. According to the transcripts from your previous tribunal, you pleaded guilty to your crimes. Your fate is already decided, but you must observe formality. Worry is pointless."

He couldn't help the sardonic laugh. "I still have plenty to be concerned about, Commander, other than my fate."

"You speak of the *human* girl." She lifted a curious eyebrow.

Talon took advantage of the distraction and faced the commander. "You sound disapproving of my companion."

"They're weak, and your affection misguided. Best to forget the girl and pass into Nymaera's arms without such shame."

"Come now." Talon offered a half-hearted smile. "You're young and shouldn't be so close-minded regarding interracial relationships. One of our people's brightest scholars suggested we should set aside our racism to solve the problem of our declining population."

She sneered, clearly having heard the argument before.

"Of course," he added, "it might also help to stop executing our own people."

Her lips pursed, and she shook her head. "Better to exterminate the weeds then let them spread throughout the garden. Besides, there's an alternative to death."

Talon flinched. He'd never choose Slumber if it were his decision. "Exterminating only works if those tending the garden are free of corruption."

Lovakesh shrugged and changed the subject. "The girl is fine. She is well taken care of in the east wing. Mouthy, though. Perhaps I'm doing you a favor by separating you." She smirked.

Talon heaved a sigh. "Can you tell me if she's being charged?"

"I believe she will be. That dagger belonged in the armory here in

Quel'Nian. Though, we're still attempting to determine how it came into her possession, as it was never recorded as missing or stolen. I don't know the details as I'm not her assigned exponent."

Talon cursed and twisted the toe of his boot in the moss. Banishment was now a best-case scenario if the auer found Amarie guilty. The mainland's habit of cutting off thieves' hands originated from the auer. But humans usually got it over with quickly.

"You should spend your time appealing to the gods." The commander disrupted his dark thoughts. "Beg for safe passage. You will meet Nymaera soon."

"Isn't my exponent supposed to help me challenge the accusations I face?" Talon muttered, and she gave him a dry smile.

"Arguing that you didn't violate the terms of your banishment feels like a futile endeavor considering your obvious presence here. Fealty to the gods is the only advice I can offer you. I hope for your sake you are gifted the choice of death. Though I suspect some of the Elders will demand the worst fate for you."

"Can we get this over with then?"

She narrowed her eyes, a crease forming between her eyebrows. Her military stance never altered during their conversation, hands at the small of her back. "Hasty. Too much time spent with humans?"

He tightened his jaw, refusing to dignify the question with an answer.

Lovakesh spun on her heels, stopping in the doorframe to converse with someone Talon hadn't known was there. Moving one hand to the handle of her chakram, she gestured to Talon with a jerk of her head. "After you."

Misty rain clouded the air when they emerged from the dormitories, down shallow steps. Lovakesh offered a tawny cloak from a hook beside the door without words, and Talon took it. He stayed beside Lovakesh as they crossed the intricately decorated courtyard towards the Sanctum of Law. There, the Council of Elders delivered justice.

The sanctum's ostentatious structure was meant to impress the few outsiders who set eyes on it. The hollowed-out stump, as wide as at least two galleon ships positioned bow to aft, hardly resembled the tree it'd once been. The roots and low branches created delicate overhangs and balconies, lined with woven railings and glittering lanterns. Dense foliage curled skyward, supporting the crystal roof, surrounded by an asymmetrical collection of spires. Taller and thicker at the front of the building, they tapered down towards the back. Glowing with a soft green from within, it painted the raindrops and canopies around it with its light.

Sheltered from the rain, Talon stood on the front steps and pushed back the hood of the borrowed cloak.

Beside him, Commander Lovakesh did the same and acknowledged the two male soldiers positioned at either side of a thick curtain of greenery serving as the sanctum doorway. She brought her three middle fingers to her forehead and then lowered them towards the guard on the right.

"We're expected. Open the way, if you please." She received a respectful nod from the guard.

Armored the same as Lovakesh, the guards had the addition of a spear in one hand. The one she'd spoken to lifted his weapon's base a foot from the ground, then slammed its steel pommel down with a whisper of power that tingled Talon's skin.

The vines covering the doorway wrapped around each other and parted, revealing the way through.

The chamber's familiar energies suffocated Talon as he stepped inside. Memories flooded him, as if it'd been only yesterday when he'd last crossed the threshold. The ceiling grew impossibly high, under the largest of the crystal spires. Natural wood formed a circular atrium no larger than most taverns, but empty.

Four guards stood positioned evenly apart with their backs to walls, spears in hand. They stared ahead at nothing, but Talon felt their gazes on the back of his head when he wasn't looking.

A spiral of mossy roots composed the floor, protected by a layer of glass to prevent treading feet from disturbing the design. Buttresses of tree trunks protruded from the wall, twisting up to support the steep slopes of the crystal spire. Glowing motes lit the room in an eerie pale green, making the structure seem to breathe with life.

Stepping to the center of the room, Talon stopped above the pattern, fighting to keep his breath even.

Lovakesh walked past him. She rapped a knuckle on the wooden door ahead, carved with a depiction of the rare araleinya bloom.

His gut twisted as he thought of Amarie, who he named after the flower.

Commander Lovakesh disappeared through a small opening in the doorway.

A wave of lethargy washed over him, energy ebbing from beneath his feet. It lapped at his Art, and Talon wouldn't have noticed if he hadn't experienced it before. The gradual drain left his knees quivering. With nearly all auer able to access the Art, the precaution of the chamber had always existed, a tradition everyone experienced before tribunal.

Horror struck Talon.

They will do this to Amarie. Is her connection different enough to keep her power secret?

Exhaustion rippled through him, anxiety numbing his skin. The pool of energy within his soul had been sucked dry, transposing into physical weariness.

The flickering motes brightened with a satisfied pulse, a rustle passing up through the leaves on the walls.

Talon exhaled through gritted teeth as the drain ended, struggling to keep standing. Armor shuffled towards him, the guards' spears tapping on the ground as they stopped on either side of Talon. He'd relied on their help before, almost fifty years ago, but refused to now. With a huff, he lifted his chin to observe the wooden doors swing open. Without being ushered by the guards, he entered the sanctum.

The impressive hall encompassed the rest of the old tree stump, with arched ceilings supported by flying buttresses of trees and vines.

Along the far side, like a crescent moon, inset curved steps led to a platform. Balconies hovered above and behind for observers, though they were mostly empty.

Talon felt remarkably small as he approached Commander Lovakesh, who stood within an inlaid gold circle on the floor beside another swirl of roots.

On the raised crescent platform sat nine auer elders. Each occupied an elaborate, high-backed chair.

The chamber smelled of sweet flowers, another disguise for the sinister reality of what was to come.

The arch judgment stood from the tallest Art-grown seat at the center. His jet-black hair, styled back and falling to the top of his neck, donned a woven oak crown. He glared down at Talon, his honey eyes darkened at the outer rims by age.

Elder Erdeaseq had passed judgment on Talon before and served the council for at least a thousand years prior to that. As one of the few elected to the position, Talon held a little more respect for him.

"Talon Di'Terian. You come before the Council of Elders to face judgment for crimes against your people." The arch judgment's voice boomed through the hall, refined within the flowing Aueric language. "Your case is unique, as you have been sentenced for most of these atrocities already. But you defy those punishments by standing here before us. To further your apparent disregard for our law, we found you practicing the very Art we sentenced you for. Your hubris has no bounds."

Talon eyed the arch judgment and tried to assemble his thoughts. It felt pointless to argue. Little chance existed for escape or mercy. Even in his desire to waste their time, delay Amarie's tribunal, he wouldn't violate the policies of the sanctum. He turned his head to Commander Lovakesh and muttered his response to her.

Her eyes narrowed, but then she rolled them. "The accused wishes to convey that he did use forbidden destructive Arts before, but not this time. He insists all power expelled was life-preserving—"

"It matters not." Another elder stood.

The arch judgment glanced at the woman with wavy white hair reaching the silver belt on her waist. An ivy wreath sat above her fathomless black eyes.

The arch judgment sat, and she nodded at him as he passed the tribunal to Kreshiida, one of the eldest among them.

Talon had hoped she'd reached the end of her incessant life during his absence.

"Arguing whether Talon Di'Terian used a forbidden form of the Art during this particular visit to our sacred homeland is semantics. His crimes warranted his death the first time he stood before us, so I see no point in humoring him with the illusion of life beyond this sanctum. It's tedious and asinine." She didn't wait for another to rise before she plunked back into her chair.

The others exchanged looks before several leaned over the arms of their chairs, murmuring to each other.

Talon whispered again to Lovakesh.

"The accused offers no contradiction to the statements, for he understands the previous will of the council against him and his sister, Alana."

Talon hurriedly whispered to her again.

She tilted her head at him, her eyes suspicious, but she maintained her duty and spoke for him. "As well as the judgment passed on his parents, Terlion and Jindeihe Di'Terian."

The arch judgment's jaw twitched, his mouth slightly agape.

A new wave of whispers erupted between the elders, and Talon's brow knitted. His breath caught as an eternity passed.

Slowly, the arch judgment stood, and as he did, silence descended within the sanctum. "This council knows nothing of the judgment you speak of. Terlion and Jindeihe never stood trial. Their lives were unceremoniously ended the eve of your departure from these lands. We didn't discover them until you were already gone, but you face the charges now, as you are accused of their murders."

Talon's eyes widened, shock shuddering through his body.

Murders?

His insides clenched, and he curled forward. "No," he gasped before he could control it and his knees met the ground.

The realization hit him like a blow to the chest.

Alana.

She'd been the one to tell him and Kalstacia of the council's judgment on their parents. Told them of their parents' deaths. But they'd been more nasty, bloody lies.

Talon remembered how enraged Alana had been on their arrest. She refused to acknowledge her parents' visits to the dormitories, since their father, Terlion, had been the one to report their crimes, forsaking his younger children. He couldn't bear the shame to his family, damning them without knowing he'd lose the eldest because of her compassion.

Alana's last interaction with their parents came after Talon had climbed into the carriage meant to take them to Ny'Thalos, carrying what he could take. He couldn't bring himself to face his mother's eyes again, and Kalstacia stayed at his side. His mind clouded with grief and shame, he didn't notice anything out of place when Alana returned.

The truth stung. Alana had gone to say goodbye and ensured it would be a permanent one.

How could she?

The evil it took to kill her own family would have consumed her.

It has. She's beyond saving.

As the ringing in Talon's ears cleared, tears heated his cheeks and the murmur of voices broke through the din of his mind. Too weak to stand, he remained on his knees, unwilling to open his eyes. He wrestled to control the emotions roaring through him, tugging at his hair as he struggled to breathe.

"Based on this reaction, I move that the crime of his parents' murder be removed from his charges." A new voice.

"Agreed," murmured several others.

"Talon Di'Terian."

Talon forced his eyes to open and look at the arch judgment.

Empathy lined the elder's eyes. "We will not hold you accountable for your sister's actions. This crime will rest solely on the shoulders of Alana Di'Terian. But all other crimes still stand, as you previously admitted guilt." His gaze shifted as the empathy passed. "Along with the new violation of your banishment. The penalties to be considered by the council are Amaranthine Slumber or swift execution. We require time to deliberate and offer this moment as a last opportunity for you to express contradiction to your charges. We're familiar with your crimes, but do you wish to hear them again?"

Talon shook his head, rising into a shaky stance. He turned towards Lovakesh to whisper his response.

"With the discovery of the truth of his parents' demise, the accused requests new consideration regarding the crimes previously admitted."

The arch judgment raised a hand to silence the murmurs within the hall. "Continue."

"The accused doesn't deny the use of forbidden Arts on our sacred lands. It's a crime driven by the fear of being an odrak, and he regrets his actions. The remaining crimes belong solely to his sister. Alana Di'Terian abused the familial bond of her brother to lessen her punishment by sharing blame. An irrational sense of blood loyalty drove the accused to protect his sister, though she didn't deserve such sacrifice."

Lovakesh tilted her head at Talon after hearing the rest of his request. "Talon Di'Terian hopes the council's acquittal of the more heinous crimes may inspire mercy. He accepts he violated the terms of his banishment and acknowledges he doesn't deserve complete forgiveness. However, he prays it may sway the council from the sentence of Amaranthine Slumber and consider only execution."

Slumber was shrouded in more mystery than death and rumored to be worse. Those sentenced wouldn't die and be granted the peace promised in Nymaera's Afterlife. Instead, they were haunted by dreams and nightmares of a life they couldn't live, preserved in sleep for the length of their sentence. When woken, the sleeper suffered a loss of who they'd once been. Born anew, they were reintegrated into society in often menial roles. Their absent memories left their soul with a hollow that could never be refilled.

The arch judgment nodded. "It'll be considered. You're dismissed. We'll summon you when we've made our decision."

Chapter 3

Amarie stood in the center of her dormitory, staring at the door keeping her from finding Talon. The looming fear of his execution occurring before she spoke to the Council of Elders made her unable to sit.

Let's hope they're as slow as I remember.

She clung to the hope, even if she suspected Talon's fate would be a simple decision.

Uninterested in the sustenance provided within her simple accommodations, she wandered in and out of her Art, tempted to use it to escape her cell and its facade of civility. She held no doubt about her own fate. There hadn't been time for her to come up with a better plan than presenting the dagger to the commander.

It's been hours. Why is this taking so long?

Amarie made a face.

Because they're slow. Just like I was hoping.

As she ran a hand through her hair, her frustration mounted. She opened her mouth to yell another protest, but closed it when vines rustled and split the doorway.

An auer man stepped through, and she narrowed her eyes. Two formally armored guards stood behind him on either side. The man wore long robes as if a scholar, his empty hands clasped together in front of him. By human standards, he appeared to be in his thirties despite the long white hair, the top half tied back behind his head.

"Where's Talon?"

A frown touched the corners of his thin lips. "Perhaps it would be wise to focus on your circumstances." He spoke in Common, rather than Aueric, and the words sounded clumsy. Blinking, he looked bored. His ambivalence only further frustrated her.

"My circumstances pale compared to Talon's. I must speak to the council before they pass judgment on him."

He sighed and tilted his head, looking down at her. "Talon Di'Terian's fate won't take long to decide, but it won't come to pass before you meet with the elders."

A breath of relief escaped her, and the auer shook his head.

"Shall we discuss your predicament then? We could start with your name, seeing as you've refused to provide it so far?"

"No. I appreciate your half-hearted attempt to guide me, but with all due respect, I don't need it. Can we go?"

"My name is Fal'harian." The auer glowered. "I'm your exponent, and we shall review the procedures you will follow before visiting the Sanctum of Law, despite your incessant impatience."

Amarie gritted her teeth.

Procedures?

He continued before she could argue. "It's highly likely Talon Di'Terian's hearing is still in progress and arriving early will accomplish nothing. It'd be best to prepare you properly, and I'd appreciate your cooperation on the matter."

Reluctantly, Amarie embraced what little patience she had left and listened to the rules.

Fal'harian sounded skeptical of her containing the ability to control the Art, but explained the tradition of the draining chamber, anyway. The thought of them stealing her energy made her stomach twist. Considering the sheer depth of her power, she doubted the chamber's ability to take it all. Nor was she keen on the auer learning the truth of the Berylian Key.

But if it's necessary to save Talon...

Amarie frowned and opened her mouth to protest that Fal'harian would speak to the council for her.

"It's a sign of respect for the council," he interjected. "Criminals aren't worthy of directly interacting with our revered leaders. And until you're proven innocent, you'll remain unworthy."

The rest of the expectations took too long to go over, and Amarie resorted to nodding to everything, hoping it would end sooner.

Finally, they exited her room together, escorted by the guards. Walking through the wide hallway with doors on either side, Amarie narrowed her eyes at another woman. A brown braid ran along the side of her head, revealing her human lineage. Auer only had hair of white or black, and the shades between.

The woman waved a minute gesture at the door she'd emerged from, the vines promptly responding to her use of the Art and weaving together. She turned from the room, close to Amarie's, and briskly walked towards them, but Fal'harian and the guards didn't react to her presence. She looked similar in age to Amarie, but shorter and leanly muscled.

For a moment, their eyes met, and Amarie's pace slowed. One green. One topaz yellow. Strangely bright, almost like an auer's would be, but without the narrow pupils. She'd never seen a person with different-colored eyes.

A blink, and the woman disappeared into the hallway behind her.

Amarie shook her head, pushing the curiosity of another human in Eralas from her mind to focus on her task. She needed to free Talon, and only so many ways existed to accomplish such a feat.

As they walked outside, her eyes darted to a pair of auer entering what appeared to be another dormitory building to the north. Neither looked back, but the dark-haired one reminded her of Talon, and she resisted the temptation to call out.

She refused the offered cloak, looking at the clouds as rain delicately coated her face.

Fal'harian pressed a hand to her back, urging her towards the main entrance of the Sanctum of Law. Her exponent spoke briefly to the guards, and their spears slammed the ground.

She reminded herself to breathe as the vines parted and she stepped out of the rain into the dreaded draining chamber. Her heart quickened as Fal'harian guided her to the center. Looking down, she closed her eyes to fight the dizziness elicited by the swirling pattern.

An invader crept into her soul.

It was gentle, but unpleasant as it lurked through her. Her muscles twitched, but her hiding aura held fast. The auer had witnessed her in meditation, so giving them nothing would be risky. She loosened her hold for a single breath to allow a drop of her power to escape, and the intruder gobbled it up, suddenly seeking more with greater intensity.

Amarie gasped at the unexpected force and hardened her aura to stone, pushing every controllable ounce of her power into the action. Feigning fatigue, she wavered and stepped back. The motes of light above her head flickered brighter, satiated by the power she gave. She refused to let any more go, and relief came when the demand stopped. Her breath dropped into her faster, driven by lingering fear, but she hoped Fal'harian would assume it to be exhaustion.

Fal'harian had no idea what potential danger he led before the esteemed Council of Elders. Even in her current state, with her limited knowledge, her Art rendered her immune to other traditional practitioners. Including the council. She could take their lives with a touch, pushing her reservoir of power into them until the overflowing energy scorched them from the inside out.

Amarie didn't wish to harm anyone, though, and she eyed Fal'harian. She promised herself it wouldn't come to violence, and her words would be enough for them to see the truth.

The sanctum's size drew her gaze upward as she crossed towards the swirl of roots she was meant to stand on. The shining glass spire roof fractured the view of grey clouds and green canopy, creating the appearance of a kaleidoscope.

Her attention dropped to the elders, taking in the appearance of each of them one at a time.

They already looked irritated with her.

I can guess why.

"Your chosen tactic in encouraging Commander Lovakesh to arrest you has put us all in a rather annoying situation." The human dialect flowed more naturally from the arch judgment than it had from her exponent. According to Fal'harian, the first auer to address her would be the leader of the council, sitting in the center of nine elders. "Your stubbornness in withholding your name has proven pointless, since you granted us the tool needed to track down one of our people who knows you, Amarie Xylata."

Finding her remaining patience, she whispered to Fal'harian.

He sighed before relaying her single-worded response. "Good."

The elders scowled and exchanged glances.

Amarie leaned to Fal'harian again, who stumbled over her words.

"I'm glad you located Piete'lian." He recited the name of the auer who'd gifted her the dagger.

This is ridiculous. And painfully slow.

Grinding her jaw, she spoke aloud, voice echoing through the sanctum. "I'm sure he cleared up the issue with my dagger, but I require your attention to a more pressing matter."

Her exponent's eyes widened in horror. He leaned toward her to hastily whisper something, but she shook her head.

"Fal'harian." The elder to the far right spoke in Aueric. "Did you not inform your charge of the law?"

Fal'harian stuttered the beginning of a reply, but Amarie interrupted.

"He informed me." Amarie shifted into the Aueric she'd learned during her previous stay in Eralas. It felt odd considering how long it'd been, and she struggled with the language, but could tell they understood her. "But I'm perfectly capable of speaking for myself."

All eyes widened. Before she could continue speaking, the female elder sitting on the far right of the tribunal shot to her feet. "We will not tolerate this insolent behavior, Sovjet." The elder spat the Aueric word for humans, which sounded suspiciously like their term for dog.

The arch judgment abruptly stood, receiving a glare from the current speaker. Silence passed through the council before the angry female elder slowly sat with an indecipherable grumble.

The arch judgment's faded honey-colored eyes moved over

Amarie. "This council doesn't appreciate your callous waste of our time. As is appropriate, considering your anxious human ways, we've already agreed on the sentence for your deception and unprecedented scheme to remain at the side of the accused traitor, Talon Di'Terian. You'll be removed from these lands, and your property returned as you board a ship to never return. Banishment from Eralas is the punishment chosen by the council, to be swiftly—"

"No." Amarie's voice resounded, and her exponent closed his eyes, his shoulders slumping. Silence chased her blatant dissent. "That's *not* what needs to happen. Talon Di'Terian is only here because he was—" She sighed as they cut her off.

"Fal'harian, reign in your charge." The elder at the opposite end stood, anger in his black eyes.

Fal'harian sucked in a breath and reached for Amarie's shoulder. A whisper of Art radiated from her exponent, its purpose indiscernible.

Her eyes shot to Fal'harian, her jaw set, daring him to follow through.

His reach faltered, and doubt crept over his expression. He'd underestimated her, and she wasn't about to let him hinder her now.

Amarie brought her gaze back to the elders, her pulse pounding in her ears. They needed to hear her.

Whatever it takes.

"Listen to me." She raised her voice. "Talon doesn't deserve death, and I won't let him make that sacrifice for me—"

Another male elder stood, one who hadn't yet spoken, and interrupted her. "Talon Di'Terian is a disgrace to our people and to grant him death would be merciful. You've dishonored this council's process, and we've had enough of your arrogance! You should pray your contempt doesn't sway this council to harsher punishment for the rejanai you so foolishly defend."

Panic flooded Amarie.

This can't be the end. They need to listen.

Mutters broke out between the elders, and the one who still stood nodded before he waved a hand. "Remove her!" he shouted, and her mind raced as guards scuffled behind her.

No. Talon can't die. I can't fail him.

The guards' hands closed on her shoulders and arms, tugging her backwards. She wrestled from their grip, stumbling off the swirl on the floor. More murmurs rose from the auer observing from the balconies of the sanctum.

"Don't touch me," Amarie growled, shoving one guard away.

Her pulse deafened her to the rasps of swords being drawn. She steadied her stance.

Talon won't die because of me.

Her mind insisted she could still save him, her last resort quickly becoming her only option.

Fear danced with desperation, creating a monsoon of potent energy. Heatless azure fire erupted from where she stood, fanning outwards. The guards jumped back with startled shouts, lifting their spears. The arch judgment shouted a sharp command as Amarie extinguished the flames with a gasp. Everything around her froze, the guards waiting for the word to strike.

Amarie focused for only another breath before she released her hiding aura. Unlike how she'd shared her energy with Kin and Talon, enveloping one other person, she let go of all hold. She dropped the veil keeping her power secret.

The invisible force washed over the entire sanctum, dormitories, and nearby courtyards like a tidal wave.

For the first time in years, she could finally breathe weightless breath.

The guards staggered back, and she watched the crash of realization radiate through them. With their natural affinity to the Art, no one would be excluded from her display.

The elders' attention locked on her in a mixture of reactions, ranging from shock to confusion. All but one, who sat hunched in his chair to the right of the arch judgment. Age had warped his body, shrouded in a thick curtain of long light grey hair. His eyes didn't move to acknowledge her, but focused on his peers with the glimmer of a smile.

Silence reigned within the sanctum, as the Art-powered motes beamed in response to her energy. They shone and vibrated with a low hum, revealing just how pale her exponent had grown.

Amarie straightened her corset and shirt, displaced by her struggle against the guards, and centered her feet again in the root circle. Her heart raced.

At least I have their attention now.

The oldest elder, the one who hadn't looked at her, broke the stillness. "Oth'ir, Relphain."

The two guards behind Amarie turned their attention to the elder, their armor rustling as they shook as if waking from a dream.

"Stand down and approach. I have pertinent instructions you will carry out immediately." The elder's voice echoed strongly within the hall, contrasting his aged body. Eyes, too black to notice any color, watched the guards as they obediently approached.

Quiet fell again, but none of the elders averted their gaze from Amarie. The surprise had faded, making room for other emotions, like fear and greed.

The pair of guards ascended to the elders' platform and crossed to the still-seated figure. The elder encouraged them so close that Amarie couldn't even see the movement of his lips.

Her stomach tightened, her hands stretching as she loosened her fists. She tried to remain patient, despite the screaming of her mind.

The guards nodded before straightening again. One glanced at Amarie, but they both moved to the back of the platform and vanished through a doorway she hadn't realized was there.

The old auer's black irises met Amarie's, and he studied her.

"Elder Ietylon?"

Ietylon waved a hand to dismiss the arch judgment, eliciting a fresh wave of surprise across the elders' faces.

The arch judgment's jaw flexed, but instead of retaliating, he glared at Amarie.

"Law Guard," Ietylon called, and the door at the back of the sanctum opened. "Clear the galleries. Escort the occupants to the south dormitories."

Chatter drifted down from the galleries, the people shifting and grumbling as they were herded towards the exits. The sanctum drifted back into an eerie silence.

"Come here." Elder Ietylon beckoned Amarie with a withered hand.

Her feet surprisingly steady, she approached. Power coursed through her veins, daring her to use it while it remained unhidden. She ignored the stares of the other council members as she climbed the steps towards the old auer.

"Elder Ietylon, please explain." The arch judgment's stance shifted as Amarie ascended to the platform. Fear tainted his tone, and she met his gaze as she cautiously stepped past him.

"In a moment, Erdeaseq." Ietylon dismissed the arch judgment's title, and with it, his authority. He held his hand out to Amarie, palm up. "May I?" A glint of curiosity danced in his gaze.

A smile twitched her lips, but she quickly controlled it, accepting his offered touch.

His boney hand gripped tight as the auer's Art prodded hers, examining in a thoroughly practiced way. He closed his eyes and took a breath. "Thank you, child."

At his gesture, Amarie ventured back down the steps, but she didn't return to the circle where she previously stood. Instead, she stayed close to the risen platform.

Erdeaseq stood stiffly beside his chair, a hand gripping the back.

"I suspect you have a purpose in displaying your true nature before this council." Ietylon gave her a knowing smile, speaking in Common. "Please, speak it."

The arch judgment eyed Ietylon but settled back into his seat.

All the elders remained sitting, silent, watching her.

Although it pleased Amarie to speak freely, she wondered about the cost of her openness. "I wish to reason with you." She used a softer tone, glancing at the other elders. "Talon Di'Terian isn't the disgrace you believe him to be. He's brought me to your lands to protect me, my power, from those who wish to abuse it. He's teaching me to better my ability, to control the immense gift I've been given. I reveal my true nature to you now because I wish to offer a resolution we all might find acceptable." Amarie paused, but when no one had anything to say, she took a deep breath and seized her opportunity. "I request you release and clear Talon Di'Terian, and his eldest sister, Kalstacia Di'Terian, of all charges and previously laid sentences." She swallowed, eyes flickering to the other elders to gauge their reaction.

"Preposterous." The elder who'd ordered her taken away narrowed his pale-amethyst eyes. "To reverse judgment, especially that previously confessed to, is impossible."

"Hush, Lo'thec." Ietylon received a fiery glare.

Lo'thec shifted to rise, but the arch judgment's stare silenced him, begrudgingly returning his attention to Amarie.

"While you may speak the truth about Talon Di'Terian's intentions in returning, it doesn't lessen the severity of the crimes he's accused of." The arch judgment remained sitting, inviting a more casual atmosphere.

"Do you even know Talon Di'Terian's crimes?" The airy voice belonged to a female elder beside him. "These crimes you ask us to pardon so readily?"

Amarie looked at the female elder and tilted her head. "With all due respect, do you? Everything you believe him responsible for is more likely the wrongdoing of his sister, Alana. I believe the good he's done since leaving Eralas and the lives he's saved are worth more than the assumed transgressions committed during his childhood. I urge you to consider the larger picture, instead of focusing solely on your desire to punish Talon. You must know who, and what, I am?"

"On the contrary." The arch judgment turned his gaze to Ietylon as he spoke. "I don't."

"She's the Berylian Key." Ietylon donned a wistful half-smile, which Amarie absently returned.

"What?" The arch judgment gasped, his exhalation quickly followed by murmurs from the rest of the council.

"There's no mistaking the power. It feels a particular way." Ietylon looked at Amarie. "It flows uniquely and hums with all the ancient power of the ley lines which ran through it before the Sundering. I was fortunate enough to visit it once when I was young, before it broke apart."

"The Berylian Key is a myth. You're growing senile, Ietylon."

A sardonic laugh erupted from Ietylon's lips and he glowered at Lo'thec. "At least I'm not foolish enough to have forgotten what this world used to be, what Pantracia used to be. And I recognize strength when I feel it pounding against my own power. Are you so naive, Lo'thec?"

"Infighting will do us no good." The arch judgment stood. "We've learned enough from our people's past mistakes to accept what is presented before us. This council acknowledges your power, Amarie, as the Berylian Key, trusting in Elder Ietylon's observations. But you demand much of us. Retracting the judgment placed on Kalstacia and Talon Di'Terian is no minor ask. You should know, Talon requested reconsideration of all crimes, except for those centered on his use of destructive Art. The severity of Talon's defiance of his banishment is still grounds for death, regardless of his intentions. This council must maintain order among our people and cannot forgive such blatant contempt."

Something in his eyes encouraged Amarie not to interrupt, and he slowly continued. "However, out of respect for the power you've shared with us, we *are* open to conversation. Tell us what it is you offer in exchange for all you ask."

"In no light manner, I offer my allegiance." Amarie swallowed. "With my power, my lifetime will rival that of an auer, if not exceed it. This offer extends the entire duration. I'll be an ally to Eralas, and in times of need, you may call on me. Not only can I spend mass amounts of the Art myself, but I can fuel your practitioners from an endless source. I'm happy to oblige a demonstration, if it is necessary, but you'll win any war you fight with the Berylian Key on your side." She paused as whispers began among the elders. "I don't wish to become your enemy. But if you decline my offer, I will interpret your decision as an act of hostility." She whispered her last words with regretful resolution.

"You dare to threaten—"

The arch judgment raised a hand. "We hear your offer. And your warning. We must take time to consult before we may grant a final decision. In the meantime..." He looked at the rest of the council. "You may walk from this sanctum and go where you wish until we summon you back for our verdict. Talon Di'Terian must remain, which we implore you to respect. He'll be well cared for."

Amarie nodded once, focused on the arch judgment. "I understand."

"Patience will be necessary, child." Ietylon offered a reassuring smile. "As this council may not work in the time typically expected by most humans. While your power may allow you to live for some time, I'm not blind to the glow of youth within your eyes."

Amarie couldn't help but smile. "Patience has never been one of my virtues. But I know it'll be necessary. I only plead you don't waste any time in reaching a decision. My training must continue, and Talon is the only one suited for the role. While I may not be practiced in the use of my Art, I'm adept in the transfer of energy. I'd be honored to oblige if you ever wish to feel it in your veins instead of at your fingertips."

Ietylon smiled wider and gave a soft laugh. "You indulge the vanity of an old auer. Your offer is much appreciated, child. I will keep it in mind while admiring the power of the Berylian Key from a distance. You may take your leave. But Fal'harian..." He turned his head towards Amarie's exponent she'd forgotten was there. "Please remain for a moment. I wish to speak with you."

Fal'harian had slunk back, watching the strange events unfold before him. He nodded furiously, daring a glance at Amarie.

Amarie gave a sheepish look to the elders. "To his credit, I was a rather difficult charge." It only took a breath to wrap her power tightly back inside herself, hiding her secret.

Each elder straightened their backs against their elaborate chairs, feeling the absence.

Amarie bowed her head, meeting the eyes of the arch judgment a final time before she spun and walked alone from the sanctum.

Chapter 4

After enduring a week of torture from Uriel's twisted Art, Kin discovered a distinct lack of interest in fulfilling his master's tasks in a timely manner. His torture, rather than murder, caused seeds of doubt to blossom. Uriel would never kill him. He was the creature's key to the throne of Feyor.

Then I'll make him suffer for trying to use me for my birthright.

Alana disclosed her discovery of Lasseth Frey in Olsa, and Kin used the travel distance to procure substantial delays. The most direct path south meant they passed by his family estate, and he decided the stop would benefit his cause. His previous departure from his childhood home had been abrupt and unexplained. Kin warned Alana that his parents may grow suspicious if he didn't reassure them.

Alana could do little to sway his defiance.

The Parnell estate thrived with the colors of early spring. Melted snow filled the streams with fresh bubbling water, bringing life back into the luscious farm-filled valley. The vineyards brightened with green leaves rustling in the wind from the mountains, and ivy flowers bloomed on the old stone fences.

Kin and Alana walked side by side down the gravel drive leading to the two-story stone mansion. It loomed like a sentinel over the rows of grapevines. At the center stood the main foyer, housing a glittering crystal chandelier visible through the windows over the large oak doorway. From the foyer ran two wings, one west towards the tree line, and the other east towards the flooded stream.

He couldn't remember the last time he'd walked his family's

gravel drive, having arrived months prior on horseback with Amarie. Alana and he had less conventional means of travel, thanks to the Art. Kin didn't need his parents to learn of his ability to shift into a raven. And Alana seemed equally interested in them remaining ignorant of her unnatural mount, a winged beast summoned from the depths of a hell no mortal should access.

So they walked.

Alana with a simple pack slung over one shoulder, and Kin with nothing but what he hid in the various pockets of his black cloak. Even with the heat of the sun on his back, he kept it firmly in place.

The foyer smelled of the wildflowers his mother always arranged in the copper vase on a lonely table beneath the chandelier. Large windowed doors at either side of the wide stairway led to the gardens, which held bitter memories.

Has it only been two months?

Kin's mother hurried down the stairwell from the west wing. "Kin!" Lindora used a sing-song tone, rushing to gather her son in her arms. Barely as tall as his shoulder, she sported grey hair braided in a tight bun. A grin adorned her face, accentuating the wrinkles that came from a joyous life, deepened by sadness in her later years.

Kin blamed himself for the newer lines, having rarely visited his parents since his service to Uriel began. He naively hoped to keep them isolated from his darkness.

"I was so worried when you all left without a word." Lindora acknowledged Alana with a brief smile, but her eyes held an edge of suspicion. A look that only a child would know of his mother.

Kin relished in the comfort of his mother's arms. He eagerly embraced her in return, lifting her to her tiptoes.

Lindora squirmed from his grasp, holding his jaw. "Kin?" Her soft brown eyes showed her astute awareness of his compromised emotional state. "What's the matter?"

"I'm fine, Ma," Kin lied, squeezing her shoulders. He gestured discreetly with his eyes in Alana's direction and hoped his mother would catch on.

Lindora pursed her lips when he refused to truly answer but gave no indication of whether she understood. She looked at Alana, gliding towards her. "It's a surprise to have you back so soon."

Alana beamed, but Kin rolled his eyes. Her delight looked genuine enough as she exchanged a hug with Lindora.

Lindora stepped away, placing a hand on her hip in her usual inquisitive fashion. "And visiting at the same time as Kin? I didn't realize you two were traveling together again."

"The gods have deemed it necessary, it seems." Alana's voice still held the same bell-like chime.

Lindora nodded with a smile as her gaze moved behind them, to the front doorway. "Where's Amarie?"

Kin had prepared himself for the question, but it didn't stop the stab in his gut at hearing his mother say her name.

Alana's hand closed on his upper arm in feigned comfort, and her nails bit through the grey fabric of his tunic.

"Another will of the gods." Kin lowered his gaze. "She's gone to Nymaera. She's dead."

Lindora's breath quavered and Kin knew her eyes filled with tears without having to look.

Alana patted his shoulder and Kin fought his instinct to pull away. "I'm sure you can imagine, Lady Lindora. I couldn't leave our Kin alone after such a loss. I knew it best to bring him home. To aid the recovery of his spirit."

Lying bitch.

"Of course." Lindora pulled Kin into another hug.

Despite her small stature and human arms, he couldn't help but feel a little safer there. He squeezed her as she stroked his back and whispered calming phrases against his chest.

Lindora released Kin to run her hands over the stubble on his chin. "I'll make your favorite for dinner tonight, my darling. You and your father can play those old tile games you loved so much. To distract you if you'd like? He's only in—"

"That's all right, Ma." Kin tried to give a reassuring smile. "I'd actually appreciate some time alone to process. But dinner sounds wonderful."

"Of course." Lindora wiped a tear from her cheek. "Your room is always prepared for you, you know that. I'll go to the kitchen and make sure everything is perfect for tonight."

"I'll assist you, if you don't mind the company, Lady Lindora."

Lindora smiled her assent to Alana before looking at her son. "I'll make you some tea, Kin, and bring it to your room."

Good. I'll get a moment to talk to her alone.

Kin climbed the eastern stairs towards his room, anxious to breathe without the air reeking of Alana. The hallway opened into the circular foyer in front of his room and two others. Memories betrayed him with a baleful glance at the door of the guest room he and Amarie shared. The thoughts of that night's events burned inside him, creating a fresh ache. She wasn't dead, but he missed her desperately. He needed to adjust to the grief of missing her.

We'll never be together again.

Nothing in his bedroom had changed since he'd left at seventeen. The space was clean, maintained for the days Lindora hoped her son would return, everything still in its proper place.

The whole room was dark with mahogany and stone. The exposed rafters of the high ceiling donned an unlit pair of chandeliers Kin never used. He'd preferred the lanterns because he could light them himself. Three windows on the far wall were open, overlooking the babbling stream at the end of the vineyards, ripe with greenery. Thick moss-colored curtains framed their height, taller than him, rippling in the spring breeze sweetened by fresh buds. An old bookshelf stood next to two armchairs between it and the windows. The chairs faced the countryside view, with a little table between.

Closing the door behind him, Kin locked it out of habit before he remembered his mother's promise of tea and unlatched it again. He drew the cloak from his shoulders and tossed it across his four-poster bed, piled with fur blankets and pillows. Approaching the windows, he unbuttoned his sleeves and pushed the thick fabric up to his elbows. He hoped the nostalgia of home would distract him from thoughts of Uriel.

Leaning with his palms against the windowsill, the scars on his back tightened, accompanied by a distant ache. With a steady breath, he urged his muscles to relax. They seized again without warning in response to a gentle knock at the door and a test of the knob.

"May I come in, darling?"

Kin turned his head and nodded at Lindora. His mind whirled, contemplating what he wanted to tell his mother. He wished he could tell her everything. Weep into her lap like when he was a child.

The ceramic tea set clinked as Lindora set it down on the small table before joining him at the window. Her hand, worn from working in the vineyard alongside their staff, closed over his.

Kin paused, glancing down at her touch.

Why wasn't this life enough? It should have been enough.

He didn't need the Art, much less the throne of Feyor. He wanted to be a simple winemaker's son again.

Glaring at the tattoo on his forearm, he considered slicing it from his flesh.

"Kinronsilis," she whispered, returning his gaze to her face. She gave a tight smile, stroking his hair as she always did when he was young. "Tell me. What's weighing so heavily on you?"

"Everything." Kin closed his burning eyes. Anguish flooded as the image of Amarie's limp body flashed in his mind. The heartbreak in her eyes as he told her they couldn't be together. Amarie's father dying in his arms, and his inability to save him or comfort Amarie while she wept over Kalpheus's body.

Kin endured it all only to be punished by Uriel for his deception. He'd prayed for death then, but the morbid hope faded away. He needed to watch Alana and Uriel, to make sure they never found Amarie. To keep them distracted with falsehoods so they never learned the truth of the Berylian Key.

"Tell me." Lindora led him to the chairs. "Tell me everything, the truth. Please." She poured the tea and, as it steeped, pushed her large chair closer to the other before settling into it. Her hand came to rest on his knee as he sat.

"I wish I could. But it's better if you don't know. Trust me."

Lindora squeezed his knee. "I do trust you. But I'm your mother. I'm the one who should protect you, not the other way around. Give me some credit."

Kin couldn't help the little laugh that came, and he shook his head. "Maybe, but some things would hardly make any sense to you."

"Why? Because I welcome Alana into my home?"

His eyes narrowed, and Lindora's knowing smile revealed he'd failed her test.

She continued before he could interrupt. "I know Alana is hardly what she presents to us, even if she has your father fooled. I don't understand her intentions, but her friendship with us is misleading. She's focused on you and you alone. She doesn't care a rat's wit about your father and me. Her purpose was a mystery until she told us about your lineage."

Kin tried not to look completely astonished. "So you don't trust Alana?" He sipped his hot tea.

"Hells no," Lindora sputtered as if insulted. "I tried to persuade you away from your infatuation with her. Why else do you think I was encouraging all those pretty young girls in your direction when you were sixteen? She never looked at you the way Amarie did."

"I thought you were eager for grandchildren."

Lindora shook her head with a sigh and took a gulp of her tea. "You should know by now, my dove, I'm an incredibly patient woman. Otherwise, I doubt I'd love your father as much as I do." A warm smile played on her lips. "And don't think you can distract me by focusing on that auer. There's more. Maybe you can start with why you've been reluctant to return home over the past ten years?"

Kin hovered in an impossible situation, seeking a confidant to help him process what he wanted, needed. But he had no one. Talon would have normally served in the role, but he was inaccessible for many reasons.

"I'd hoped to spare you. I didn't want you and Father to feel you had to clean up after my mess, like when I was a child."

"I suspect there's little I can do to help with whatever mess you speak of. But I'll listen and love you, regardless."

"That devotion will be tested when you learn what I've done." Kin frowned at the tea in his lap. They had no blood connection to encourage her love, and he hardly deserved it after all his misdeeds.

After a slow breath, Kin explained how Alana manipulated him to take the power from Uriel. He hadn't known the details of service at the time and how he'd become a murderer. Become a villain, lost in the power. He recounted meeting Amarie and how she'd unintentionally helped him realize the fallacy of his allegiance. Carefully steering around the truth of Amarie's power, he refused to burden his mother with that knowledge.

"She died, Ma." Kin blinked back tears at the memory of holding her lifeless body. "I blame myself for this curse. If I hadn't gotten so wrapped up in this selfish—"

"Kin." Lindora tightened her grip on his wrist as she knelt before him. She seemed so small, but her touch calmed his churning stomach as she wiped away the tears on his cheeks with her handkerchief. Her eyes rimmed with wetness, but none fell. "None of what you have endured is your fault. You were put into impossible situations by those around you. Yes, you could have made different decisions. Yes, you may have lost yourself and done unimaginable things. But it all leads back to this man. This master. He's the only one who can truly be blamed. You must remember that. Amarie's with Nymaera now, and he's to blame, not you."

Kin grimaced, flinching from his mother's touch. "But that's just it. Amarie's still in danger because she didn't stay dead."

Lindora's eyes widened, a sharp breath accompanying her grip of his hand. "She lives? How is that possible?"

He nodded and kept his voice low. "I can't explain the details, but if my master finds out..."

"You believe he'll go after her?"

"She's what he's been looking for, but he doesn't know it yet. I can't be near her because of the danger I would bring. I'd lead him right to her."

Lindora fell silent for a moment, watching his face. "But you wish to be with her. Does she feel the same way?"

"She hates me now." Kin sighed. "And it's best that way regardless of how much I love her. I'd fooled myself into believing the two of us could become something."

"It looked to me like the two of you *had* become something. Maybe things will change? Love doesn't easily die, my dove. Perhaps there is hope."

A bitter laugh escaped Kin's chest. "Hope." The word sounded foreign. "My dreams of a family with Amarie mean nothing if I can't keep her safe."

Lindora tilted her head. "Until you've exhausted all options, you need to hold on to your desire for that family. Keep it at the forefront of your mind and strive for nothing less."

"You make it sound so simple." He shook his head. "But what do I do?" The question continually burned in him after the final lash of Uriel's punishment. "There's no end to service, and I'm too valuable for him to kill."

He felt like a child again as his mother took him into her arms and held him. Her spiced scent from her time in the kitchen, mingled with wildflowers, filled his nostrils.

"I can't give you those answers," Lindora whispered. "I can't pretend to understand the intricacies of the Art or whatever has been done to you. But you've found light within all these shadows, and I'm proud of you." She cupped his face and looked at his eyes. "Follow that light as long as you can. Perhaps it'll show you a way out?"

She sounded so naively hopeful that Kin couldn't help but smile, but he shook it away with sudden fear. "Alana can't know. She needs to believe you're still ignorant, and Amarie..."

Lindora huffed a laugh, running her hands through his hair. "You've seen the dinner parties I host, haven't you?"

"Of course, you love those parties." Kin furrowed his brow.

Lindora wagged a finger. "I hate them. I'll be perfectly capable of hiding my distaste for that *woman*, even though I'd rather pluck her eyes out." Her face turned to a nasty scowl.

"Violence doesn't become you, Ma," Kin playfully scolded. He squeezed her hand, willing himself to part from her. "You should probably go before she gets suspicious. I'll see you at dinner."

Lindora frowned but gathered the tea settings back on the tray. "Are you certain you don't want me to stay?"

He shook his head. "I'd like some time alone. We can talk more tomorrow." Standing, he helped gather the dishes.

She pursed her lips but took up the tray.

Kin walked with her and opened the door for her.

"Never mistake my love for you." Lindora met his gaze. "You'll always be my son."

Kin's heart swelled, banishing some numbness from his chest. He tightened his jaw and nodded. "I love you too." Having sought the power to be worthy of love, the irony of it struck him. Neither his mother nor Amarie's love for him had depended on his Art. Yet, it served a purpose as long as the Berylian Key remained an interest to Uriel. Protecting Amarie and her power would forever be his focus. Once she was safe, he'd find his own escape.

There must be a life beyond this one, and Frey almost found it.

Before heading to the dining hall, Kin stopped by his father's study and fed him the lies he'd planned.

They entered the large dining hall together, sharing a comfortable silence.

Alana circled the set end of the long banquet table, pouring wine, and Lindora emerged from the kitchen. That night's dinner involved no staff, because only his mother could cook Kin's favorite meal.

Kin hadn't seen any of the usual help around the house since he'd left his room. Something to be grateful for. Interaction with other people felt impossible.

Lindora carried a serving plate, filled with steaming squash and spinach surrounding a perfectly cooked pink fish topped with lemon.

The smell made Kin almost forget everything except the fact that he was home. He stepped towards the table, but Alana intercepted him and held out a glass of shimmering white wine.

Kin accepted it with a tight, forced smile as his father rounded the table to take his usual seat.

"Lindora mentioned this new blend is one of your best in years, Hartlen." Alana purred, filling his glass as he settled into his chair.

Lindora placed the meal at the center of the table before she bent to kiss her husband's clean-shaven cheek.

His gaunt face had stronger lines, far different than Kin's features. Sun-worn wrinkles creased his face like Lindora's. His skin still held youth within it, only slightly pocked, but heavily freckled with thin lips and a cleft chin. Grey and white streaked hair curled tightly around his head, kept short.

Kin couldn't have looked less like his father, something he never thought much about as a child.

"Lindora always likes the white wines." Hartlen smiled as he offered his glass to meet hers in a toast while she sat across from him. "Hard to disappoint her. Every year she says it's better than the last."

Alana laughed and sampled the wine with an exaggerated murmur of pleasure. "I don't know, I think she might be right on this one," she said, taking another sip.

Kin resisted rolling his eyes, taking the empty seat beside Alana.

"See." Lindora smiled, gently elbowing her husband and reaching for her glass.

Hartlen stood to help serve their meal, the conversation dropping into casual tones.

"I'm glad to see the two of you traveling together again." Hartlen swallowed another decadent bite, cheeks flushed from the abundance of wine he'd consumed.

Kin opened his mouth to speak but stopped after a glance at his mother.

Lindora's brow furrowed and body straightened as her features tensed. Cheeks flushing, more so than they should with the single glass of wine she'd been nursing the entire meal, her body wavered.

"Ma?"

Her eyes met his and looked distant as she made a little questioning sound.

"Lady Lindora?" Alana's voice came with an edge of concern. "Are you feeling well?"

"I'm fine." Lindora lifted the back of her hand to her forehead. "Just a little lightheaded. The wine, most likely."

Hartlen put a hand on his wife's shoulder and turned in his chair to look at her, but she brushed off his touch.

"I'm fine. I think I just need a little air."

"I'll join you." Kin pushed his chair back as a wave of worry filled his chest.

She's never sick.

"You'll do no such thing." Lindora stood with her palms pressed to the table. She made the demand without the expected eye contact, keeping her gaze on the table as she wobbled again.

"Ma?"

She lifted her bloodshot gaze to meet his, and his throat tightened. "I want you to enjoy the meal." Lindora drew in a shaky inhale. "It's just a bout of dizziness, it'll pass."

Hartlen pushed back his seat, his chair groaning against the floor, as Lindora teetered when she stepped away from the table.

The older woman's legs gave out beneath her before her husband could escape his chair. Her body hit the hardwood floor with a thump, followed by silverware clattering and Alana's chair grinding out from underneath her.

Kin leapt and slid over the banquet table, toppling over a chair as he rushed to his mother's side. He reached Lindora first, lifting her into his arms and nestling her head onto his lap. His fingers brushed her fiery forehead, coming away damp with sweat. She radiated heat, and Kin hadn't noticed from across the table how saturated with perspiration her thin day dress had become.

"Ma?" Kin shook the limp form in his arms. He held his fingers to the vein at the side of her neck, finding her pulse rapid and uneven.

A groan vibrated through Lindora's parted lips, but her eyelids only fluttered.

Chapter 5

Talon roused from a restless sleep when a surge of familiar power collided with his soul. It yanked him from slumber with a gasp as his energy automatically reacted to the pulse of Amarie's. His arms reached out to embrace her and pull her from the nightmare she might be having that loosened her aura enough to envelop him. But memory harshly returned, and his eyes shot open while his mind whirled for answers.

What's happening?

Fear rippled through his gut as he stumbled to his feet. Voices murmured beyond the walls of his room, but he couldn't make out the words. With a flicker of his power, he activated the light motes on the walls to confirm his solitude within the dormitory.

The thrum of the Berylian Key's energy hovered in the air like an invisible haze. It felt painfully distant. He tried to trace Amarie's location, but the wards in the building blocked his attempts. Only able to confirm her presence to the west, near the Sanctum of Law, a rock hardened in Talon's stomach.

Despite trying to force it, sleep eluded him after that. He stared at the woven branches composing the ceiling above him. The wave of Amarie's energy dissipated, and he assured himself that nothing horrible had befallen her. Closing his eyes, he scratched the stubble on his cheeks as he imagined the thousands of reasons he no longer felt her power. He prayed it was only because she reconstructed her hiding aura.

A shout on the other side of his sealed doorway startled him alert, and he opened his eyes. His grogginess suggested he'd fallen back asleep amid his rampant thoughts.

Another yell, and the voices grew louder within the halls. A change of guard, he guessed, but the racquet continued as more people entered and exited their rooms.

Talon sat on the edge of his cot, staring at his unmoving doorway, even after the chaos beyond calmed.

Answers never came, and they left him starkly alone for days. The auer who brought him meals never spoke, keeping their eyes averted despite Talon's insistent questions.

The tedium of restless sleep and lackluster days continued for at least a week, but he couldn't be certain. His room had no windows, so he guessed the days based on the number of meals brought.

Despite the traditional solitude he suffered awaiting judgment, the guards granted him amenities when he requested them. Regardless of his lack of company, he refused to lapse on his usual routine.

The room remained fastidiously tidy, his face clean shaven.

On one particularly lonely day, he'd grown frustrated with the length of his hair and cut several inches off. The change, as he stared at himself in the little mirror, somehow reminded him he still had some control.

Talon fashioned himself a desk and took to writing to pass the time after that. It wasn't a hobby he ever enjoyed, but cataloguing his life suddenly felt important. Destined to die, recording his experiences so that someone might benefit was all he could do. He wrote letters to Amarie, to Kin, to his sisters.

His scrawling surmounted to a small stack of journals, arranged on the corner of the desk as Talon attempted yet another letter to Amarie, assuming she was alive. He used mismatched phrases of Aueric and Common, trying to describe what she meant to him. He begged her to stay in Eralas, despite whatever hate she might hold for the council. She needed to stay safe.

A rustle of leaves startled him, and he jumped, barely catching the ink well before its contents spilled across the desk. He corked it before he lifted his head to acknowledge Commander Lovakesh, who took her usual wide stance with her hands behind her back. She wore the armor she always did, appearing the perfect picture of an auer commander.

Her presence could mean only one thing.

Talon hurried to button his pale-green tunic, which he'd left open in his solitude. Running a hand over his hair, he tucked the sides behind his ears.

"It's time." Lovakesh's expression was impossible to read. "The Council of Elders awaits you."

Anxiety he thought he'd overcome washed through him. He turned back to his unfinished letter to Amarie and wrote a hasty conclusion and apology. After signing it, he spread pounce on the surface to dry the ink so he could fold and tuck it into the front cover of the top journal.

"I have a question, Commander." Talon stood to face her.

"Ask." The commander glanced at his bare feet.

Talon sighed and reached for his boots, knowing she likely wanted to proceed with the walk to the sanctum. "Amarie." He pulled a boot on, and Lovakesh quirked a dissatisfied eyebrow. "Is she alive?"

"Yes. I suspect you have a request for me as well?"

Relief accompanied his loud sigh, and Talon took a moment to revel in the good news. "Could you ensure she receives my journals then? And that the letters are sent as appropriately as you can, but only after they have carried out my sentence. I trust you'll respect my privacy?" He didn't want Amarie to receive his letters before his death, fearing she'd try something foolish like she had in getting arrested.

"I'll see to your request." Lovakesh nodded.

Stepping from the dormitories, Talon blinked in the sunlight he hadn't been privy to for days. It shone through the opening of the canopy above the Sanctum of Law, its roof glittering like facets of a jewel. The gardens were more occupied than he expected for the morning, and a pair of guards stood in front of the entrance to the observing balcony. They argued with a disgruntled auer who they refused entry.

Talon narrowed his eyes and unconsciously slowed his step before Lovakesh's hand on his shoulder hurried him ahead. She didn't utter a word of greeting to the guards at the doorway, but it opened the moment they arrived.

They're rushing.

Talon tried to wheeze in a breath during his automatic stop in the draining chamber. But he stood in the center for only a breath before the large wooden doors leading into the sanctum opened. The dim chamber remained inactive, and he stared at Lovakesh with his mouth agape as guards ushered him forth without ceremony.

Dread followed the uncertainty of the change in procedure.

Lovakesh entered but stopped inside, next to the door.

A new exponent?

Talon's chest tightened as he eyed an unknown figure standing where Lovakesh should have moved to. A strong feminine form, dressed in black breeches with laces up the sides, stood within the ring of inlaid gold. Hugging the top of her hips and waist was a tight black corset over a plain white shirt, loose on her arms and ending at the elbows. Dark-auburn hair flowed loosely down her back, holding a familiar wave as Talon approached his place behind her and to the right.

"Amarie?" He couldn't believe it when he saw the outline of her profile and the flash of her deep-blue eyes as she met his gaze. Lovakesh had told him she was alive, but it was different to see her standing there. Absolute proof of her safety.

What is she doing here?

Talon never wanted her to hear the shameful acts he stood accused of. Feeling like a broken shell of himself, he'd hoped to spare her the foreknowledge of his sentence. He'd poured everything he could into the journals. Those were to be his legacy with her, not a memory like this.

As intensely as he gazed at her, Amarie shifted her attention to the council. Her jaw flexed, her chest rising and falling at a faster rate than usual.

He opened his mouth to speak, but the arch judgment stood and raised a hand.

"Talon Di'Terian." The arch judgment's voice reverberated through the sanctum, but this time he continued in Common. "You come before the Council of Elders to face judgment for your crimes. We acknowledged in our previous session that your case is unique, and it appears to be growing more so with the presence of this human at your side." The arch judgment's gaze turned briefly to Amarie. He gave her a respectful nod, which she returned in a manner far beyond customary.

Talon fought to keep his breathing even as he looked from Amarie back to the elder.

"This council has thought diligently on the reality of what you stand accused of, but also your pleas for consideration. In addition, we must consider Amarie Xylata's words on your behalf, as well as her *generous* offer. Please understand that the strictest of confidentiality applies to this tribunal." He narrowed his gaze behind Talon at Lovakesh and her guard. A faint shifting of armor followed.

Talon glanced back, watching them all leave. With the viewing galleries empty, he and Amarie were alone with the council. His heart thundered. "Amarie?" he whispered as he turned to her. "What—"

"It's all right." Amarie didn't return his glance. Her chest stilled as she held her breath. With her hands clasped together in front of her, he almost missed how they shook. Her anxiety only compounded his, and his stomach lurched.

"Talon Di'Terian." The arch judgment's voice made him jump. Elder Erdeaseq cast a prolonged look at his fellow elders. They each turned towards him and nodded, showing final assent, though some gave it more hesitantly than others. "For the murder of Elder Jeq'Te and espionage against our law, this council finds you innocent. For the use of destructive powers, including the Art of summoning, this council still finds you guilty. And finally, regarding your defiance of your banishment, we find you guilty."

Talon's heart sank lower with each verdict. Even though they forgave the crimes he hadn't committed, the other two were enough for mortal punishment. He turned again to Amarie, wishing she'd vanish and never hear the proclamation of his inevitable death.

"The proper justice for these crimes is well known among our people, *however...*"

Talon's eyes widened at the word he never expected. His shoulders tensed in apprehension.

"We've considered the offer made by Amarie Xylata on your behalf. In which, she agreed to pledge her power as the Berylian Key to Eralas and this Council of Elders. With the agreement, she will serve and make ready her power for Aueric use when the council deems it a time of need. With no requirement to remain on this island. In exchange for such an alliance, we agree to pardon Talon Di'Terian of all crimes, as long as he agrees to refrain from the use of destructive Art while in the boundaries of Eralas unless it is necessary while training Amarie Xylata in the use of the Art and the power of the Berylian Key. This continuation of training will be required under the terms of this agreement. The pardon and its terms will also be extended as requested, revoking the title of rejanai for both Talon and Kalstacia Di'Terian."

Talon took in each word and as he attempted to process one idea, he was bombarded with another. Everything swam with the word pardon and his sister's name. But dread tainted the relief at the realization of Amarie's pledge. He'd rather die than have her bound in such a way. It was bad enough that they even knew of her power. He turned to Amarie, his insides warring between maintaining a disciplined stance before the council and reaching for her to beg her not to give so much.

The arch judgment paused, gazed locked on Amarie. "How do you find these terms?" He spoke to her while patiently gathering his hands in front of him.

"I agree."

"Then it is done." The arch judgment nodded and settled into his chair. "Talon Di'Terian, you are hereby pardoned and freed of the title rejanai. The same ruling applies to Kalstacia Di'Terian." He smirked at Amarie and shrugged as if all formality was gone. Waving a hand, he added, "You're free to go. We will be in contact to establish the procedure for when we call on you."

The words resounded in Talon's mind as he remembered to breathe, and he spun to Amarie.

She finally looked at him, and her smile broadened to a grin meant only for him.

Formality and expectation be damned.

Talon stepped to her, wrapping his arms around her waist. He met her smile with his lips, pressing them hard to hers in an eager kiss.

A gleeful sound escaped her as he did, and she returned the embrace. A touch he never thought he'd feel again.

Talon parted from her reluctantly, tracing her jaw with his fingertips. "Amarie. You shouldn't..."

She touched his cheek and shook her head. "Yes, I should. I told you I had other ways, and I'd do it a thousand times over." Leaning back from his grasp, she turned to the elders with a smile and again addressed them directly. "Thank you."

A look of amusement crossed Ietylon's face, utter disgust on some others', but Talon didn't care, tightening his hold on her waist and burying his face within the sweet scent of her hair.

"Let's go." Amarie took his hand.

He offered no resistance as she led him out of the sanctum.

Having been waiting on the other side of the door, Lovakesh's eyes widened as they exited, and she followed them outside. Turning towards Talon and Amarie, she assumed her usual posture, the initial surprise wiped from her face. "I assume your request no longer stands?" Her eyes flickered to where Talon held Amarie's hand, her lips tightening into a thin line.

"Correct." Talon squeezed Amarie's hand, glancing at her. The whole world lightened, like gravity somehow no longer applied. A feeling like the buzz of alcohol. The excitement, coupled with fading anxiety, created a rush of adrenaline that made him strangely giddy. He had to focus to gather his thoughts. "But if I could ask, Commander, I'd appreciate it if those things could be delivered to the dwelling you found when you initially arrested us?"

She nodded curtly. "I'll see it done. If you'll excuse me."

The change in her demeanor gave him a greater sense of belonging than he'd had in nearly fifty years. He faced Amarie, not caring that they'd only made it halfway through the front courtyard of the sanctum. He touched her chin, holding it between his thumb and index finger. "Amarie. Why..." He couldn't find the right words.

"Do you have to ask?" Amarie's eyes glistened as she touched his face. "I swore I'd protect you."

"But this?" He turned his head to nuzzle against her wrist and soak in the feel of her touch. "It's too much. There will be consequences neither of us can predict."

Amarie shrugged. "A problem for another day. Nothing would've been too much."

"I owe you everything I am. I could never have imagined being able to stand here, openly, in my homeland again."

She tilted her head, her deep blue eyes delving into his soul. "I'm honored to give that back to you. You'll have a harder time hiding your affection for a *human* now." Her lips twitched in a smirk.

Frowning, Talon playfully guided her chin back and forth. "Don't make light of what you've done. I know the depth of your sacrifice even if you brush it off. I'll never be able to repay you."

Amarie changed the direction he moved her chin into a single nod instead. "You don't owe me anything. Your safety is the only thing I desired. I'm not making light of what I've done. I know the gravity of my promise. But it's worth it." She touched the side of his neck, fingers twisting in a loose strand of his shortened hair. "You've done so much for me. I think it's finally fair that I could do something for you."

A smile curled his lips, despite trying to remain serious. He covered it by succumbing to his whims and kissing her again. He pushed all his gratitude into the tender affection.

As she responded, she wrapped her arms around his middle and pulled him close. He could feel her muscles quiver against him, her nails biting into his back as she withdrew from the kiss and hugged him. Even her breathing shook as her head rested on his chest.

He remained there, unwilling to let her go as he ran a hand through her hair. His lips formed kisses on the top of her head.

"I was so afraid they'd kill you," she whispered against him, gripping a handful of his shirt at his back.

He didn't have a response. While he'd been afraid for himself, a greater weight had terrorized him. Burying his face in her hair, he closed his eyes to fight the emotion threatening him. "I feared they'd already done worse to you. I didn't want to live anymore if they had."

"They wouldn't let me see you while they deliberated." Amarie kissed his neck. "Otherwise I could've reassured you. If I'd had a way…"

"I know." He leaned his head against hers, listening to her breath, matching the rhythm with his.

They remained like that, oblivious to the others in the sanctum gardens, until Amarie finally loosened her grip and drew away to look at his face. "I care about you. More than I can possibly say."

Immediately, he wanted to pull her into him again, but he froze. His heart thundered. Words felt inadequate. Touching the back of her hand on his jaw, he entwined his fingers with hers. "And I care about you, too, my araleinya." He kissed the back of her hand, and she grinned, her lower lip pinned under her teeth. "Come." He wrestled from the trance her eyes put him in. "There's a city I'd like to show you, one I'd also like to see again myself. Then we can go home."

Home.

Such a strange word to use, but over the past weeks, the little dwelling he'd created in the base of an old banyan tree became just that. And Amarie belonged there with him.

She nodded and took his hand. "Viento and Lynthenai are stabled nearby." At least she hadn't been confined to the dormitories like him. "You can show me around the city all you like, but be warned I'm having trouble paying attention to anything else right now."

Talon laughed, and it felt remarkable. "I'm relieved that I'm not the only one feeling overly romantic." He walked with her away from the Sanctum of Law, towards the outskirts of the city. If it wasn't for the occasional bridge that spanned the distance between mammoth cypress trees and the wisp-like orbs of light among the vines, it might have been easy to miss the city's presence. The trees' roots arched, creating hollows for shops and houses. Some branches formed stairways granting access to higher dwellings nestled within the trees. The worn streets wove for miles like a spiderweb, with the Sanctum of Law at its heart. Talon headed south, towards their home.

"You cut your hair," Amarie pulled his attention to her.

"Just a little. It was getting too long."

Amarie tugged his hand, turning to walk sideways, and sun glinted off the dagger once again at her thigh. She followed his gaze and smiled sheepishly. "I didn't steal it. In case you're wondering. It was just the only thing I could think of."

"I guessed as much."

Auer sauntered down the streets in the merchant district, conducting their business with rhythmic ease as if they'd done the same thing thousands of times before. Their lethargic pace contrasted the urgency of human traders.

Curious looks followed them as they walked, but he reminded himself they weren't something he needed to fear anymore. Instead, they were directed more at Amarie, being human, and their displayed affection. Talon wouldn't hesitate to announce his love for her to the entire city, their prejudices be damned.

"Can I ask how you acquired it, then?"

Amarie shrugged and shook her head. "It's not all that exciting. I lived here for several months after I rescued Viento from Helgath. I made friends and earned the respect of one of the equestrian trainers outside the city. I helped him with a stallion he was having trouble with. To thank me, he gave me the dagger."

Talon smiled in amusement and nodded. "That explains a lot about Viento's stubborn streak. He's Helgathian," he teased, and she laughed. "Do you want to visit your old friend?"

"No," Amarie blurted, barely letting him finish his question.

Talon furrowed his brow but changed the subject. "When you lived here, did you ever visit the Lenoneishé Gardens?"

Amarie shook her head. "I didn't. I can't say I had much ambition to visit a garden when the entire island is a giant one."

Talon laughed, shaking his head. "This is just a street." He gestured to the flower-rimmed road, which would have upstaged some of the grandest gardens on the mainland. "Imagine what requirements we impose to call something a *garden*. Lenoneishé was one of my mother's favorite places to visit. Would you like to see it?" He raised her hand to his lips and watched her face as her smile widened.

Chapter 6

Even as Amarie walked the streets of Quel'Nian, heaviness burdened her chest. She'd lived in tortuous uncertainty for a week, leaving her constantly nauseated. Her pulse still seemed faster than it should have been, and she squeezed Talon's hand.

He's safe. They can't change their minds.

Trying to calm her stomach, she took in a deep inhale of the fragrant island air. During their time apart, she'd seen small portions of the city and only left once to retrieve their horses.

The weight of her vow paled compared to the threat of losing Talon, and no regret tainted her mind. In the week without him, she learned what he meant to her. How her life would look without him in it, and how shattered her heart would be if the Council of Elders took his life.

And how it would devastate Kin to lose his closest friend.

Amarie watched Talon as they walked, but he looked at the city. His jade eyes held peace as they took in even the simplest things.

A child walking hand in hand with her mother, a shop lined with roses and an intricate mural created by Art-fed ferns.

He never let go of her hand, his grip occasionally tightening as he took in each sight that he probably believed he'd never see again.

Amarie found greater joy watching him than she did looking at the sights herself.

Crossing into an area of the city where smaller trees grew further apart, Talon glanced back at her with a smile.

The street ended at an archway formed of two cypresses, whose branches met and wove together to create the curve. The air quieted as crowds thinned and they were suddenly, blissfully, alone.

As they stepped onto a mosaic crystal path, the air in the Lenoneishé Gardens hummed with energy radiating from the flora crafted by the Art. The path followed no particular direction, curving in loose patterns. Trees grew in precise, abstract designs, carved, yet not carved at all. The sun glimmered through the thin canopy above, warming Amarie's skin and casting prisms of light off the path.

They passed singing creations floating free of the ground, their vines encircling orbs of water trickling into a pond. Walking over a crystal bridge, Amarie peered through the structure at schools of orange and red fish swimming through the stream below. Beyond, the ground flattened, and the gardens took on a different life.

The trees rose into pruned shapes with glinting water eyes and outstretched wings. A beautiful battlefield stretched before them, floral draconi and auer, frozen in a memory of times long past. A vine-covered beast silently roared with its mouth wide. Unlike the wyvern Amarie had seen in Feyor, this resembled a veritable dragon. With a strong cat-like shape, thorns spiked over its back and framed its jaw and head. Serpentine face and neck curled to confront its unmoving adversaries.

Amarie looked up, her head barely as high as the floral dragon's crouched belly. She imagined the creature's size to be accurate, but she'd never laid eyes on one.

"I used to pretend to be one of these warriors," Talon whispered as they stopped.

Amarie smirked, stilling the playful remark threatening to escape her lips, and replaced it with, "I used to pretend I had a pet dragon, and he'd fly me away from... everything."

Unbidden, Kin's teasing voice resonated in her mind. The night they met, she'd told him she planned to obtain a dragon and joked about naming the beast after him. *And will Kin be your protector or your mount?* Her stomach flopped, and she wished she could share the moment with Kin.

He'll never be here.

"If only dragons still existed," Talon mused.

Exhaling, Amarie shook her head. "I bet they do."

"Maybe they're smart enough to stay away from the mess we've made of the world." Talon smiled, turning to meet her gaze.

"Can you blame them?" Amarie shrugged and laughed. "I can understand wanting to escape."

"Funny, it was the opposite for me." Talon touched her cheek. "I feared being left behind and missing out."

Her shoulders finally relaxed as she examined Talon's calm expression. Relief washed over her again. "So, you wanted to join the fray, and I wanted to run." Forcing her gaze from him, she eyed the dragon. "Do you still feel that way?"

He took a deep inhale before he answered. "It's changed now." He drew her attention back to him with a hand caressing her waist. "I've found my purpose." Pausing, he pulled her closer. "What about you? Do you still want to escape?"

Amarie's throat tightened, her hand resting on his chest and feeling the beat of his heart. "I have nothing left to run from. It's the most unsettling feeling I've ever had, honestly. My life is... perfect. But perfection is fragile, and I can't help but wonder if something is going to come along and ruin—"

Talon's thumb grazed her lip. "Let's go back to the part where you said perfect." He smiled, and it sent a flutter through her gut. "I'm tired of living in fear. So, let's not anymore."

Amarie nodded, kissing the pad of his thumb before he moved it away. Her arms slid around his shoulders. "All right. I can do that."

Can I? Is this really perfect?

"Thank you." He kissed her lips and they felt odd. "There's something else I wanted to show you." Slipping his hand into hers, he tugged her towards another archway. Beyond it stood a domed structure of white oak.

Amarie smiled at the back of his head, banishing her doubts and darker thoughts.

I should be happy. I will learn to be happy.

They crossed the threshold together. The circular room, lit by pale purple motes lining the top of the walls, housed a shallow pool. Above it, a sphere of water hung suspended, specks of light dancing around it like fireflies. Its surface pulsed, producing the occasional drip. The pond's mirror surface flickered each time. Roots encircled the top of the orb, collecting into a single, closed bud the size of a fist, downturned as if it looked at its reflection.

"I felt it only appropriate." Talon drew Amarie towards the water's edge. "My araleinya."

Amarie studied the rare bud and wondered if she'd ever see it open. A smile touched her lips, and she looked up at him. "What color will it be?" Her voice barely carried over the still air.

Talon stepped behind her, slipping his arms around her waist. He kissed the side of her head. "I'm not sure. I've never seen it. I'm too young, and no one talks about it. They say it's meant to be seen and not explained. That's why all depictions of it only paint it as white. But I've heard it's not."

Amarie leaned against him, her hands resting on his. "You've never seen it, yet you believe it a fitting name for me?" Turning within his embrace, she kissed his chin.

"You mistake my meaning. The name isn't for your beauty. I name you araleinya because of your rarity. You're the most precious and unique of beings." Talon kissed her jaw, trailing down her neck.

Amarie's eyes closed, taking in the delicate touch. The heat of his lips made her head swim, and she brought her mouth to meet his.

Talon is a good man, and he cares about me. I need to forget Kin.

His powerful arms drew her tight against him as the kiss hungrily renewed. Her fingernails traced his scalp, tangling with his hair as she lost focus of where they were. It felt so secluded, with no sounds other than the distant trickle of the stream and whisper of leaves.

His mouth invited her to lose herself in him, and she pressed her tongue against his with a tilt of her head. His hands ran along the curve of her back and down her hips. The distraction of his touch didn't prevent her from sensing the movement of energies.

Pulling away, Amarie watched the chamber's only doorway grow shut with a whisper of Talon's power.

Talon's mouth pressed to her neck, kissing towards her collar.

She smiled and closed her eyes, focusing on the sound of his breathing. "Afraid to be seen with a human?"

He answered by nipping her skin, bringing his lips closer to her ear and making a lovely purring sound. "Hardly. I'd be happy to open the way again and continue if you'd rather?" He teased the bottom of her ear lobe with his tongue.

"Mmmm." Amarie leaned into him. "Leave it closed, even if it's a tad... presumptuous." She nuzzled against his neck and grinned, enjoying his scent.

Talon hummed in her ear again, tracing the length of her body with his hands. "I wouldn't want to overstep my bounds." His fingertips played with the bottom of her shirt, and he added, "Again."

Amarie pulled away enough to meet his striking green eyes. "I said presumptuous, not *wrong*."

"I see." Talon traced the top of her breeches with featherlight fingertips, making her shiver. "Then I pray you forgive my presumption and allow me to give in to what I've craved for so long."

Amarie nodded, his eyes boring into her. "Consider yourself forgiven. It sounds like a worthy motivation."

He gave a playful little frown. "Quite worthy, I would think."

Rising to her toes, she hovered her mouth near his. "Prove it."

Talon closed the gap between their mouths, pushing feverishly against her lips as their tongues danced. He held her, a calm within all the heat as he dug beneath the layers of clothes to touch her skin.

Her eyes shut and she caressed the muscles of his chest and shoulders. She wanted him, even amid her doubt. Her heart sped as he unfastened buttons.

He took his time, painstakingly so, encouraging her hips against his. Each time Amarie tried to help remove a layer, he stopped her. He was deliberately torturing her, yet she drowned in the decadence of each moment.

Talon guided her down onto luscious grass near the pond as his hands explored her newly exposed curves. He'd stripped away every layer from her upper body before she had an opportunity to rid him of any clothing. His needy hands roved across her stomach and up her ribs to cup her breast as his tongue played at her neck.

The combined sensations elicited a hasty inhale. She sought to pull his shirt over his head, wanting to feel the warmth of his skin against hers.

He rocked his hips against hers as he wrestled free of the tunic, tossing it aside. Leaning down, he nuzzled into her neck, beginning a new series of kisses. "Weren't we trying to go slow?"

Amarie laughed. "Are you complaining, my auer?"

"I'd be a fool to." He drew away, his tone turning serious. "But do you want this as much as I do?"

Amarie trailed a fingertip over his lips to his chin, then up his jaw. She nodded. "Definitely. I want you."

And maybe I'll finally stop thinking about someone else.

Talon lowered his body, their chests touching, and brought his lips to hers for a passionate kiss. As his hips shifted, she wrapped her legs around him. He traced her jaw and pulled from the kiss to speak. "And I so desperately want you."

Amarie grazed his lips with hers, loosening the tight hold on her hiding aura. It engulfed him, drawing him into her sea of energy.

A groan reverberated through Talon, and he slid from the kiss. Running his hands down her abdomen, his lips eagerly followed. Her body scorched as his mouth closed on the tip of her breast, evoking the arch of her back. His tongue responded to her soft moan, encouraging her spinning mind to blur as his kisses resumed their journey down.

Amarie grasped his shoulders, fingers twisting through his hair while he freed himself from the remainder of his clothing.

He returned, fingers playing along the seams of her breeches. In a single, agonizing motion, he peeled them off as his mouth played around her waist. His tongue teased a gasp from her as he explored lower.

Closing her eyes, Amarie's mind took her to a steamy night.

Her back pressed against a wall before Kin placed her onto a vanity, his mouth on her as Talon's was now.

She sucked in a breath, eyes opening. But a garden surrounded her, rather than the guest bedroom at the Parnell estate. Tightening her grip on Talon's shoulder, her nails bit into his skin as she tugged him to return his lips to hers.

He obeyed, sliding his body along hers to meet her mouth.

Strands of his hair tickled her cheeks, the scent of him and his smooth face washing away thoughts of Kin. Talon's energy danced with hers with a greater intensity than she'd felt before. It surged around hers, playing a game of chase. She'd never seen the full extent of his power, and its strength took her breath away.

Banishing her ability to think on it any longer, Talon's power caught hers, wrapping together as he pushed into her, filling her. She gasped and their bodies fell into rhythm, breath speeding in tandem with each rising moan.

Amarie held his shoulders before sliding her hands down to his backside, each of his thrusts bringing stars into her vision.

Talon's mouth stifled the cry of bliss as her body erupted with euphoria. Her hips pressed against his movements as the ripples tore through her. His speed escalated, and she whimpered as his mouth left hers, his face burying into her neck. He groaned, lips vibrating against her skin, and plunged deeper. Savoring her neck, his pulsing slowed as he rode their waves of pleasure.

Their power ebbed against each other, but that too faded with kisses softening and breath recovering from the elated rate.

Talon's hands gentled, tracing appreciatively over her skin. As he drew away, her eyes met his.

A smile touched the corners of her mouth, captivated. No haste propelled her to rise from his embrace.

"This isn't exactly how I pictured my day unfolding." Talon watched his fingers caress her shoulder before meeting her gaze again. "I'd never dreamt of such perfection, my araleinya."

Her heart quaked, and she smiled as his lips touched her jaw and she found the word she's struggled to say before. "I love you, Talon Di'Terian."

"And my heart will forever belong to you."

The bliss shrouded a strange foreboding in the pit of her stomach.

I'm not meant for peace.

Doubt tainted even that moment as Talon kissed her again.

But I will enjoy this. As long as I can.

Chapter 7

Tugging blankets over his mother, Kin watched the slow, unsteady rise of her chest. Stray hairs stuck to her sweat-dampened forehead, and his heart collided with the inside of his ribcage. His fingers tracked her rapid pulse.

Hartlen stood on the opposite side of the bed, eyeing Alana as she wrung out a cold cloth.

Kin touched Lindora's cheek. "She's fire hot."

"I'll see what I can do for her fever." Alana slid closer.

"Haven't you done enough?"

"Kin." Hartlen scowled at his son. In the strained silence that followed, he touched his wife's arm.

Her eyelids fluttered, but she didn't wake.

Alana glided around them and leaned over the bed next to Kin, extending her tanned hand towards Lindora's face. As it passed him, Kin snatched her wrist, and she paused. "Kin. Let me help, please." Her tone seemed earnest, her eyes flitting to Hartlen.

Kin wanted to tear Alana's sinister heart from her chest. He fought the instinct to use the Art to pin her against the wall.

She did this.

"Son." Hartlen's brown eyes pleaded.

With a huff, Kin loosened his grip.

"I've seen this kind of illness before." Alana placed the cloth on Lindora's forehead. "It'll progress rapidly. I'll offer what healing I can to cleanse it from Lady Lindora." She stood straight, smoothing the layers of the black dress she'd changed into for dinner.

"What do you need?"

Alana rattled off a list of items for Hartlen to gather, but Kin didn't hear any of it. A list of lies.

Kin adjusted the cloth on Lindora's head, examining her ghostly pale skin.

What did Alana do to make this happen so fast? Ma was fine an hour ago.

Blocking out Alana's assurances to his father, Kin stared at the blackened windows on the far wall. He could just make out the dark shapes of tall trees on the far end of the property, blotting out the stars.

On the bedside table sat the hair pins Kin had methodically taken from his mother's hair.

He straightened the blanket again as a breeze rustled past the rich green curtains framing the open window.

Crickets chirped outside, oblivious to his plight.

Looking up, Kin realized his father had left to gather the things Alana had asked for in her deceitful pretense of healing Lindora. Hartlen didn't know the auer woman had no skill in healing.

"What have you done?"

Lindora's breath slowed, her pulse growing more sluggish and uneven.

"What's necessary to remind you of your place."

The powerful intoxication rippled through Kin's core, passing into the air around him. The shadows of the room, plentiful with the night, writhed with energy. He'd avoided using the Art since his torture at Uriel's hands, but anger drowned his reservations.

Darkness rose as he turned, blackness whipping towards Alana. She didn't struggle as tendrils wrapped around her shoulders, but her eyes widened when they tightened and slammed her into the wall beside the windows. She crashed into it with a huff. Her body stiffened as the wicked vines snaked closer to her neck.

Alana lifted her chin, white teeth forming a nasty smile. "Kill me, and you'll kill your mother too."

A rumble reverberated deep in Kin's chest as he stepped forward. His hands closed into fists, holding the invisible threads of the Art. Alana made no move to touch her power, but Kin's spine straightened in anticipation. Although she was superior in ability, he wouldn't go down easily.

"Fix her." Kin's fingernails bit into his palms. "Undo what you've done to her."

"Now, if I did that, what would you learn?" Without warning, power surfaced and surged through Alana's limbs. The temperature of the air plummeted like an Isalican winter.

Kin's shadows froze in place, crackling. Goosebumps rose on his arms, but the manifestations of his Art were the target. Noise crescendoed in a bone-rattling cacophony, the dark tendrils splintering into sharp obsidian fragments. They dropped like black icicles, shattering against the floor.

Alana landed on her feet and snapped her fingers.

The sound bounced through the room, escalating into a high-pitched ring. The lanterns in the room sprung to life, their flames larger than they should've been, turning the room into a shadowless space in the span of a breath.

"Unlike you, my *sae'quonei*." Alana purred the nickname she'd given him, meaning 'little one' in Aueric. "I remember my duty and strive to fulfill it. So, you will stop this ridiculous stalling and resume your task, or I'll be forced to remind you that you still have much to lose." Her nearly pupil-less eyes panned to his mother.

"Bitch." Kin stepped to block her view. "You dare threaten my mother, when she's been nothing but kind to you?"

"I'm not the one jeopardizing her life, you fool. *You* endanger her with your insolence and childish antics. Her life is in your hands, and if she dies, it's because of you."

Kin's insides raged, his only option to obey.

I should never have returned home.

Of course Alana would use his parents against him. Guilt overcame the fury.

"Morning, then." Kin loathed succumbing to her. "If we leave tonight, my father will be suspicious."

Alana smirked and shrugged. "That's tolerable."

Kin's obstinance faded as their journey toward Lasseth Frey resumed. Defeat dulled his spirit, unwilling to risk his mother to be a thorn in Alana's side. The auer found every opportunity to mention Lindora and her weakened state, adding to Kin's anxiety.

Because of their ability to fly over the mountains, they arrived in Arboral in three sleepless days. Soaring over the dense forests of the valley left Kin wondering which nearby settlement Amarie once lived in. Her uncle had raised her near Arboral after her mother's death, only to die himself when she was fourteen. The sleepy city, nestled against the base of the Olsa mountains at the country's border, might have proved a good place to grow up if she'd been more fortunate.

Arboral had once been a fortress, but the infrastructure had been partially torn down, the materials repurposed for residences. The trees grew tall and thick, smaller cousins to those in Aidensar. The dense canopy provided a plethora of shadowed spots to retake his human form outside the city.

An open meadow stretched in front of them, dried stumps peppered throughout it. The distant thunk of an axe suggested progress continued. The rooftops of the inner city were thatched, but the outer ring of structures boasted new clay shingles. Charred husks of abandoned buildings to the east gave context to the city's concern for fire resistant roofing. Packs of grygurr roamed the wilds of Olsa's mountains and were the likely culprits for the damage.

Sunlight glinted off the metal helmet belonging to a poor guard stuck roasting in the top of a rickety watchtower. He glanced towards the pair emerging from the tree line, then settled back beneath the railing.

Kin stood facing the open iron gate of the city when Alana struck him in the chest with a rolled piece of parchment.

"I have *faith*," her tone demented the word, "that you can handle this from here."

Kin unrolled the scroll and found a graphite-sketched face staring at him. Little agitated lines repeated over and over to create the density of Lasseth Frey's thick jaw, sunken eyes and withered features. With a sigh, he re-rolled Alana's drawing and tucked it inside his cloak. "Yes." He didn't bother masking his disdainful timbre. "Where will I find you when it's done?"

"Whatever tavern is closest to the east edge of the city." Alana clipped her words, mirroring his annoyance. "Be there by sundown."

Kin looked at the elongating shadows.

Mid-afternoon already.

"Shit." He didn't bother with another word before storming through the city gates. Once, he would've enjoyed the challenge of such a task, but he found no pleasure in it now. Amarie, and encouragement from his mother, had reawakened his desire to find another way.

Lasseth's secrets would provide Kin with answers, like how he'd evaded his master for so long. Normally, defectors were efficiently captured and punished, much like the famed Helgathian military. Shades had a greater disadvantage, trackable by the tattoos on their forearms.

Kin tucked away the Art deep within himself. He couldn't risk his master seeing his plan to question Lasseth about how he escaped.

Finding him proved easier than expected.

Kin wove through the crowds, eyes locked on Lasseth's hobbling figure. His head of shaggy white hair stood out among the rest. Keeping his distance, Kin used his height to his advantage, looking over the heads of townsfolk going about their daily business.

The streets narrowed the closer Lasseth walked to the densely packed city center, his attention shifting from cart to cart. He carried a worn knapsack on his hip, weighted by something within, but he hadn't stopped to buy anything.

The former Shade's pace quickened.

Did he notice me? But then why isn't he running?

Walking purposefully, Lasseth zigzagged through the streets with determined strides.

Kin shook his head and pushed through the crowds to get closer to the old man. The moment he closed the gap between them, a cart rumbled across his path and forced him to skid to a stop. With an exasperated sigh, he peered around the cart to reclaim his sight of Lasseth but couldn't find him again until the cart moved on.

The old man raced down an alleyway the next block over.

"Nymaera's breath." Kin rushed around the back end of the cart to pursue. Ignoring the agitated shouts of townsfolk, he shoved past them at a sprint. He rounded the corner into the alleyway, catching himself before he slammed into the wall. The dimness of the alley left him blind, and he blinked rapidly to help his eyes adjust. Looming shadows framed boxes and barrels propped against the walls.

Kin faced a dirty brick wall, a dead end. Certain Lasseth had entered moments before, he looked up. There wasn't a route to the rooftops, and even he couldn't have made the jump.

Great.

Checking the crates and barrels as he walked to the end of the alley, he found each uninhabited.

Touching the rough back wall, he scoured it for any signs of a hidden door. His fingers located a groove in the cold bricks. With a low growl, a mixture of victory and frustration, Kin heaved against the wall beside the seam with all his might. Much to his relief, the wall gave way and pivoted open without triggering a trap. Stone ground against stone as Kin created a big enough opening to pass through. On releasing the heavy wall, it rumbled back into place.

He peered down another dark alleyway and spurred his legs to move.

Why do I get the impression this is merely the beginning?

Kin's boots echoed hollowly on the ground. Looking down at a trap door, his eyes widened. With an awkward hop, he jumped to find safety on the iron grate beside it. His balance jeopardized, he had no chance for recovery as the iron gave out. He knocked his jaw against the rim of the trap as he fell, vision flashing a blotchy white. Hitting the ground on his shoulder, he grunted and blood filled his mouth. His arm throbbed. Rolling onto his back, he rubbed the muscles still tender from the dislocation months prior.

The memory of Lungaz and Amarie's daring rescue spiked in his mind, but he shook it away with the pain. He rolled to push himself up, spitting out the blood.

Dim light shone through the open grate above. It wasn't far up, and he scrambled to his feet to reach for the lowest bar. Before his hand could close on the rung, the metal snapped shut.

His fingertips stung as he forced them into the tiny spaces of the grate. Skin tore with tiny lacerations while he tugged on the sharp edges. The metal held firm. He gave up the attempt and looked around at where he'd landed.

A rounded tunnel stretched to his left and right, composed of stained stone. Trenches of flowing water ran along the sides of the pathway. Farther down the left side of the tunnel, the water sloshed through more grates. The stark darkness made each direction impossible to see down more than a few feet.

Kin rolled his eyes. Lasseth would know better when creating a potential trap for a Shade. Dissolving to shadow and leaving through the narrow slits in the grate was likely how the old man hoped he'd escape.

So don't be predictable. He's probably down here.

Instead of reaching for his power, he turned left and walked. Groping through the dark, he ran into another dead end. More grates, with water filtering through, and the distant chatter of rats. The temptation to reach for the Art grew. It would've made the dank tunnel easier to navigate. Fighting off the urge with a stubborn grumble, he touched the wall, searching for anything unusual.

Recoiling from a small crevice, he hissed. Warm blood trickled from a cut on his finger, but he returned to investigate a broken lantern. Taking it gingerly from the wall, he made his way back to where he'd fallen.

Kin dug into his cloak. He withdrew a small glass lens Amarie had given him after watching him struggle with flint one afternoon.

"You're making that look way harder than it is." Amarie smiled, failing to hold back her laughter. She crossed her legs, sitting up from the frosty tree trunk she leaned against.

Kin grunted, throwing the flint into a shallow snowbank beside him. "The grass is too damp. It might be easy for you to do it, but my Art doesn't work that way."

Amarie tilted her head. "I never mentioned the Art. I don't use mine for that, either."

He looked up, admiring the rosy tint the cold added to her cheeks. He couldn't help but smile back at her as he stood. The snow crunched beneath his boots as he walked towards her, eyes locked with hers. "Will you enlighten me, then?"

Taking his offered hand, Amarie rose to her feet.

Her skin warmed his, and he refused to let go.

"I thought you'd never ask." Shoving her free hand into the inner pocket of her cloak, she presented him with a lump of clear glass in her palm. "How do you think I started the fire yesterday so fast?"

With her so close, Kin debated the necessity of fire to create warmth. "What am I supposed to do with glass?"

"It's fireglass." Amarie pulled her hand from him as she glanced teasingly at his mouth. "I'll show you."

She turned towards the firepit, but Kin caught her before she could move away. He slipped his arm beneath her cloak, wrapping it around her waist and pulling her close. Unable to resist the temptation, he touched the pink on her cheek. "I should properly thank you then." He drew his lips close to hers. "Though I don't know why you waited so long to show me."

"You look cute when you're focused." She pinched her lower lip between her teeth.

"Like you, when you do that." He ran his thumb over her

captured lip. She leaned into him, and he couldn't resist any longer. Kissing her, the entire world melted away.

She laughed as she withdrew, pushing firmly on his chest. "No distractions. This only works while the sun is out."

His gaze followed her as she crouched next to the pile of dried grass. Holding the fireglass above it, she rotated the thick, inch-wide disk until it projected a beam of sunlight onto the center. Holding it steady, she waited.

"Really? The sun is going to start a—"

When the pile smoked, Amarie smiled and finished his sentence for him. "Fire?"

The flicker of flames snapped Kin from the memory. The wick of the lantern sprung to life while he held the piece of unassuming glass in the beam of sunlight creeping through the grate. As the cracked lamp chimney fell into place, a shiver ran down his spine. The winter with Amarie felt a lifetime ago.

The opposite tunnel beneath Arboral led to a cave-in. The boulders and rocks looked impossibly heavy, and a steady stream of water bubbling out of the stone two feet from the ground didn't bode well for what was on the other side.

He got the distinct feeling that Lasseth was off somewhere having an ale and a good laugh imagining this.

Withdrawing his sword, the steel rasped against its sheath. Uriel's power roiled in the chasm Kin had banished it to, chiding him for refusing it. He ground his jaw. The less control he gave it, the less he gave Uriel. He needed to believe in a life without it. Besides, Lasseth knew Shades, and everything Kin encountered in these tunnels could be a trap.

Kin wedged his sword into a crack, prying the stones apart enough to get his fingers beneath. He started at the top of the cave-in, working his way by the light of the lantern. By the time he'd dug a hole large enough to fit through, he was drenched in sweat and his hands bled.

With a grunt, he crawled through the narrow opening into a new tunnel, flooded with stinking stagnant water. He turned back to retrieve the lantern, lifting it to eye the flooded tunnel. Light glimmered off its dark surface from another distant tunnel.

Kin braced himself as he wrapped his cloak around his neck and shoulders. The water came to just above his knees, and the rank smell made him want to gag. Lifting the hem of his cloak to cover his nose, he stepped carefully on the stone beneath the surface.

Light flickered in the right passage, its origin hidden by a steep incline. Desperate to get clear of the filth, Kin followed it. He kept a hand on the wall as he stalked out of the water, his stealth impeded by the squelching of his soaked boots.

Touching the pommel of his sword, the cold metal brought relief to the injuries on his hands. Kin eyed a lonely lantern, placed strategically on a protruding brick. Looking down the tunnel, he sighed. Another glowed, farther down and around another corner.

I'm being lured somewhere. Like a damn rat.

He growled and picked up his pace through the higher-arched tunnel. The brick work and layout were too specific for sewers. Perhaps it had once been more. Coming to yet another lantern beside a caved-in passage, he glared at the dead end. He kicked the rubble, and a stone echoed as it tumbled from the wall, rolling down the ramp behind him.

It stopped partway, gritting against the ground beneath the sole of someone's boot.

Kin withdrew his sword, whirling around. Adrenaline spiked and he lifted his weapon to meet the oncoming glint of steel from his attacker. It took both hands to brace the blow, and the lantern fell from his grip. It exploded into a pool of orange and blue flames as oil coated the ground. He side-stepped, his wet breeches steaming.

Orange light accentuated Lasseth Frey's gaunt face as Kin deflected the old man's attack, and steel clashed with stone.

Lasseth stepped back, arcing his sword towards Kin's exposed right side with shocking speed.

Forced to cross himself with his own blade, Kin braced the flat side against his right forearm to block the attack. He kicked out and hooked Lasseth's ankle with the toe of his boot.

The old man shifted back to catch his balance, using his lowered stance for another swing at Kin's middle.

Kin disengaged, but his boot caught on Lasseth's ankle and he hit the floor, knocking the air out of him.

Lasseth roared, driving his blade towards Kin's throat.

Wide eyed, Kin rolled into the pool of fiery oil. He ignored the searing heat as he spun on the slick ground, using the momentum to slam his boot into Lasseth's knee.

Lasseth collapsed, crying out.

Kin lunged to his feet, whipping his smoldering cloak to the ground. He slapped out the flame clinging to his thigh. Surging forward, he kicked the former Shade, sending him sprawling away from his weapon.

Lasseth huffed as he hit the ground and scrambled along the floor. Hands groped as he pulled himself to the wall. He reached into a hole in the stone and withdrew a knife, flinging it directly at Kin's chest.

He barely had time to let loose what he'd buried. The shadows at his feet sprung from the ground like stalagmites to guard him. The knife thunked into the tendril passing over Kin's left side, redirecting it. It clattered down the steep ramp, disappearing. With a whisper of will, Kin pushed the shadows into the darkness behind him.

"I was wondering how long you'd hold out." Lasseth grunted. "Shade of Uriel."

Kin narrowed his eyes, anger filling his chest for what Lasseth forced him into doing.

Instead of attacking again, the old man leaned against the wall and gripped at broken ribs, wincing.

"You say his name like you don't fear him." Kin picked up his cloak. "He's your master too."

"Once, but no longer," Lasseth growled, tensing. "Are you the only one pursuing me?"

Kin studied him, retrieving his sword from where it'd fallen before sheathing it in an act of good faith. "No. Alana has been tracking you. I suspect for months. She led me straight here."

Lasseth cursed, wincing as his shoulders slumped. "Then perhaps the time for fighting has passed."

"I won't lie, Lasseth." Kin forced his own body to relax. "My task *is* to return you to Uriel, and Alana is here to make sure it is done. But I hoped we could talk first."

"Talk?" Lasseth rolled his shoulders and wriggled his way higher on the wall. A dry chuckle came to his lips. "Would you seriously have me believe that one of the fiend's nascent Shades is already getting cold feet? And Uriel's bitch is hanging around to make sure you get the job done. Though your rank seems impressive for one who still looks so young." Lasseth gestured with his eyes towards the tattoo on Kin's arm, exposed in the lantern light. "Your master must be growing more generous."

Kin twisted it to look at the fourteen geometric shapes denoting how many tasks he'd completed.

Lasseth turned his right wrist out, pulling the sleeve of his black tunic to reveal where his own mark had been. Beneath a thick spiderweb of scars, Kin counted nine vague shapes.

"And to think, I was the most experienced of his Shades when I left." Lasseth tugged his sleeve back into place. "If I'd continued, I would've died before my twenty-fifth birthday, and greedily, I sought more life."

Numbers ran through Kin's mind as he considered what Lasseth was implying. It seemed impossible. Lasseth looked at least seventy.

"How old are you?"

Lasseth raised an eyebrow and laughed before stopping with a hiss, clutching his ribs. "Certainly not what I look. Thirty-six."

Kin's brow furrowed.

How is he only nine years older than me?

"Uriel's power made you age faster?"

Lasseth tilted his head. "You speak his name. Only the foolish do."

"Like you? I no longer fear what he may do to me. Now, please." Kin stepped forward but stopped when Lasseth flinched. "I need to know more about him if I'm to accomplish what you have. Tell me what his power's done to you."

"My youth is one of the prices I paid." Lasseth nodded but pursed his lips. "You must be freshly recruited if you don't know the consequences yet."

Kin shook his head, trying to sort his thoughts. "No. I've served for ten years."

Lasseth gave a low whistle as he straightened his back from the wall. "Then we have plenty to speak of, indeed." He eyed Kin's sword one last time. "I don't know which is more naive of me... believing you're earnest or accepting the fate you're tasked in fulfilling. I've dodged Uriel's followers for too long and I'm weary, but talking to you will give me a few more hours." He walked past Kin, a new limp in his gait.

Lasseth glanced back at Kin following behind. "What's your name, Shade?"

"Kinronsilis."

Lasseth hummed. "The Lazorus child." Kin's heart stopped, but the old man continued. "Seeing as you're walking beside me, instead of lost to Uriel's original purpose for you, tell me about the shadow fiend's new face."

Chapter 8

"I'm going to Quel'Nian today." Talon looked across the bed at Amarie, who lifted a tunic from the pile of clothes they'd washed the day before at the stream.

Over the past week, they'd enjoyed the quiet of the forest together, but he needed a change. His mind tormented him with the importance of the day, despite the pleasant distraction of the song Amarie hummed.

"Kalstacia is arriving, and I'd like to tell her the truth about our parents in person. Then perhaps go to the burial caverns together." He didn't look forward to telling his oldest sister that Alana had murdered their parents, especially considering Kalstacia's sacrifice. But she deserved to know. He also owed her an explanation beyond the hurried note he'd sent, tied on the leg of a messenger owl.

They'd agreed to meet at their family's old home, which had been given to Talon after his pardon.

Amarie offered a faint, reassuring smile as she put down a folded shirt. The breeze from the bedroom window caught her hair, and loose strands, free of her ponytail, touched her face as she nodded. "All right. Would you like me to come with you?"

"It'd be best if I speak to her alone first. Explain the details of our pardon. But she'll want to meet you." He stacked the folded clothing on shelves he'd constructed along the wall beside the bed. With access to the wares of the city, the little dwelling resembled a proper home with linens and pillows. It was comfortable, but Talon would've slept on a solid rock slab if it meant he could hold Amarie at night.

She nodded again and slid the small stack of clothing onto her shelf before walking over to him. Her bare feet made no noise on the soft ground as she wrapped her arms around his waist.

He returned the gesture without a thought.

"I'd love to meet her." Amarie looked up at him. "Do you think you'll be back tonight?" Her tone was gentle. They hadn't spent a night apart since his time confined within the dormitories, and he had no wish to deter from the routine.

"Most certainly." Talon touched her chin and gave her a kiss. "Promise me you'll be cautious if you practice while I'm gone." He suspected she dove dangerously deep into her Art during his rare absences. The distance removed the danger her power posed to him, but it still made him nervous. Hunger for knowledge wasn't always conducive to training with the Art.

Her deep blue eyes blinked at him, and she smiled. "I promise."

"Mhmm." He hummed, bemused, with pursed lips. "Just be careful." He waved a hand as he stepped away and crossed into their front room. "I don't want to come home to find you've *redecorated* the house by flipping it upside down, or something."

Knowing she could accomplish such things with her power felt daunting. Especially considering how hard it was for him to shape everything around them.

"I'll be sure, if that happens, to flip it back before you return." She followed him. "Though I may need your help refolding the clothes."

Talon laughed as he retrieved a bowl of berries from their dining table and popped a berry into his mouth. Offering the bowl in her direction, he grinned. "That would be appropriate, as I'm far better at folding than you."

She accepted the bowl and shrugged. "It's possible you're more inclined to the life of a house husband, and I, one of the adventurer. We needn't fold clothes in my way of life."

"House husband?" Talon scoffed at the phrase, raising an eyebrow. "Now that's a term I never expected thrown in my direction. But I suppose we could construe my distinct manners and class as such when compared to your barbaric ways of balling clothing and proclaiming it *folded*."

Amarie's laugh resounded from her throat, a sound he'd become fond of hearing. "I'm sure there are many aspects of your current life you didn't expect." She set the bowl of berries on the table and he helped himself to another. The briefest look of discontentment crossed over her face before disappearing beneath a smile. "You didn't seem to consider my ways *barbaric* when I failed to fold your precious clothing after relieving you of it," she taunted with a mischievous look.

"House husbands are no fools." Talon's joy swelled with the banter. "Even *we* must admit that folding has its time and place. Those moments, my araleinya, are not the place, nor the time."

Amarie walked towards him, but then continued past without the kiss he'd expected while casting a baleful glance at the bowl of fruit.

Following, Talon caught her hand as they slipped through the widened front doorway. He kissed her fingers. "Are you feeling all right?" He banished the teasing tone in his voice. "You haven't been eating much."

Amarie shrugged, a smile lingering on her lips. "I feel fine. Just not hungry this morning. Perhaps the warmer weather."

Talon furrowed his brow.

She'd tell me if something was wrong.

He released her hand, looking in the river's direction. Whistling, he waited only a moment before his white mare cantered from the woods. "Don't wait for me if you get hungry. I probably won't be back until the afternoon."

"Don't worry, I won't waste away while you're gone. I hope your visit goes well. Do you think you could bring home some of that tea that I like? I ran out yesterday."

"Of course." Something felt off, and Talon watched her carefully in the hopes her behavior might enlighten him.

Lynthenai butted her head into his hand, dissatisfied with the lack of attention, and urged him to scratch beneath her chin.

"Go." Amarie touched his face. "You're imagining things to worry about." Kissing his freshly shaved chin, she smirked. "Everything is fine. I love you."

"I love you too." Talon forced his nerves to quiet, giving her another kiss before mounting his horse.

Amarie held her hand up in a wave before heading towards the river as he departed for Quel'Nian. He'd visited it a handful of times since his pardon, mostly for supplies. Each time, Talon awed at the beauty of the city, grateful to walk the streets again.

The sunny spring day inspired cheerful songs from birds and the chatter of people on the streets. Despite the years since his banishment, hardly anything had changed. The streets still ran the same course through the grown homes and businesses, the structures diligently maintained. The air hummed with the omnipresent force of the Art, which brought him a sense of belonging.

Entering the residential neighborhoods, he led Lynthenai down a familiar narrow road. The controlled buzz of power faded, slipping into wilder energies.

Lynthenai halted in front of an overgrown hedge.

The two pristine properties on either side made the dense wall of foliage look like a mistake.

His memory insisted it used to be two short rose bush fences with a delicate archway guiding visitors to his family's front porch. With a sigh, he dismounted, walking onto the mossy stone walkway.

His horse's ears pricked forward, and she shifted away from the doorway at the center of the hedge. Kalstacia's familiar energy lingered from recently shaping it.

Stepping through, Talon closed his eyes to allow himself the nostalgia of what it used to be. Once maintained by his father, a pair of pomegranate trees flanked the entryway to the worn steps of the front porch. The grass had formed intricate patterns among their roots, leading to his mother's flower beds. Narrow banyan trees, woven together, created the porch's roof. Above that, open vine-draped windows lined the second floor.

The Di'Terians had been considered a big family, growing their home into a two story 'monstrosity' to house their three children. No one suspected that the children, considered a blessing from the gods by their neighbors, would end up bringing such shame.

Blinking his eyes open, his memories drowned beneath the dense greenery strangling the old homestead. Little was distinguishable, other than the vague structure. The untamed grass tickled Talon's knees as he walked towards the figure standing before the pomegranate trees. They'd exploded with life and great bushels of green blossoms, laden with ripe fruit. They tangled together at the center, forming the approximation of an arch.

Kalstacia stood with her arms crossed over her abdomen. She looked so much like their mother, his heart ached. Pitch-black hair fell to just beneath her ears, curling against her jawline. A pale blue dress hugged her frame, and the loose sleeves, with a cut-out shoulder, formed a bell-shaped cuff near her elbow. Her fingertips moved back and forth over their mother's silver-laced belt around her waist, constructed of material like the armor of the auer military. It had been a gift the day Kalstacia sacrificed herself for her siblings.

Talon tread through the grass, crossing to stand beside her, but she didn't turn to greet him. He examined her profile, the curve of her small nose and the pressure between her thin ruby lips.

Her chest rose in a deep inhale as she opened her jade eyes, like Talon's but rimmed with a hint of purple she'd inherited from their father. "I hoped someone would've cared for it," she whispered.

Her tone eased the tension in Talon's shoulders. "Me too."

The sun glinted against a plated silver necklace, resting with a downward point at the top of Kalstacia's sternum. It was etched with flowing patterns and scrawling Aueric words.

"You've been reinstated with the Menders' Guild?"

All auer, once they reached their three hundredth birthday, chose a path to contribute to society. Kalstacia chose the Menders' Guild, becoming one of Eralas's most revered healers. Then she had given it up to save her younger siblings.

Kalstacia touched it, and the way she did told him how much she'd missed the feeling of its weight. "Yes," she said with an exhale, looking at him. They have granted me the opportunity to regain my rank, which is something I hardly expected. And while I don't wish to sound unappreciative, how *did* you accomplish our pardon?"

"As much as I'd like to take credit, I accomplished nothing. It's a long story." Talon sighed as he ran a hand through his hair.

"One I need to understand in full." Kalstacia lowered her hands to her sides. "You're keeping something else from me, though, I can tell. Speak it."

Talon frowned and averted his gaze. He never understood how Kalstacia could read him so easily, even though they'd never been particularly close. Talon had suspected Kalstacia knew about his and Alana's forbidden practices all along.

"Alana." Talon frowned. "She lied."

"That's nothing new. What lie are you referring to this time?"

With a painful knot in his stomach, Talon told Kalstacia of their parents' murder. Of Alana convincing him to take responsibility for her crimes to lessen her punishment. Of her actions beyond their lands, her manipulation of him and countless others, including Kin.

Kalstacia listened without interrupting. Her jaw tightened, and a tear rolled down her cheek as truth after truth found her ears. Closing her eyes briefly when he finished, she took a deep breath. "We no longer have a sister." She steadied herself on the trunk of one of the fruit trees.

Talon nodded gravely, touching his sister's shoulder.

She quivered beneath his touch but turned to face him. Finally, they embraced, her tears dampening his tunic.

Talon held her as long as she allowed, trying to offer what strength he'd regained with Amarie at his side.

Kalstacia slowly broke away, heaving a sigh as she looked back to their old family home. She swallowed a lingering sob and shook her head. "Our home shouldn't look like this."

"The council has restored the property to our family name."

Talon nodded at the overgrowth. "It's yours, if you want it."

Kalstacia eyed it. "Always leaving me with all the work," she said dryly, a hint of a smile returning to her lips.

"I have faith in your ability to restore it far faster than I'd ever be able to."

Silence settled between them, and Talon wondered where Kalstacia's thoughts had taken her.

"I'd like to meet her."

"Amarie wants to meet you too."

"But not today," Kalstacia continued, touching the tree.

Power passed from his sister to the tree trunk, and it reacted to her energy. The leaves shivered and a handful of fruit dropped with thumps to the ground.

"Of course." Talon nodded as he picked up a pomegranate. "You're always welcome. We've made a home together on the other side of the western river."

"Together?" Kalstacia's voice took on an interested tone.

Talon's cheeks heated, and he cleared his throat. "Yes." He braced himself for the possibility of his sister's disapproval.

Kalstacia lifted a hand and smiled as if apologizing. "No need for details, brother." She smirked and picked up more of the fallen fruits to hand to Talon. "I can come to my own conclusions. I look forward to meeting her even more now."

Talon sighed and shook his head. "I'm grateful you'll be distracted for a while then. I'll come visit soon." He shrugged his armful of pomegranates. "And thank you."

After leaving his sister, fruit stashed in his saddlebags, Talon allowed merchants and their wares to distract him as he passed through the city. The craftsmanship surpassed anything he'd seen on the mainland. Time wasn't as pertinent to auer as to humans, and they celebrated laborious processes in creating fine goods.

A leather crafter caught Talon's attention and he indulged in picking out a gift for Amarie.

When Talon finally arrived in the clearing of their home, dusk approached. The day seemed surreal. After a leisurely afternoon in the markets of Quel'Nian, he was returning home to a woman he loved. His heart pounded as he caught the first note of Amarie's voice floating through the forest. His eyes settled on her form from afar, and he drew back Lynthenai's reins.

Amarie stood with her back to the little house built among the roots of a banyan tree, her hair tied up behind her head. Her profile stood out against the dark background, but her attention remained elsewhere. Her hands moved in front of her as she manipulated the Art as though she'd been doing it for years, rather than weeks.

He let her song caress him as he silently untacked Lynthenai.

She sang an Aueric ballad he hadn't heard from her before. The lyrics spoke of love and nature. While the melody echoed from her lips, her eyes focused on her task.

Energies coalesced before her. She'd acquired water, fire, dust and light between her hands. She manipulated one to the other, with no obvious goal. She formed shapes and used the other elements to change them. Fire melted ice, water quenched fire, and the light grew green shoots as the dirt moved before her. The whole thing took up no more space than another person would, growing and weaving within itself.

Talon maintained his distance, watching and listening. He could feel the strong pulse of her power, pulling substantial amounts from within herself. Far more than she ever did while they were together, for reasons he understood. The connection between Amarie and her power was still fragile, and she could quickly lose control.

Pulling her hand back, a new sprout erupted from the ball of soil floating in the air. It developed into a small plant, with roots dangling beneath it. The fire knitted into a white-hot sphere, and water dribbled down the mature greens as they grew taller. In a breath, she released the power from her hands and the entire creation dropped into her waiting palms.

The energy dissipated into the breeze, all gone except the plant.

Still singing, she brushed the dirt off the carrot she'd grown.

Viento lingered nearby, looking expectantly at her and the vegetable, likely not the first grown on his behalf.

Lynthenai betrayed Talon's silent observance when she cantered to join them, playfully nuzzling Viento's neck as if trying to push the black stallion away so she might get the carrot instead.

With Amarie's connection safely tucked away, Talon stepped closer with less concern.

Her gaze settled on him, and her mouth shut to end the song prematurely. The end of the tune brought a sudden emptiness in Talon's chest.

Amarie looked sheepish, even with the smile that lingered on her face. Breaking the carrot in half, she shared it between the two horses before approaching Talon.

"Please, don't stop singing on my account." He took her hand, drawing it to his lips.

She watched him, and the hint of tension faded from her face. "It reminds me of you. Helps me focus."

Talon smiled against her skin as he kissed her fingertips. "I'll take that as a compliment." He stepped into her and wrapped an arm around her waist. "Though, sometimes, I enjoy the idea that I make it harder for you to focus, like how you affect me."

The memory of her song left a buzzing against his soul, igniting a desire deep in his gut.

Her smile grew. "I said the *song* helps me focus," she said coyly. "Your touch tends to have the opposite effect." Her pulse sped under his fingertips, remnants of her power still whirling in her veins. The lingering pressure intoxicated him as it pressed against his senses.

"That's good to know." Unashamed, he caressed the bare skin beneath her shirt. His mind and body aligned in their want to feel the warmth of her.

Her chin lifted. "Do you enjoy hearing me sing?" Her eyes glittered with specks of pink and purple as she engulfed him within her hiding aura. Like a wave of warm water, it swirled against him in greeting, and his power answered.

Talon's breath quickened as the energies intimately entangled. "Yes." He brushed a kiss on her neck. "Your voice is enticing." The flow of the Aueric language was only the beginning of why he became thoroughly entranced whenever Amarie took to music. The pitch of her voice, and the way she swayed the notes into a delicious hymn, made his entire being hum.

Talon's hands traced her perfect curves, self-control slipping away. He nibbled her earlobe, receiving the reward of her soft inhale. "There are other sounds you make that I find equally enticing." His whisper elicited exactly what he'd hoped for, a whimper of a moan as she pressed her body against his. He responded with a satisfied murmur when her lips hungrily met his.

They fell into each other, finding the way to their bedroom, a tangle of bodies and power melding perfectly for an evening that passed without awareness of time. He relished in her, as he usually did, drowning himself in the sounds of Amarie responding to his touch.

Recovering from their ecstasy, they remained entwined and naked in each other's arms. Breath calmed to a relaxed pace, but their energies still danced, unwilling to fully part.

Talon tucked a loose strand of Amarie's hair, clinging to the perspiration on her jaw, behind her ear. "I love you." Her eyes shone with the power of the Berylian Key, fascinating him.

Her lips sought his again, kissing him deeply before pulling away with a peaceful smile. "And I love you." Her warm hand stroked over his bare chest.

Talon wondered how he'd lived for so long without such an integral part of his existence. Encouraging her head to rest against his chest, he tightened his hold on her. Lavishing in the way her power felt against his, he groaned happily. The two coexisted perfectly together, leading to a familiar craving for more. He sought to quench the greed with a deep inhale of breath and a renewal of their kisses.

Thoughts of all he would give to protect her, coupled with the sound of her breath and feel of her skin, eventually lulled Talon into peaceful sleep.

Chapter 9

A cool breeze brought Amarie back into awareness, a kiss pressing against her lips. Her mouth responded without her opening her eyes.

She felt so at peace. The thrum of her Art pulsed idly in the surrounding air. As their mouths parted, she blinked and met Kin's pale blue eyes. Her heart swelled, entranced by the feel of him within her aura and her arms.

Warm rays of sun trickled through the canopy and onto the bedroll they shared, surrounded by crisp grass. Beyond the trees, the surface of the lake glittered in the morning light.

"Good morning, my love." Kin's baritone voice rumbled as he kissed her again.

The taste of his mouth evoked a deep response from her, her hands playing across the dusting of dark chest hair. His bare, muscular arms surrounded her with his sun-kissed scent. Their lips moved naturally together, a short scruff of beard scratching her chin. They surrendered to a rhythm that left her wanting more as he withdrew.

His eyes followed the line his hand drew down the opening of her corset. As he lifted himself above her, she took in his features. A head of thick, dark-brown hair cut short at the sides and just long enough on top for a lock to fall over his forehead. His eyes, like steel, pierced her soul, seeing every part of her.

Kin rolled to his side beside her, propping his head up while he continued to tease along the hem of her shirt. His irises lightened further, watching where his hand touched her abdomen.

"Why did you leave me?" Her voice drifted on the air, far away.

Kin's eyes flickered back to hers, holding deep pools of regret. "Because I love you too damn much," he whispered. He flattened his palm against her abdomen, holding it there. "You aren't safe with me."

His words echoed in her mind as his eyes transformed in hue to a bright green after her blink. Finding herself looking at Talon, his lips moved and the auer's voice came instead of Kin's.

"I'll protect you in whatever way necessary, I promise."

Amarie squeezed her eyes shut and willed herself to see the truth. *Please come back, Kin.*

"I haven't given up." Kin's voice returned, and she hastily opened her eyes to see his face once more. His index finger traced a slow circle on her stomach. "I want this, and I'm fighting for it."

She calmed again, just from being able to see his face.

"I meant it when I said I'll always love you." His lips turned into the sideways smirk she'd grown so accustomed to seeing. "There's no greater truth than that for me. All I do is for my love of you. *You.* Not your power. And there's nothing in this world that will change the way I feel for you. Not distance, not time, and certainly not your care for another man. We will *always* have this." He flattened his hand again, fingers playing with the fabric of her shirt.

"But you left me." Doubt crept into her mind. "You chose your other life. You said we could never be together." She sat up, his gaze following her.

He smiled, melting her anger. She wanted to let it go and forgive him, every nerve in her body wishing to be back in his arms and feel his mouth on hers.

"I did leave. And I did say that, and for now... it's still true. But I'll find a way to change it." Kin sat cross-legged across from her. "No matter the cost, I'll protect you." His mouth moved, but the words echoed with Talon's tenor tone humming oddly over Kin's.

"Kin," she breathed, her surroundings blurring. "I miss you."

He brushed a strand of her hair aside, tucking it behind her ear. Guiding her face closer, his lips parted, and he kissed her.

The weight of the world lifted from her shoulders, her heart thudding in her ears as her hands found his bare torso again.

Kin pulled her onto his lap, and she stayed there as their lips parted from each other's, only enough so he could rest his forehead to hers. His breath tickled her pinned lower lip. His grip tightened around her waist, and she wanted to stay within his embrace, surrounded by the scent of his skin.

"Where are you?" she murmured with an exhale, hands sliding up his neck and into his hair. "I want to see you."

"I'm somewhere you can't follow." Sadness filled his tone. He pressed his forehead harder against hers. "Please, don't try."

With a gasp, Amarie opened her eyes.

The bed beneath her brought her back to reality, coupled with the distant pressure of Talon's hand against her forehead. She blinked at his silhouette in the hazy morning light streaming through their window.

"I'm sorry." Talon kissed where his hand had been. "I thought you might have a fever. You're pale and your breathing was shallow." He slipped away from her, sitting upright. The blanket covering them both fell to expose his bare chest.

Her mind strove to catch up to where she was, her heart aching with the loss of Kin all over again.

"You can go back to sleep, my araleinya. I didn't mean to wake you."

Amarie struggled to shake the cobwebs of the dream, of Kin, from her mind. She watched Talon's spring green eyes intently, using them to discern fantasy from reality.

"Talon," she breathed. His brows knitted together, and she hurried to wipe the confusion from her face. "It's all right, I'm fine. I was just having a strange dream, I think. I'm up now, though."

He smiled, taking her hand and squeezing it before he stood, still naked from the night before.

Heat rushed to Amarie's cheeks, and she averted her gaze as she sat up, lifting the blanket to cover her chest.

Thankfully, he didn't notice, choosing a clean pair of breeches from their laundry. He tugged them on before turning back to her. "Would you like some tea? I picked up the one you like, and you still look a little pale. Are you sure you're not sick?" He circled the bed, touching her forehead again.

Amarie shrugged. "I have a bit of a headache." She ran a hand through her loose hair and took his hand. Unwanted feelings of guilt ran through her, even as she reminded herself that she'd done nothing wrong by moving on from Kin. "Tea would be lovely, thank you."

Talon leaned over and placed a warm kiss on the top of her head before exiting through the curtain of vines towards the kitchen.

Her gaze stayed on the vines as they settled, her heart twisting. She loved this man, this auer, yet not how she loved Kin.

How is it possible to love Talon and still desire Kin?

Closing her eyes, she covered her face with her hands, emotion welling within her. Kin wasn't coming back, no matter how many times her dreams tortured her.

Amarie opened her eyes and looked at where Talon had lain beside her in their sleep. She smoothed her hands over her hair, taking a steadying breath.

This is where I'm meant to be. Here, in Eralas, safe with Talon.

The love between them satiated her, and the thought made her smile.

Rising from the bed, she dressed in clean clothes, and Kin's words from her dream reverberated through her. *And certainly not your care for another man.* Had he known she and Talon would become more than friends? Had he planned it that way, to help her move on?

As she strapped her dagger to her thigh, she wondered if she'd been given the whole story. Talon had been the one to suggest going to Eralas together, right after Kin left.

Why didn't he suggest it sooner? Perhaps before my death?

Amarie rolled her eyes and shook her head. She opened her mouth to call out and ask Talon the question, but stilled her voice.

Do I really want to know?

Her stomach twisted. Sighing, she frowned.

Kin is my past. Talon is my future, and he'll tell me the truth.

Reaching out, she parted the vines and stepped into the kitchen as Talon lifted a steaming mug from the table.

"I was about to bring this to you." He offered it forward, hesitating when he caught her eyes, and his lips pursed.

"I want to ask you something." Amarie accepted the mug from him, staring at it.

"Anything." The tension in Talon's arms melted away, and he touched her chin before retrieving the second full mug.

"Why didn't we come here sooner? To Eralas?" Amarie lifted the hot drink to blow on it.

"I don't know if we could've made it here any faster. We came straight here as soon as we could."

Amarie looked down at her tea, gritting her jaw. "I know we came here immediately after you suggested it, but why didn't you suggest it earlier? Why did we go to Aidensar at all, if you knew Eralas was safe from Shades?" She met his gaze and tilted her head.

Talon paused, his wrinkled brow relaxing. "Oh," he breathed, lowering his tea to the counter without drinking any. "I hadn't considered it before. Kin suggested it." He averted his gaze when he said the Shade's name.

Amarie's stomach flopped. "When?"

"The day you died," he whispered, leaning against the counter, hands behind him. He didn't look up. "Right before I found you in the river."

Bile rose in her throat. "What else did he tell you to do?"

Silence loomed as Talon considered the question.

Amarie set down her tea and rounded the table. She lifted his chin with a delicate touch and studied his face. "Talon," she murmured. "Did he tell you to do anything else?"

"Not specifically." He finally met her gaze. "He said it'd be best for me to find you instead of wait. Which is what I did. I doubt he felt he could ask for more, since he already asked me to violate my banishment. Kin knew everything they had tried me for."

Amarie's shoulders relaxed, and she closed her eyes.

Kin didn't manipulate this into happening.

Talon's warm hand grazed the side of her cheek. "Why are you asking these things?"

Amarie shook her head and kissed his palm, covering his hand with hers. "I don't know. Just feeling... I just wanted to know that he didn't... *encourage* you to be—"

"Amarie." His tone hardened as he turned his hand to squeeze hers. "No. Don't even consider that. Kin has nothing to do with what I feel for you. If anything, I felt horribly guilty, like I was preying on your emotional vulnerability. I was surprised when Kin begged me to take you to Eralas instead of ordering me to walk away and leave you alone."

A smile spread over her face. "Why do I get the impression you might not have obeyed such an order?" He smiled, and she continued. "But, in all truth, you could've sent me alone and avoided the personal peril of being here."

"I couldn't have done that. For a multitude of reasons."

"Oh?"

"What? Did you want me to recount them all?"

"Well..." Amarie smirked. "Since you're offering."

Talon shifted and cleared his throat as he lifted her hand between them. Upturning her palm, he traced the length of her fingers to count as he spoke. "I was curious. To learn more about you and the burden you carry." He moved to the next finger. "Concerned, because of what you'd just endured. Kin's departure and your experience with death. Protective, because I believed you didn't deserve more suffering. Enthralled by your resilience—"

"You're going to run out of fingers," Amarie teased, grinning.

"I can find other places to trace." He kissed her palm. "Besides, the idea of you on an island full of infamously charming auer who wouldn't properly respect you didn't sound appealing when I considered my growing attraction to you."

Amarie's smile faded. "You wouldn't have had to worry about that. Of all the people who could charm me, it wouldn't be an auer."

He lifted an eyebrow. "Not an auer? How am I so lucky, if my people are so unappealing to you?"

Frowning, she whispered, "You're different."

Talon narrowed his eyes, watching her in silence for a moment. "Am I?"

Stepping closer to him, Amarie rested her hands on his chest and nodded. "When we first met, I assumed all the worst things about you. But I was as wrong as I could've been."

"Maybe you weren't? I look back on how brutal and insensitive I was when I told you all those things and wish I could redo it somehow."

Amarie shrugged. "Maybe a little insensitive, but there was no room for you to soften the blow. You told me the truth, when no one else had. Brutal, but honest. I needed that."

Talon smiled, smaller than before. He blinked slowly, his chest rising beneath her hands in a deep inhale. "Tell me what happened? I suspected a history after your reaction in Rylorn, when I—"

Amarie silenced him with a finger to his lips. "When you made an innocent comment, and I projected unfair assumptions onto you. Yes, I remember." Lowering her hand, she continued. "I met someone when I first visited here. I was seventeen, and remarkably naive. He was Piete'lian's son."

"Piete'lian? The master of the Equestrian Guild?" Talon's eyes widened. "You said a trainer gave you the dagger, but—"

She hushed him again with another gentle touch and smiled. "Are you going to let me tell you or not?"

Talon paused, taking her hand from his mouth. He squeezed it, and his eyes looked sad. "Even as a rejanai, I remember Baetrik's reputation. It nearly overshadowed his father's. He's the one?"

Amarie cringed. "His father is a good man." She nodded solemnly. "Baetrik made me think all kinds of things, but none of them were true. I was foolish, but I'd never been courted before and I put too much faith in his promises. He lost interest after he could gain no more amusement from me."

Talon's lips pressed into a thin line. "I'd willingly become rejanai again, if it meant I could teach Baetrik a lesson."

Amarie smiled, her heart warming. "I don't need you to teach him anything. I could do it myself, but he's not worth the effort."

"Depending on how far he let his manipulation go, I think it's very much worth the effort."

Amarie sighed. "Don't make me say it, Talon. Do you think he would've stopped short of anything? Do you think he cared at all about *my* honor? Of course not."

Talon closed his eyes, leaning against the counter behind him. "Bastard," he growled, shaking his head. He opened his eyes to meet Amarie's again, brushing her cheek with his fingertips. "I completely understand now. You had every right to assume and judge when we first met. And how I behaved in Rylorn..."

Amarie shook her head. "Maybe my feelings were founded when we first met, but they weren't in Rylorn. I knew you by then, and I know you so much better now. Which is why I can say you're different. It doesn't matter what he did. It was a long time ago, at least for me. So, don't go getting yourself banished again. I need you here." She kissed his chin, running her hands up the sides of his neck.

"As tempting as it is..." Talon tilted his head to allow her mouth better access. "I'll control my baser impulses to murder him. Mostly because I desire to be nowhere but here, with you." He guided her chin up, bringing her lips to meet his in a tender kiss.

Memories flickered to her dream, but she inhaled Talon's scent and renewed the kiss with greater intensity.

He responded, sinking into the affection with her before gradually bringing it to a stop a few breaths later. "I assumed you'd want to practice the Art today, but if you'd rather return to bed, I'd be happy to oblige."

Her smile broadened, her thoughts refocusing. "A compromise, then. Practice, with an early bedtime?" She raised one eyebrow at him.

"Always the practical one of us." Talon smirked and gestured to a bowl of fruit and bread on the table behind her. "You should eat something and come outside when you're ready. I have something for you." He gave her a quick kiss and slipped away before she could stop him. Plucking his mug of tea from the counter, he took it with him through the front door, walking barefoot outside.

Her curiosity piqued. Choosing a piece of bread and popping it into her mouth, she continued outside without bothering with her boots. "You have something for me?" She stepped into the sunlight. "Did you pick up more fruit while you were in town yesterday?"

Talon poured a sack of feed into the trough he'd grown for the horses. He'd tucked in his shirt and rolled the sleeves up past his elbows. Casting her a glance, he smiled. He finished the chore, patting Viento's neck as the big horse investigated his breakfast.

"I do have some pomegranates from my family's trees, but that's not what I was referring to." Talon moved towards his saddle, which hung over the railing of their porch. He drew a blue linen sack from the full saddlebag. Inside, metal jingled together. "A gift. For my araleinya and her constant companion."

A dainty silver drawstring secured the bag closed, and she eyed it for a moment before looking at Talon. "A gift?" She hesitated, watching Talon pat Viento's side. "Why?"

"Do I need a reason? Open it."

Amarie smiled sheepishly and opened the sack, reaching inside. Her fingers found soft leather, and she pulled it into the sunlight. Her eyes settled on the bridle and her breath caught. Made from black leather, fine silver stitching lined the edges. The supple material made leatherwork from the mainland look rugged in comparison. She suspected they reinforced the silver buckles with the same strength the auer crafted into their armor.

Turning it over, she found a silver plate where it would rest along the side of Viento's head. She traced the engraved metal with her fingertip. *Viento.* She inspected the other side and bit her lip at the engraved image of the araleinya flower. Its vines created a swirling pattern up the length. It was beautiful, and her heart swelled with adoration as she looked at Talon.

He watched her expectantly, but didn't prompt a response.

"Talon. This is..." Amarie lost her words, stunned by the thought he put into the gift. "You're amazing. This is incredible, I love it." She stepped towards him and threw her arms around his shoulders before kissing his neck. His arms slipped around her waist, and she grinned into his skin. "I love you."

Talon touched her chin, lifting her lips to meet his. "Hopefully Viento likes it as much as you do."

Amarie reluctantly moved from Talon to her horse, interrupting him in his quest to fill his belly. He snorted at her, but obeyed, allowing her to remove his worn, light-brown leather bridle. She dropped it and slid the new black one onto his head while he chewed his oats. Adjusting the buckles, she made sure the fit was perfect before letting him resume breakfast.

While she admired how perfect it looked on his black coat, Talon wrapped his arms around her waist from behind. He nuzzled against her hair near her ear. "Now he's a true Eralasian horse. No more need for that Helgathian attitude of his."

Amarie laughed and leaned back against Talon. "I've never seen him tolerate anyone else like he tolerates you."

"I'll take that as a compliment."

"Thank you," she added softly. "That's the most thoughtful thing anyone's ever gotten me."

He kissed her temple. "Keep saying things like that and I'll get the wild idea to go with a saddle next. There's nothing that could amount to what you've given me. I'm blessed to have been granted the opportunity to know you, let alone love you."

Amarie closed her eyes, basking in the contentment filling her. "You're making it difficult to want anything other than to take you back to bed."

"Nonsense." Talon chuckled in her ear. "I've never known you to be so easily persuaded from practice. Perhaps I should remember this as a technique for the future." He ran his hands playfully down her abdomen and over the waistband of her breeches before resting on her hips again. "Now is an excellent time for practice, as much as it pains me. Distraction is something you need to learn to work through. Though, I rarely use this kind for my students."

"Students?" She exaggerated the plurality of the word. "You don't *usually*? I selfishly hoped this was a new tactic." She closed her eyes. When she immediately saw Kin's face, she hastily opened them again.

What's wrong with me?

Talon didn't react to the sudden tension in her shoulders and inhaled near her ear. "It's new." He took a silent step back, and the heat of his body vanished. A protesting whimper came from her lips, but he laced his fingers between hers, leading her towards the area of trees they typically practiced in. The energy there had become familiar, and Talon faced her, holding their hands between them.

"Just a pinch of power for now. Then try taking a larger handful if it feels right. I've tried to distract you before, but it's time to replicate scenarios you might encounter." He so quickly reverted into his role as teacher, it was jarring. Talon's green eyes were steady and hard-set. "Always remember to breathe."

She nodded, centering herself to her training mindset. Closing her eyes briefly, she delved into her Art, focusing her intention. As always, she separated from it before taking a small amount.

Above their heads, branches creaked. Talon stepped away, leaving the space in front of her vacant. A branch snapped down directly in front of her, accompanied by crackling vines. Leaves brushed her cheeks before the entire branch whipped back into the tree.

She couldn't see Talon, but remained facing forward, controlling her instinct to flinch as more vines flashed in and out of her vision. She maintained her breathing, forcing each breath to fall in evenly. Holding tight to her power, she broadened her stance to endure another attempt to distract her as the ground bubbled and shook beneath her bare feet.

Talon paced into the corner of her vision, his hands tucked at the small of his back. "Good. Release it and begin again."

She obeyed, letting go of the power without having it manifest, this time without closing her eyes.

Dark fire engulfed Talon's hands. He flicked it forward, and it bounced jubilantly across the grass, splitting into little jets of flame surrounding her feet. The air thickened with heat, and each breath burned her lungs. Finding the concentration to summon her Art became harder, but she succeeded out of stubborn determination and it danced into her veins.

"Again."

Tucking it away, she started over.

Talon moved out of her line of sight, treading silently behind her. As his chest pressed to her back, she sucked in a deep breath and began the ritual again. His hand stroked over her hip, down to her thigh. Drawing her hair aside, he moved his mouth in close to her ear, purposely breathing at a faster pace than she needed to maintain. The weight on her thigh lightened as he withdrew her dagger. She ignored it, urging herself into her power.

Sunlight glinted off the blade, casting a beam of light on the grass. The cold, sharp blade scraped across her skin as it touched her throat. An arm curled around her waist, yanking her against his solid body just as she gripped her power.

She grasped Talon's wrist. Images flashed in her mind of the collection room in the Delphi estate. Kin's mouth stopped her from screaming with a heated kiss. He held her against him, blade to her throat, feigning threat. His breath warmed her neck, and her skin stung as the blade broke her flesh.

Her grip on Talon tightened, her heart racing as the perfect storm of sensations ripped away her control. Her lungs burned for air, but she could only breathe her power. She gasped, drowning as the waves overtook her. Like a hungry predator, her power tore at her moment of weakness and consumed all it touched.

In a panic, she fought it. The cold steel against her skin

disappeared, and she no longer held Talon's wrist. Her vision erupted in color, streaking her surroundings with violets and blues. Something moved in front of her, but she couldn't make it out beyond a warped figure.

Talon told her to breathe, but his voice sounded far away, echoing through impossibly long caverns.

She struggled for air, but each breath only burned, bringing no reprieve from the strangulation. The ground beneath her melted away. Hovering, she reached for anything to grasp onto, but found nothing. Her voice reverberated in the trees, crying out, but from somewhere else. White light seeped into her vision, blinding her, and she closed her eyes.

Amarie wanted to tell Talon to run, but couldn't form words, overwhelmed by a shattering world she couldn't decipher. Everything around her vibrated, resonating in an ear-splitting ring.

Breathe.

She found the memory of Talon's training. The only bit she could conjure.

Taking a slow inhale, her lungs screamed with the power that accompanied the air. Her exhale pushed away her frustration, sending the energy out with it.

Use it against itself.

The surrounding energy froze at her captured breath, and she dared to open her eyes. She floated several feet above the ground, poised mid-air. The trees appeared suspended in time, their leaves unaffected by the breeze. With the pressure of the Art in her hands, she used it to shape the rampant energy around her. She forced it back into herself after another staggeringly deep breath that made her lungs ache.

Her entire body thrummed, buzzing with the massive amount of energy she locked within her veins. Light brimmed through the trees, blurring her vision. Sucking in another breath, she used it to bury the power. A growl escaped her throat, and a breath later, her knees struck the ground. She clawed at the displaced dirt in front of her, the power secured in the depths from which it'd come.

Finally able to breathe, she sucked in great lungfuls, her eyes refocusing. The ground she knelt on had been ravaged, grass and flowers uprooted, the plants twisted away in a perfect circle. Rocks were shoved aside, leaving paths through the dirt to new resting places. She'd dropped into a crater, a foot lower than the rest of the forest floor. A haze clouded the air, as if the topsoil still floated. Small pebbles thunked to the ground, gravity taking hold once more. She imagined how much worse it could have been.

Everything fell chillingly quiet.

"Talon?" Her voice shook, uncertainty filling her as she looked beyond her circle of destruction.

Silence.

"Talon?" She rose unsteadily to her feet. Vaguely aware of tears on her cheeks collecting dust, she turned towards the rhythmic thumps of a rock cascading down the branches of a banyan tree.

Twenty yards away, Talon lay sprawled on the ground, as if he'd been struck from behind.

"No, no, no." She ran, nearly tripping in her haste to reach him. Falling to her knees at his side, she dared not touch him as she surveyed his body for injuries.

His clothing remained undisturbed, his features unmarred. Head turned sideways, his eyes were closed, his face peaceful as if he only slept. No blood, no bruising, no burns.

She rolled him onto his back and lowered her ear to his mouth. Her heart pounded, tears racing from her eyes as she tried to listen for breath. Movement tickled her ear, and she pushed away her hair to be certain. He inhaled steadily, and she closed her eyes with a crash of relief. Her muscles lost strength, and she collapsed against his chest, drawing in a shaky breath.

How could I let this happen?

She caressed his face, struggling with what to do. She patted his cheek and shook him, but he didn't respond.

Retrieving a blanket, she used it to drag him home. Her power aided in lifting him to their bed, and she obsessed over positioning pillows underneath his head.

Moving his arms again, finding where she thought they'd be most comfortable, the adrenaline faded. Her stomach contracted into a familiar knot. Leaving him in a hurry, she rushed outside before falling to her knees at the tree line. Her stomach lurched, ejecting the little breakfast she'd eaten.

Dizziness kept her there, the tall trees spinning around her, and she braced herself with a nearby trunk. She'd thought her upset stomach had recovered. Her fears grew as she clutched her middle and forced herself to stand, relying heavily on the tree.

She returned to check on Talon, hoping he'd woken in her absence. But when she brushed aside the curtain of vines at the doorway, her hope vanished.

Amarie's worry intensified as the morning faded into afternoon, and Talon hadn't stirred. His breath maintained a steady pace, but nothing roused him. She tried varying tactics, including scents of mint and eucalyptus. A cold cloth to his forehead. Talking to him, begging him. But nothing worked, and her desperation escalated. She needed a healer, someone she could trust, but her contacts on the island were few.

There may not be anyone here you trust, but perhaps someone he trusts?

During visits to Quel'Nian after Talon's pardon, he'd gestured in the general direction of his old family home.

Amarie flew from the house, ignoring her churning stomach, and pulled herself onto Viento. Bareback, she kicked him in the direction of Talon's eldest sister.

Chapter 10

Lasseth led Kin to a hidden doorway, deep within the complex tunnels of Arboral.

Considering his past as a Shade, how is he comfortable in so much darkness?

Yet, the narrow underground walkways were clearly his domain.

Coming to a dead end, Lasseth approached the wall. He pushed aside a boulder, too easily for it to be real, and revealed an opening into a circular hub of several tunnels.

High ceilings sported grates granting access to sunlight from a busy street above. Pipes rigged beneath the grates caught falling water and debris, guiding it away from the living space below. Wooden beams crisscrossed the wide circular space, decorated with swooping colored sheets.

It didn't seem too unlike any other house, with furniture and a small kitchen, complete with a small aqueduct inlaid within a wall.

The three tunnels open to the space each had a door near the mouth, built of various scavenged materials.

The other four tunnels, including the one they'd entered from, were blocked with rubble.

Lasseth gestured to the musty chairs at the center of the chamber and walked to the kitchen. Reaching up to wooden shelves, he selected jars of various herbs. He set to work with one hand, the other still holding his side, unscrewing lids and combining foul-smelling ingredients.

Kin draped his cloak over a chair facing Lasseth. Sitting as a guest in the old Shade's home sent a chill down his spine. He needed to turn this man over to Uriel. His mother's life depended on it. Stalling to ask questions felt a foolish endeavor, yet Lasseth offered an opportunity he'd likely never get again. He'd promised himself he'd find a way to part from Uriel, despite the desire to protect Amarie.

Ma wants me to find a way out.

"I served Uriel for four years," Lasseth started without Kin having to prompt. He worked a mortar and pestle, grinding his concoction together. "It began when I was twenty. Young, healthy and greedy for power. It ended when I realized I looked like the village elder, my life slipping away from me. I did horrible things during my service. Things I regret and the gods will never forgive me for. The rapid aging stopped when I severed the link between myself and Uriel, but I have no idea how long I'll live." He looked at Kin. "Though your task suggests that it won't matter much longer."

"I don't understand." Kin straightened, shifting to the edge of the chair. "If you aged that fast, I should be dead considering the length of my service."

"Then Uriel discovered an exception to the rules of its power after I abandoned my duty." Lasseth heaved a sigh as he carried the thick paste to a table near Kin. "For your hands." He remained stone-faced before returning to mash more in a fresh bowl.

Kin eyed the goop but recognized the scents as ones he used to promote healing. He hadn't realized how bruised, beaten and scraped his hands were until he looked at them in the dull light. He pulled a waterskin and cloth from within his cloak, proceeding to clean them before applying the medicine. "You're saying something changed in Uriel? Changed how?"

The old Shade gave an amused snort. "Isn't it always changing? Every time it gets bored with a body."

Kin's brow furrowed, and he looked up from his hands.

Lasseth mirrored his expression. "Your confusion tells me Uriel hasn't required a new host since your service began. Even in my short term, it changed bodies three times."

"What?" Kin said with wide eyes. His stomach quaked at the idea of Uriel's face changing. "He's always looked the same. But I don't understand. You make it sound like he isn't a man."

"He's not," Lasseth grumbled. "And its body doesn't belong to it. It consumes and possesses those it chooses as a host."

"So, what is *it*?"

"I don't know." Lasseth lifted the edge of his worn shirt to smear his medicinal creation onto his bruised ribs. He winced, and Kin wondered at the futility of his efforts with what awaited him. "Uriel has never allowed anyone to witness the process, but when I abandoned my service, I'd been in the middle of a political scheme in Feyor. I'd been working to infiltrate the monarchy with the prospect of usurping. The host Uriel chose was an advisor to the throne, and it needed to be a quick transition. It had already burned through the previous host."

Kin's mind spun. Each answer Lasseth provided sprouted several more questions.

"I've had time to contemplate how Uriel's power works, considering the connection I had. The number of Shades Uriel has in service coincides with how fast it burns through hosts. The more Shades, the shorter lifetime of the host. Uriel disposed of multiple Shades shortly after taking control of the body I brought him, leaving only myself and one other because he wanted his new political pawn to last as long as possible." He pulled his shirt back down over his injuries. "Tell me, Kinronsilis. How many Shades serve Uriel now?"

Political pawn? He was preparing to take the throne of Feyor...

Kin tried to process all the information, calculating the years Lasseth spoke about, almost missing the question. His brain throbbed to find the answer. "Twenty-two." He rubbed the ointment into his hands. "Including myself."

Lasseth straightened. "So many?" He chewed his lip, stepping closer to Kin. "Seems impossible. Maintaining eight caused the rapid deterioration of an otherwise healthy host in less than a year. Not to mention, the very same corrosive effects happening to those of us who carried the mark. Very curious indeed. It seems this new host swayed Uriel from his carefully laid plans. Who is it?"

Kin didn't know how to answer the question. He tried to imagine the life his master's body might have had before.

Who was he? Did he have a wife? A family? Or did Uriel destroy that part of him too?

His stomach soured, thinking more on what Lasseth hinted at. Uriel had invaded the Feyor royal family through the acquisition of a political figure. As his mind jumped to foreboding conclusions, his body numbed.

"I don't know who Uriel is now, but what was his original plan?" Kin swallowed the bile rising in his throat.

"Uriel is a fastidious planner." Lasseth sat in the chair opposite Kin. "It often had its hosts planned out generations in advance. It's obsessed with power, whether physical, Art, or political, and would manipulate itself into situations where it would gain the most. Somehow, it acquired access to the Feyorian prince's twin, even though the country had been unaware of your existence. Everything was almost in place for it to transition, but it must have discovered a better option while lurking in the monarchy."

Kin's gut flopped.

Was I meant to be Uriel's host?

Whoever Uriel inhabited now must have had incredible power to sway him from the Feyor throne.

Kin had always suspected nobility, but now wondered if it was more. And considering the change in the drain on both the host and Uriel's Shades, there was certainly more to the host's power.

A pang of unexpected sympathy hit him, and a new question surfaced.

"What happens to his hosts? Do they die when it takes over?" A foolish part of him hoped for respite for the man who'd spared him such a fate, even unknowingly.

Lasseth pursed his lips and shook his head. "They die when the creature is done abusing their bodies. I cannot be certain what fate has befallen the man behind the face it currently wears. Has the host aged or withered at all during your service?"

Kin shook his head.

"Interesting." Lasseth settled back in his chair. "And terrifying. Considering the strength Uriel has now, I fear what it would be like if it gained more, yet I'm certain it's not satisfied."

Kin tried to focus as his mind wandered to Amarie. Talk of power and Uriel's drive to collect it... He'd been terrified for her before, and now...

He would seek her as a host and be unstoppable.

Glancing at the ceiling and the waning light through the grates, he cursed his limited time. Alana would be waiting for him.

"How did you sever your connection? If I go a few days without touching the Art, I feel like I'm dying. Yet you've gone years. How?"

"Oh, it felt like that for a while." Lasseth shrugged. "The drive to take it up is like an itch you can't scratch for years. Even now, I feel it from time to time. The moment you used your Art to stop my dagger was one of those moments I contemplated reaffirming the connection. It hasn't been completely severed but blocked to make access hard enough to encourage me not to take it, and enough to keep Uriel from finding me. Though clearly Alana found another way. That bitch is still playing lap dog to Uriel, huh?"

Kin ignored the question. "How did you block the connection?"

Lasseth gave a wry, knowing smile. "Trying to do it yourself? It's no good, the one who did it for me is gone. She helped me through the first year or so of withdrawals, but she died. She killed herself rather than be taken by the Shades who came for her." Sadness shone in his eyes, a grief Kin recognized. He'd felt it when Amarie died.

"How did she block Uriel's power?"

The old Shade shook his head once. "She was unique. And that got Uriel interested enough to send Shades after her. She had a power unlike anything I've ever seen, and I still struggle to explain it. An ancient power. She's the only Rahn'ka I've ever known to exist."

Kin narrowed his eyes, his heart thudding. "Rahn'ka?"

Lasseth shrugged. "She told me the name stems from the Aueric language. It has something to do with the energies of souls and how it all connects. Never made sense to me. She was zany because of it, all the souls around her chattering in her head. But she reached right into me and found the corruption and bound it up. She said she couldn't remove it, or it'd kill me, so she did what she could, then helped me through the pain that followed."

"What... else could she do?" Kin's mind whirled as he delved into his memories. He experienced a unique power once before while completing a task. Thinking of it suddenly made his stomach flutter. Out of embarrassment, he'd never mentioned his devastating defeat to anyone.

"All sorts of things. It was the most beautiful, yet terrifying Art I'd ever seen. Once I saw her pull a bandit's soul right out of his body. Killed him dead in a breath. A pale, blue and white light shimmering out of him before she let it drop."

It can't be a coincidence. It sounds like what that man in Lazuli tried to do to me.

"And she's the one who separated you from Uriel's power?"

Lasseth frowned but nodded.

Kin didn't have time to consider what it all meant now. "Thank you." He stood. "And I'm truly sorry for what must come next."

Lasseth closed his eyes and settled deeper into his chair. A dry smile played on his lips. "Too much to hope for a little more time?"

Kin glanced up at the fading daylight trickling through the grates and gave a solemn shake of his head.

"Promise me one thing?" Lasseth said, his eyes dark.

Kin hesitated, guessing at what the request might be. He couldn't promise a clean death. During similar tasks, he'd buried the guilt, but this time it stung beyond measure.

Lasseth didn't wait for Kin's response. "Keep what I told you about Uriel secret. I have a feeling it'll be the greatest weapon against him. I pray to the gods you are the right one to pass the knowledge to."

Kin chuckled dryly. "Me too." With a slow inhale, he reached for the power he'd avoided all afternoon.

Lasseth Frey didn't flinch as shadow consumed him.

Unable to take his raven form due to Lasseth's imprisonment amid his shadows, the journey to Uriel would've been tedious without Alana. The minor discomfort of the Art constantly pushing against his soul while joining Lasseth in the blackness was still better than riding behind Alana.

Her mount, a massive, bat-like corrupted with webbed wings, conveyed them all.

Kin shuddered each time he saw the summoned creature, formed of vile energies from the pits of hells mortals were never meant to know. It looked like an odd amalgamation of a leopard, horse and bat with matted auburn fur.

Alana didn't shy away from summoning, despite it being condemned by all practitioners of the Art. Punishable by not only her own people, but by the human nations as well. Corrupted had minds of their own, and rogue monsters who'd slipped their leash killed without prejudice.

Baellgaith, as Alana affectionately called the creature, cooed like a dove whenever she scratched his ears. The bone-rattling sound made Kin's skin crawl, despite not truly having any while in the shadow realm under the creature's beating wings.

When they arrived at the base of the Dykul mountains days later, the moonlight painted the familiar skeletal form of the ruined temple.

Baellgaith's claws bit into the crumbling stone steps, the grating sound rippling through Kin's shadows as he scrambled away. The beast purred at Alana as she whispered instructions.

Black tendrils stretched outward, carrying Kin and his prisoner towards the front doorway. Kin focused his power, swelling into his human shape as the corrupted leapt away with cat-like grace, vanishing into the overgrowth.

The darkness surrounding Kin flicked away like burned leaves. He left Lasseth in the shadow, trapped at the bottom of his cloak. Without looking at Alana, he climbed the entry stairs and pushed through the crooked doorway.

Uriel waited, the sputtering bonfire glowing behind him. His shadow danced on the worn marble, cracked by the passage of forgotten time.

Kin performed the familiar routine, despite the new shudder of fear down his spine. His master was a creature of more faces than he'd ever thought. He studied the features of the man who'd tortured him, trying to imagine who he might have been before. For a horrible moment, he saw himself standing in the man's place, unable to control any of his own actions.

Coming to a stop midway to the altar, Kin released Lasseth, who fell from shadow and hit the ground with a grunt.

Lasseth stubbornly pushed himself to his feet. He didn't turn to Kin before confidently walking the remaining length of the temple towards the creature he, too, had called master.

"Lasseth." Uriel's shadows twitched. "It's been too long."

"Get it over with, you fiend," Lasseth growled, earning a flash of anger from the master's eyes.

Black swelled like a wave, knocking Lasseth forward. He hit the ground, knees striking the cold floor with a pained exhale of breath. Lashing vines flowed up his body, wrapping around his neck.

"I don't wish to rush this." Uriel sauntered down the steps.

Lasseth's back arched, Uriel's power forcing his head back.

"Though." Uriel paused, contemplating Kin with a curious glance. "I have other business to attend to first." With the twist of his hand, the writhing shadows swallowed Lasseth, dragging him into their depths as if he'd never been.

"My task is complete." Kin strode towards his master. He averted his gaze with a bow.

"Yes." Uriel hissed, twisting his bracers as if they were the source of his irritation. "So, you shall have another."

Kin's chest tightened at the idea, even if expected.

The dulcet patter of boots echoed as Alana entered from behind, but Kin didn't turn to look at her. He could imagine the smug expression on her face, her arms crossed over her burgundy vest.

"Speak it, and it will be done, Master." Kin bowed his head lower, hoping it would distract from his clipped words.

Uriel hummed and rocked back on his heels as he locked his arms behind his back. "I'm certain it will be." He paused. "You will bring me the Berylian Key."

Kin wavered as if the words physically struck him, and he sucked in a breath to stabilize himself. But his lungs wouldn't work. All breathing failed. He was suddenly grateful his eyes were locked on the ground and prayed the master wouldn't see his horror.

"Do you understand the task before you, Kinronsilis Lazorus?" Uriel's tone darkened.

"No," Kin stuttered, trying to regain his composure. He wanted nothing to do with the Berylian Key, for it only pointed him in one direction. "Do you refer to a Berylian Key *shard*, Master?" He forced his gaze up, pushing his fear from it. "Such as was my task before?"

"No." Uriel's shoulders tensed. "I mean *the* Berylian Key. I have been granted the knowledge that gathering the shards has been a fool's errand. The Key is already whole. You will bring it to me."

It.

Kin clung to the distinction. Uriel didn't know. He didn't understand the Key was a human. He didn't know that it was Amarie.

Kin furrowed his brow in feigned confusion, using it to hide his tumultuous emotions. He wanted to refuse. Say no and force Uriel to kill him for defiance. Kin was tired of the games, but there was still the matter of his mother.

He turned to catch Alana in his peripheral vision, then nodded and bowed again. "I understand my task, Master. It will be done." The words stung like acid on his tongue.

An eruption of pain ran down his forearm, and he tugged his sleeve away from the tattoo. He glared at the new solid triangle close to the bend of his elbow.

"I believe you'll enjoy this new power I'm giving you. It was one of Trist's favorites."

Kin rubbed at the ink, avoiding his master's eyes.

"Alana will continue to monitor your progress." Uriel's tone shifted to declare a change of subject. "Until I'm satisfied that you are performing as expected."

Kin restrained the growl in his chest. Alana's hovering would make it far more difficult to avoid the task and begin his pursuit of escaping Uriel's power.

"It will be done, Master." Alana stepped forward to stand beside him. "It's appropriate, Kinronsilis, that I inform you of a connection we're already aware of between yourself and the Key."

His heart stopped as he turned to Alana.

"Your dead lover." She smirked. "Amarie."

"What?" Kin didn't have to feign surprise due to merely hearing her name aloud.

"Don't pretend to be naive, you must have suspected something with the number of shards the girl carried." Alana crossed closer to the altar steps.

"What are you suggesting?" Kin glowered. "Why would she have shards if she already possessed the Key?"

"Deception. To hide the truth." Alana toyed idly with the bottom of her blood-red shirt protruding from under her black vest. "If no one could assemble the shards to find out they did nothing, the pointless task of searching for the pieces would forever continue."

Kin's mind sought for options to spin anything in his favor. "If that's true, then all of this could be done if you hadn't interfered in my business and pushed Amarie away. I might have found the truth and the Berylian Key."

Alana's eyes flashed as Uriel's attention turned to her. He seemed amused by the heated argument, rather than concerned.

"What of Trist?" Kin asked before Alana could interject. "She was the last to see the girl alive."

"Dead." Uriel shrugged. "It's unclear whether she obtained the Key before perishing so thoughtlessly."

"It seems death follows this Key wherever it goes, then." Kin swallowed. "I'll relieve the power of the Key from whoever holds it."

"Just bring it before me." Uriel sighed in irritation. "I tire of your ineptitude. I hope you can prove Alana's suspicions wrong." He turned and walked into the shadowed archway behind the bonfire, leaving Kin to face Alana alone.

Her emerald eyes did nothing to hide her fury. "You dare attempt to blame your inability to complete a task on me again and—"

"You'll what, Alana? Haven't you already done enough? Lasseth Frey will receive *justice*. What more could you possibly want?"

She pursed her lips and stalked closer. A clawed hand reached up and ruby painted nails bit into his chin, forcing him to bend his head towards hers. "Obedience."

Despite every inclination, he didn't pull away. He held her gaze, meeting it with a rage of his own. The entirety of his suffering belonged to her. She served Uriel and perpetrated the evils she did. Kin glared into eyes that rejoiced in the wickedness they saw.

Alana held him strong, silence heavy between them. Both obstinately waited for the other to give in.

She backed down first, to Kin's surprise, blinking before giving him a sickening smile. Still holding him tight, she placed a kiss on his lips.

Grabbing her wrist, he yanked her hand from his jaw and stepped away. The feeling of her mouth nauseated him, bringing back the nightmare of when she'd controlled his will in his estate's garden.

"Oops." Alana grinned as she lowered her hand. "I thought you might appreciate the comfort, my Sae'quonei." She pouted, pushing past him to follow Uriel. "It's never easy when a boy loses his mother."

Eyes widening, Kin stopped breathing. The pounding of his heart overtook his senses, the outer rim of his vision blurring. "What?"

"She died the moment she drank her beloved white wine." Alana glanced back at him over her shoulder, a wicked smile on her lips. "I'm sure it's been days now. You should see your father, but don't take too long. You have a task to complete."

Kin's throat seized, and he closed his eyes.

Ma.

His knees gave out, striking the ground with a thud.

Chapter 11

Honeysuckle and jasmine vines stretched across the ceiling above Talon. The tiny bud of an unborn flower became his guide from the darkness. Everything else blurred around the single blossom and he attempted to blink away the haze. Failing, he closed his eyes again to ease his throbbing head. A groan rumbled in his throat as his body roused.

All of him hurt. Every muscle and bone, and his skin felt white hot.

Something cool touched his forehead, and he tried to focus on the relief it brought to banish the pain. Water dripped down his temples. The low hum in his ears altered to indiscernible female voices.

Light flickered across the room, the glow passing over his eyelids. A melodic voice whispered sweetly, and soft hands touched his arm.

A jumble of images pervaded his attempts to remember. Flashes of the colorful, magnificent power responsible for disrupting his own. For knocking him out cold. It'd left an imprint on his soul. The sensation reminded him of Amarie, of her power caressing his when they made love.

Amarie had appeared shaken that morning, affected by her dream. And despite her denial, she'd felt ill for weeks. Hardly eating since his pardon and lethargic. Regardless, he pushed her during their training. The Art wouldn't wait for her to feel better or be in the right mood. He hadn't restrained himself, hoping she'd developed enough to handle his distraction attempts.

The moment she grasped too much, her power flooded the air,

seeking an escape. He ran, just as he promised he would, but didn't get far enough to stop the Berylian Key from using him like a lightning rod.

I should be dead.

A spark of surprise stirred with the recognition.

She regained control.

An accomplishment on its own.

His headache seemed like a negligible price. It could have been far worse. As he breathed deeply, he focused on each of his limbs to seek damage but found nothing but an expected amount of soreness.

"Talon..." Amarie's voice penetrated his mind. "Is he awake?"

"He's awake," a second voice confirmed.

"More aptly... he's alive." Talon's tongue stuck to the roof of his mouth. He tried to open his eyes and lift his head, but everything spun. He quickly shut them again and flopped back onto his pillow with a groan.

Amarie whimpered, and the grip on his arm tightened as she collapsed against his chest.

"I'll give you a moment alone." Kalstacia's voice. The cloth remained, but the pressure behind it disappeared and the light on his lids swayed again as she exited the room.

Talon ran his hand through Amarie's loose hair, her head rising with his chest as he inhaled deeply. He touched the wet cloth with his other hand, lavishing in the relief it brought to his pounding skull.

Amarie lifted her chin, though her touch on his arm didn't leave. She pressed a cup to his lower lip, encouraging him to sit up just enough. "Drink."

Closing his lips on the rim, Talon obeyed. The water soothed his parched throat. "How long?"

"A day." She set the cup aside. "It happened yesterday. I'm sorry."

Talon could tell she wanted to keep talking but closed his hand on hers to stop her. "You don't need to apologize." He examined her bloodshot gaze, deep and raging, like the sea. He brushed her cheek, trying to catch the tears that had already dried.

"Amarie, I'm fine. There's nothing to be sorry for. You probably saved me," he whispered, caressing her jaw with his thumb. "You regained control, didn't you?"

Her jaw flexed, but she nodded as her hand slid to his chest.

Talon let a little sound of satisfaction leave his lips as he replaced his head atop the pillows. "See." He patted the top of her hand before he lifted it to his lips. "Just a few bruises is all."

Amarie scowled, but her chin quivered. "I thought you were dead."

"But I'm not." Talon squeezed her hand. "And we both knew the risk when I agreed to teach you. *I* know the risk. Regardless of what could've happened, it wouldn't have been your fault. But it doesn't—"

Her lips interrupted his words with a kiss, and his mouth instantly responded. The affection alone had the power to banish all his pain.

The clearing of a throat came from the doorway, and Amarie's lips left his barren, prompting his eyes to open.

Kalstacia stood between parted vines, holding a steaming bowl. A strange smile graced her features, which might have been mistaken for a placid look of indifference, but Talon knew better. "Apologies. I thought since you were awake, you should eat something, sae'moroq." She carried the soup to the bedside table.

"Sae'moroq? Little..." Amarie looked at Kalstacia, head tilted.

"Brother."

Talon eyed his sister, then the soup, and his stomach growled. Taking hold of Amarie's hand before she could pull it away, he tried to sit up.

Amarie gripped tighter and helped him.

Grateful for not needing to ask, he slid back to lean against the wall at the head of the bed.

Kalstacia offered him the bowl, forcing him to let go of Amarie. "Would you like me to heal your bruises?" This routine between them was thoroughly practiced. She asked even though she knew the answer, which was why he suspected the soup was already full of natural healing ingredients.

"That's not necessary." Talon gave her a half-smile. "I'll heal with time."

She nodded, a deeper conversation taking place between them.

Talon had an adverse reaction to the Art when it involved healing. It would work, but his body paid the cost in stomach-shattering pain and nausea. It'd initiated the belief that Talon was an odrak.

"Perhaps a slight energy boost, instead?" A look of uncertainty played on Amarie's face, tainted with a hint of fear. Not of her Art, but of the rejection she likely expected from him.

His instinct was to deny it. The Berylian Key's power had caused his blackout. Logically, it seemed unwise to expose himself to it again. But the look in Amarie's eyes fueled a more substantial desire that banished his logic. Instead, he smiled and nodded.

She needs to know I'm not afraid of her.

With a subtle movement, she touched the side of his leg. Her furrowed brows relaxed, and she poured energy into his body. It buzzed under his skin, seeping through his already charged veins. Unable to prohibit it, he gasped, blinking rapidly as the pain in his body subsided. The bruises didn't heal, but he became less aware of them as his body's natural energy stores filled. And he remained conscious, proving his concerns frivolous.

Kalstacia narrowed her eyes as she stood beside the bed.

Renewed, he straightened without help and dug into his food. It warmed him and quieted his stomach.

Amarie's gaze flitted to the bowl of vegetable soup and then back to Talon's face. She smiled and squeezed near his knee where her hand still lingered. "I think I'll get something to eat myself."

Eager to keep her near, Talon offered his bowl. The idea of her eating thrilled him. "We can share?"

Her smile faltered, and her nose wrinkled ever so slightly. She shook her head with a smile. "I need to feed the horses first. I'll be back soon, I promise." As she rose from their bed, she bent over to kiss his forehead.

He smiled despite his disappointment, and she disappeared into the front room. Taking another spoonful of soup, he glanced at Kalstacia, who watched him with a patient look and her arms crossed.

"That wasn't the way I expected to meet the girl responsible for our return home." Kalstacia switched to Aueric, forcing Talon's mind to struggle to keep up for a moment. "Quite inconsiderate of you."

Talon scoffed, nearly choking on a bit of carrot before he swallowed. "My mistake. I'll strive to remain conscious in the future."

"What is she?"

Talon cringed at her directness. Gulping down his bite, he turned to his sister and set aside the nearly empty bowl. "I believe you mean *who*. She's still a person."

"Typically, I'd agree." Kalstacia glanced at the doorway. "Though I've never experienced power of that magnitude in any single living being. Did you know it manifests as heatless flames when she's emotionally distraught? It's fascinating."

"Could you stop talking about her as if she's one of your little experiments in the Menders' Guild?" Talon growled. "Yes, I know. And I find it wholly un-fascinating and entirely heart-wrenching."

Kalstacia blew out a sighing laugh. "You were always the most empathetic of us Di'Terians. Comes with being the youngest, I suppose. Exposed too young to the human world and all their cares."

Talon shook his head again and ran his hand through his hair. "Unlike you, I don't see empathy as a weakness."

"No, it's always been your strength."

Silence grew between them.

Kalstacia patiently waited with her arms folded loosely against the thin material of her dress, the sun catching the silver menders' necklace.

"It's not my place to tell you." Talon broke the silence. "Amarie is entitled to her secrets, as much as anyone else. If you wish to know, you can ask her yourself. Just remember, she's a person, not an experiment."

She lifted her hands in mock surrender.

"I was hoping to ask you something," Talon continued, eyeing the door to ensure Amarie hadn't returned.

Kalstacia's brow knitted, and she followed his gaze. "What is it?"

"I'd appreciate it if you'd speak with her. She's ill, but she won't talk to me about it. Perhaps she would speak to you as a mender, and you could help?"

"I thought you said she's entitled to her secrets?"

Talon clenched his jaw.

Kalstacia smirked. "If she's resistant to tell you, I doubt she'll be forthcoming with me. But I'll try. Because of what she has done for us. And because of who she is to you. Your niané."

Talon's cheeks flushed. He hadn't used the Aueric word for love with Amarie. Not aloud. Niané surpassed love, proclaiming the merging of two souls, two pieces unable to exist without the other. And when Kalstacia spoke it, Talon couldn't deny how perfectly it resounded in his heart.

"Thank you, Kalstacia." Talon took her hand.

"Don't thank me yet." Kalstacia patted his knuckles. "I have some questions for you too. Ones I don't think you'll like." Talon frowned, but she continued. "I've had time to think further on the events you told me of. The truth of our parents and Alana's treachery. I imagine she'll be upset when she finds out about our pardon, which they have denied her."

Talon winced at the thought of his older sister. He rocked from the bed to his feet, stalking away from Kalstacia, but her questions followed him.

"Does Alana know about Amarie?"

"Why would that matter?" Talon stopped, his mind still groggy despite Amarie's gifted energy.

"It matters quite a bit." Kalstacia placed a hand on her hip. "Alana is a vengeful creature. If she discovers that Amarie played a part in our return home, she might seek her out. Not to mention, you care for the girl. I doubt a woman who murdered her own parents would hesitate in manipulating your lover against you. Or worse."

Talon chewed his lip. Kalstacia wasn't wrong. And the situation put Amarie in an entirely different dangerous situation than Kin's master. Alana could seek her for her own means, regardless of Uriel's bidding. And Alana could return to Eralas as easily as Talon had. If she avoided capture, even just for days, she'd have plenty of time to wreak irreparable damage.

"When did you last see Alana?" Kalstacia interrupted Talon's chain of thoughts.

"A few months ago. But she probably thinks Amarie is dead."

"Then pray it remains that way," Kalstacia muttered. "I don't want to imagine what might happen if Alana found out, especially considering the resources she's amassed in the last fifty years. She's only fallen deeper into darkness. Did you know she sent corrupted with messages to me? Little vulgar imps with bat wings, as if she enjoys tormenting me with the constant reminder of the Art responsible for banishing us all."

Talon could only nod. He received messages in the same manner, from various ingvalds. Out of brotherly loyalty, he'd always answered. Alana never failed to find him, no matter how far he was from her. She'd once sent an ingvald to the furthest northern reaches of Isalica to urge him back from where he'd sought solitude.

What would happen if she found me now? And with Amarie?

His stomach sank faster than an iron anchor in the sea.

"We'll talk more on this later." Talon waved a hand, eager to end the conversation that was making him wish he hadn't eaten. "When I've had more time to recover and think on it."

Kalstacia watched him for a moment, then sighed and nodded. "Very well."

"Speak to Amarie? Please."

Kalstacia nodded and patted her brother on the shoulder. Without another word, she slipped through the doorway of the forest dwelling, leaving Talon alone with his thoughts.

 Chapter 12

Amarie wished she could curl up in bed with Talon and share the meal, but she needed fresh air. The fragrant soup hit all the wrong notes, further aggravated by the guilt weighing within her.

Talon will enjoy the time to talk with his sister, anyway.

Stroking Viento's neck after filling his trough, her eyes lingered on the fine leatherwork of his new bridle. She smiled half-heartedly. If only her life with Talon could be simple.

Her stomach calmed, but she didn't dare re-enter the house. She feared Talon asking more questions about the lack of appetite she hardly wanted to think about. Her suspicions about the cause only led to one incurable conclusion.

Kalstacia emerged from the front door of the home, drawing Amarie's attention.

"How is he?" Amarie dusted her hands off on her breeches.

"He's fine." Kalstacia approached the roomy paddock fence. "Already aware enough to be worried about you."

Amarie frowned and shook her head with a scoff. "He'll spend the better part of the next few days trying to tell me this wasn't my fault."

"While I don't understand what happened, I trust what my brother says." Kalstacia came to stand beside Amarie. "Would you like to walk with me?" Her gentle tone almost masked the underlying insistence.

Surprised, Amarie shrugged and nodded. "All right." Turning to walk beside the auer, she fell quiet until they entered the tree line. "Is something on your mind?"

"Not on *my* mind, particularly. Other than to thank you properly for what you've granted me. You didn't need to include me in your bargain with the council."

Amarie shook her head. "It didn't seem right to absolve Talon of guilt and not his more innocent sister. I was just trying to do the right thing. I'm grateful the council listened to me."

"As am I. The *right thing* is something so few think of. I'm ashamed to admit that I've rarely seen it prioritized."

Amarie's smile widened, and she recalled Talon once having a similar outlook on good deeds. "Your brother has embraced it." She looked at Kalstacia. "He helped save several human lives from a pack of grygurr in Aidensar."

Kalstacia raised a thin raven eyebrow. "Now that doesn't sound particularly like my brother. Empathetic, yes, but foolish enough to risk unnecessarily? No. Perhaps his company at the time inspired him?"

Amarie's cheeks heated, and she laughed. "It's possible, I suppose."

"Talon told me that if I hoped to learn more about your power, I needed to ask you directly." Kalstacia motioned vaguely with her hand. "While I'm curious, I don't need to know. As it would feel like I'm unfairly questioning the person who granted me the ability to return home. I merely thought you should know we discussed it."

Amarie paused before responding. The Council of Elders knew who she was, and she suspected Kalstacia would keep the secret as adamantly as the elders. "I'm not sure how familiar you are with history." She chewed on her bottom lip. "Have you heard of the Berylian Key?" Confiding in someone still made her nervous, but sharing the secret with Kalstacia felt right.

"I have." Kalstacia's brows furrowed for a moment, and she turned to look Amarie up and down. "Forgive me, but you—as in your soul and being, and not a mythical object of stone—are the Berylian Key?"

Amarie's eyes widened at the fast conclusion. "I am." She briefly allowed the energy within her to color her irises with the vibrant tones of beryl. "I was born with the ability to house the power, as my mother was."

Kalstacia made an interested sound and scratched her jaw. "I suppose we have plenty of time to discuss it, if you don't mind my curiosity? Part of my duties in the Menders' Guild is as a librarian of sorts, and I've always been fascinated with the origins of the different aspects of the Art."

Her casual attitude had a calming effect, and Amarie smiled. "I don't mind. I've always wanted to learn more about it myself. I even stole the first edition of an Aueric text from Capul awhile back, hoping it held insight to my family."

Kalstacia laughed, covering her mouth with her hand. "That was you? I was frustrated when I arrived at the Great Library this past summer to discover security measures had been increased because of a theft. I had to redo all that tedious paperwork."

Amarie gave a sheepish cringe. Thoughts of her partner in crime that day dared to haunt her, but she shook her head to refocus. "Sorry about that." She chuckled. "I still have it. Would you like it?"

"I'd like to read it, if you're willing to part with it. Perhaps we can assist each other. I don't have to fill out quite as many forms to access our libraries in Quel'Nian." She turned more directly towards Amarie but kept a respectful distance.

Amarie tilted her head as Kalstacia continued.

"I have something else to inquire about. Though, this comes at the request of my brother." She clasped her hands in front of her. "He's concerned you haven't been feeling well and may be trying to conceal the symptoms from him. If I may be so bold, I'm an accomplished healer and would be more than happy to offer my care to you. I'm not sure the extent of your illness, as I don't delve without permission..."

Amarie nodded, not surprised at Talon's concern, but surprised he'd send his sister. Though, for some reason, Kalstacia was easier to talk to, and she silently commended his decision. The cloud of Kalstacia's Art hovered about her, encouraging peace.

Heaving a deep breath, Amarie looked down at her boots. "I appreciate the offer, but I suspect my ailment isn't something you can help me with."

Kalstacia frowned. She drew up Amarie's left hand into both of hers with a reassuring touch. "Amarie. My offer of assistance extends beyond curing an illness. I seek to comfort a woman I now consider a sister. May I at least confirm what you suspect? Just in case you're wrong and I could help?"

Amarie conceded with a smile. The auer's words resounded in her heart. A sister. She wondered how long that thought would last once the truth emerged.

Regardless, she nodded and tried to ignore the knot in her stomach. "I'll gladly take the comfort, if nothing else. And I'd appreciate the confirmation. You have my permission to *delve*."

Kalstacia remained intent in their exchange of eye contact, as if confirming Amarie's desires once more. Keeping her hands tight on Amarie's, she bowed her head, closing her bright green eyes. A whisper of Kalstacia's Art pressed against Amarie, flowing through her like a tickle, but nothing more. The process took only a few breaths, Kalstacia's steady exhales ebbing with the flow of her power before it withdrew, like a warm blanket being pulled away.

With a breath, Kalstacia slipped her hands from Amarie. Their eyes met, and Kalstacia's softened. "I see what you mean." She kept her tone level. "There'd be substantial pain, but if you want me—"

"No." Amarie forced a smile. "I think in this case, your comfort and... discretion, is all I need."

Kalstacia's brow furrowed, but she forced a sad smile as it relaxed. "I understand. My offer for what comfort I can provide still stands. But you know... you must tell him at some point."

"I will. I promise."

Just not yet.

They returned to the house in silence, and Kalstacia left Amarie alone outside to bid farewell to her brother before returning home. When she exited, she held the leather-bound book Amarie had stolen from the Great Library under her arm, likely having asked Talon for it. She crossed back to Amarie and gave her a firm hug. "Things will work out as they must, and I will visit again soon."

Amarie answered with a tight smile and a nod of her head. Despite her support, she still felt relieved when Kalstacia and her horse disappeared among the trees.

The aroma of the soup had dissipated within the front room when she checked on Talon. Its pungent scent replaced by brewing mint and ginger tea.

In Talon's usual tradition, two cups sat side by side on the table. Wafts of steam rose from their ceramic rims. She spied him through the doorway to their room, the vines draped to the side. He'd changed into clean clothing, his arms exposed, and his hair fixed in a low ponytail.

A smile warmed his freshly shaven face as he finished folding the blanket at the foot of their bed, then crossed through the doorway to meet her. "I made you some tea. Thought you might enjoy it after all the excitement today."

"Thank you" She tore off a hunk of bread from the loaf on the counter before choosing a mug. "How are you feeling?" She raised the mug, inhaling while she chewed a bite of bread. It smelled good and settled her insides.

"Perfect, honestly." Taking his tea to the other side of the room, Talon sat in a low, cushioned chair. He gestured to the one beside him.

She happily dropped into the other seat, despite her preference to climb onto his lap.

"I feel like nothing even happened," Talon continued. "My body likely just needed to naturally recover from the shock to my energy pool. I'd be ready to get right back to training if that was something you desired, but I think it'd be better if we both take the day off."

Amarie smiled meekly and nodded. "Of course." She pulled her ankles up to sit cross-legged. As much as she wanted to be near him, Kalstacia's new knowledge of her inner plight made her worries more tangible. Her thoughts became haunted, and her attention to the conversation waned.

Turning from his gaze, she stared out the open window. She contemplated how she'd ruin the bliss of their life together by sharing the truth. It wasn't fair, and he'd suffer because of it. It'd be better to tell him, but a selfish part of her wanted to prolong their happiness as long as she could.

Gradual awareness of Talon's focus on her interrupted her thoughts. His brow furrowed in its usual contemplative way. Silences were not unusual, though banter served a more common filler of the void. His head tilted as he cradled his mug of tea.

A strange tingling passed through her insides.

Does he know the truth already?

The slight frown suggested he did.

"Would you be up for a ride?" Some fresh air would distract her from her thoughts, and it might be good for him.

"Of course." The odd look on Talon's face didn't change, and he didn't move from his spot, despite a longer silence settling in.

Heaving a deep breath, he rubbed his jaw. "Amarie, you know I'm not one to pry, but I can't bury this any longer. Something is wrong, but I'm not sure why you won't speak to me about it. A ride is merely another distraction from whatever is bothering you."

Amarie broke their eye contact, disappointed, but not surprised that her attempt failed. Lying to him felt worse than the truth. "Something *is* wrong. And the ride is just a distraction."

Talon set aside his tea. Standing, he stepped torturously close to her and knelt on the ground, placing his hand on her knee. "I'd hoped you'd know by now, my araleinya, that you can tell me anything. Regardless of what it is, I'll still be here. I'll still love you. I doubt even the gods could change that now." He lovingly pinched her chin, and it made her eyes burn.

He didn't know what he was saying, and his adamancy only made it more difficult. She didn't dare look at him, wishing for one more untainted moment or kiss.

She closed her eyes and shook her head. "You don't understand." She finally looked at him. "Can't I just have another day?"

Talon pursed his lips, and something in his eyes she'd rarely seen directed at her before surfaced. Impatience. "Just tell me. Perhaps I can help. One day sooner I could assuage all this fear and worry that you're bottling up." He squeezed her knee. "Let me help."

"You can't help."

"What are you so afraid of?"

She stared at him, silently begging him to let it go.

He let out a sigh and shook his head. Rocking back onto his heels, he stood and rubbed his chin. He paced away before turning back again, his jaw set. "I see little point in giving it another day as I've already given it too many. And each seems to get progressively worse for you. Your fear of the secret, whatever it is, may be doing worse damage than whatever's wrong."

Urging her stomach to settle as anxiety bubbled within her, Amarie stood and set her cup down on the window ledge. Reluctantly, she faced him, balking at the undercurrent of anger in his gaze. It was so jarring she felt lightheaded.

"I need some air," she whispered.

She couldn't get past him before his hand closed firmly on her arm, turning her towards him. Talon stepped into her before she had a moment to react. Gripping her waist, he heatedly took her lips with his. The kiss came hard and sudden. Urgent and pleading. As unexpected as it was, Amarie's lips returned it. It was possibly the last time he'd kiss her. She wasn't about to resist.

The kiss renewed, and she wished it wouldn't end. When Talon drew it to a close, his worried eyes opened to meet hers.

Amarie steeled herself as she dared one last request. "Will you say it again?" Her eyes burned. "That you love me?"

"Amarie," he whispered in a sad tone, tracing a line with his finger across her jaw. "Of course I love you. You are my niané." His mouth perfectly formed the last word, playing off his tongue and setting her soul afire.

He'd never used the powerful Aueric epithet before, and amid the flames, her heart shattered to consider he'd never say it again.

Standing in his arms, the final barricades of her will crumbled. "I'm pregnant."

The words rolled out with regret, and she struggled to maintain her gaze on his.

Undeniable shock clouded his eyes. They seemed to flicker through emotions, all encapsulated in the minute dilation of his small pupil and swirl of spring greens. His grip loosened, but he didn't part from her.

"Oh, my araleinya." Talon's demeanor settled, and he brushed a strand of hair behind her ear. "Why were you so afraid to tell me?"

His reaction wasn't what she expected, and doubt rose within her.
He doesn't understand.

"Because... My symptoms began while you were being held at the Sanctum of Law."

The timing. She needed him to understand the timing.

Talon still didn't draw from her, which made the feeling in her worse. He had to realize the truth, yet his expression hardly changed. "I understand." His tone held a somber quality, but he tightened his embrace around her waist.

Wetness pooled on her lower eyelids. "You're not... upset?"

Talon furrowed his brow. "Why would I be upset?" His voice sounded raw. "You didn't know when we first grew close. And I'm fully aware of your previous relationship. A new life is something that should be celebrated, even in less than ideal circumstances. It doesn't matter to me who may or may not be the true father, only the mother." He brushed away the tears racing down her cheek and kissed the hot trails.

Her heart swelled, beating furiously in her ears.

"I'm only upset *for* you, not at you. There are bound to be complications because of the child's father and who he still serves." Talon's hand slipped down to touch her abdomen.

Amarie's mind flashed back to her dream, when Kin's hand had pressed to her stomach, and she squeezed her eyes closed. When she opened them, she held Talon tighter. "He can never know."

"No." Talon kissed her forehead. "He can't."

Amarie let out an exhale and relaxed in his arms, letting her head rest on his shoulder with her nose touching his neck. "I thought I'd lose you." A part of her still believed this would be the end of them. She hoped he'd be beside her in the morning, after he had time to process the information.

"Not because of this. I wish you'd told me sooner. I would've already been running into Quel'Nian for all those things you might crave. Assuming that's not a midwife's tale and happens." Talon eyed her playfully as he tilted his head.

She couldn't help but smile and shrugged. "So far, all I can say is there's a long list of things I *can't* eat. Or smell. Perhaps desiring food comes later. I should've told you."

"I can't imagine believing the way you did." He pulled from her but kept his hands on her shoulders. "I need time to process everything that will arise with the arrival of a baby, but my love for you will not waver. You are still my niané. My araleinya."

Her throat tightened as she gazed at his face, and she nodded slowly. "Remind me again tomorrow?" The corners of her mouth twitched.

"And perhaps the day after that, as well?" Talon teased back, and she nodded vigorously. He laughed and brought her chin up so he could meet her lips once more. The kiss began slowly, drawing a sigh from her as he moved into her.

"I'll do all I can to constantly remind you," Talon whispered between kisses. The words buzzed in her mind, making her blood heat.

"Then I'll do my best to be forgetful." She returned her lips to his. With a steadying breath, she enveloped him within her aura.

Chapter 13

Summer, 2611 R.T.

Talon stepped from their bedroom into the kitchen, greeted by the vibrant steel-blue eyes of their daughter.

The little girl smiled at him over her mother's shoulder, giggling as Amarie walked about the front room. An Aueric children's song came from Amarie's mouth, bringing squeals of delight from the baby.

Talon's mother used to sing the same tune.

He felt lighter, the burdens from his life lifted from his shoulders.

Approaching behind Amarie, he wrapped his arms around her. Peering down at the baby felt right, despite not being her blood father.

Kin would have been ecstatic with the news of a daughter. In his absence, Talon stepped into his friend's place as best as he could. Amarie and her child needed to remain a secret to be safe. The fate of the Berylian Key depended on them.

Amarie hummed as Talon kissed her jaw.

Chubby little arms reached towards him with anxious coos.

"She missed you." Amarie turned, passing the infant to Talon.

He lifted her to his hip, admiring the baby's strength and ability to support her own head.

How did she grow so fast?

Although her eyes matched Kin's, they were innocent of her father's sins. She nestled against his chest, burying her face, and his heart thudded. He loved this child more than he imagined possible and kissed her forehead as she slapped his chest.

"How precious."

Talon didn't recognize the voice. It whispered through the tune that Amarie still hummed as she went about tidying their home. Amarie didn't react, and Talon's brow furrowed, his body tense. He tightened his hold on his daughter, hugging her closer to his chest.

"Talon?" Amarie tilted her head at him, eyes flitting to her fussing child.

Talon looked past Amarie, searching the shadows for the source of what he'd heard, but saw nothing. He shook his head, forcing himself to relax. "Sorry."

When the baby calmed, Amarie resumed her humming, walking towards the washbasin. As she passed by the front doorway, Talon caught a hint of movement.

His heart leapt. "Amarie!"

The figure in the doorway surged inside, darting behind Amarie. Hands gripped either side of her head, and before she could react, they jerked her neck at an unnatural angle. A sickening crack echoed through the small space, and the hands released her.

Limp, Amarie collapsed with a thump, her lifeless eyes still locked on Talon.

Talon gasped, claws raking at his heart. He froze when acid green eyes looked at him from under the hood of the cloaked figure. The hands that had broken Amarie's neck lifted to lower the hood, and white teeth gleamed in a menacing smile.

"Surprise. Miss me, brother?" Alana nudged Amarie's body with her boot and frowned. "I'd expected that to be a little more climactic."

The kick forced Amarie's cold blue eyes upward. A glimmer of power flashed within them.

A light brightened, blinking throughout the room, and power pressed against him. Leaving Amarie, it entered the new host in Talon's arms.

His daughter screamed, deafening in his ears, and blue flames erupted. The fire burned, unlike it had with Amarie, but he couldn't move. It scorched his skin and his cries melded with his child's as he fell to his knees.

White and vivid blue encompassed everything, and he fought the instinct to release the baby. He clung to the pain as it washed through him, trying to look at Amarie.

The weight lifted from his arms, the pain vanishing with it. The ring in his ears faded to a low buzz as he gripped at the ground. Forcing his eyes open, he blinked away the blur of tears, and looked at Alana.

The baby tugged on her long black hair, kicking against a blood red dress as she whimpered. The child quieted, entranced when Alana wove a wisp of shadow.

"Alana." Talon fought for breath. "Don't."

"I never thought you so naive." Alana laughed as the child reached to touch the shadow.

Her steel-blue eyes flecked with pinks and purples.

"Did you think you'd be able to hide from me forever? We're blood." Alana turned her palm to offer a glob of writhing shadow to the child, who grasped at it.

Talon watched in horror as the blackness consumed the baby's arm, but she calmly watched it crawl higher.

"I'll always be able to find you. And you've proven to be Uriel's most effective tool without even knowing it. Thank you."

In the time it took Talon to blink away the hot tears streaming down his face, the child disappeared into shadow. His body gave way, collapsing and curling in on itself.

Alana's nails scraped on his back, entwining within his hair, and he met her gaze once more.

Her eyes were nothing but black, fully consumed by the darkness within her. "I couldn't have done this without you," she purred, then shoved him to the ground.

Talon gasped, jerking awake. His chest ached as he sat upright, sweat beading across his forehead.

A hand touched his, and Amarie sat up next to him. "It's all right," she whispered and kissed his shoulder. "You were dreaming."

Talon closed his eyes, slowly exhaling to banish the tears forming.

Amarie pulled him into her, his hand resting on her growing belly. A reassuring kick fluttered under his palm, as if the child within sought to comfort him as well.

He let out a sigh as he kissed Amarie's temple. "I'm sorry." His skin still burned from the Berylian Key's flames in his dream.

Amarie caught his lips with hers. "Shh," she murmured, guiding him with her to lay back down on his side, facing her.

Talon curled his arm around her, drawing her against his chest. He used the rhythm of her breath to help him set a pace for his.

"Do you want to tell me about it?" Her voice was soft on the night air, and her lips grazed his neck.

"I don't know if it would help." Talon hadn't told Amarie about Alana's uncanny ability to find him. Perhaps his subconscious was telling him it was time. "It just felt... real." The scent of her hair granted him some comfort.

Moving away just enough to see his face, Amarie lifted a hand to trace his jaw. "It wasn't real." She stroked his hair back. "We're safe."

Despite hearing her say it, doubt formed. "That's the problem. I don't know how much faith I have in that safety anymore."

Her brow knitted, but he could tell she didn't take him entirely seriously. "What are you talking about? Shades can't come here, and any other Art user poses no threat to me."

"Only if you're not caught by surprise," Talon countered, his mind treating him to the sound of her neck breaking. He shook his head and looked at her. "Alana is still a threat. And I'm afraid the council will be too when they find out about the baby. I'm not sure if staying in Eralas is the right decision anymore. We're too easy to find."

Amarie didn't lose her calm demeanor and join him in panic as he partially hoped. "Then we go somewhere else. Anywhere you want, where you feel we're safer. I don't care if it's here or Isalica. As long as we're together, we'll be all right."

Although her words meant to reassure, they jabbed into his chest. He wanted nothing more than to be with her, especially now. He'd allowed himself to fantasize about being a father to the child she carried and creating more life with her. Their own children. He wanted it so desperately, but none of his desires mattered if he posed a threat to her. He empathized remarkably with Kin.

After making Kin swear to leave her if it would keep her safe, what kind of man am I not to abide by the same standard?

An animal scuffled outside their home, and Talon twitched. He laughed as soon as the shock passed, shaking his head at his nerves. Slipping his arm from around her, he said, "I just need some air."

"I can come with you." She sat up.

"No." Talon smiled and nudged her chest back down. "I can handle this by myself, I promise." He leaned down to kiss her and it brought a modicum of comfort.

Amarie watched him, moonlight playing off the side of her face. "If you're gone too long, I *will* come looking for you," she playfully threatened, but an undertone of worry tainted her voice.

"I won't be long." He pulled on a pair of breeches before exiting their bedroom. He hadn't bothered with a shirt, and it proved a good decision as he stepped into the early summer air. Eralas never grew unbearably hot, and the cool shadows of the forest soothed his skin.

For the first time he could recall, Talon felt at home. He'd continued to work on the little house over the months, finally finding satisfaction in the results. He wandered towards the garden clinging to the side of the banyan tree, where Talon had painstakingly attempted to play to his Aueric roots.

An owl screeched somewhere in the trees above, responding to the scurrying creature in the branches of their home. Wings fluttered as sparrows fled, roused from their sleep by whatever animal had encroached on their territory.

Talon frowned, peering up into the branches, and two beady yellow eyes blinked back at him.

A gaunt shape hunched within the summer leaves, no larger than an alley cat. The beast's husk of a body pulsed with rapid breath. Its skin shone a dusky amber in the moonlight, speckles of orange and red along its rigid spine and floppy ears. Tail lashing, the small creature bared its rotted, needled teeth.

The ingvald's presence evoked fear, seizing Talon's chest as the frog-faced thing darted like a lizard down the trunk towards him. It would have sent him running back into the house if he hadn't seen them many times before.

As it grew closer, a set of bat wings shifted atop its body. It hesitated at the bottom of the tree, seeking his response.

The routine.

Talon lifted his arm like a falconer.

The corrupted launched itself from the tree and landed on Talon's forearm. Despite the ingvald's wicked claws, nothing pierced his skin. It cooed and rumbled with an affectionate purr.

"What is it?" Talon hid the terror in his voice. It was better to be stern with corrupted, unflinching. If they sensed weakness, they were prone to stray from their commands. It wasn't the creature he feared, but the one who summoned it.

"Your sister..." the thing hissed, voice scratchy. "Demands audience."

"Impossible. I'm unavailable."

"Is urgent. Your services required and cannot wait. You join her. Nema's Throne. Three months."

Talon pursed his lips. Nema's Throne was almost as far north as one could go in Pantracia, and it would take several weeks alone just to travel there.

As he considered, the ingvald ran up his arm and settled on his shoulder. It hunched down expectantly as Talon plucked a beetle from one of the garden plants, holding it between his fingers. Its tongue lashed between its lips.

"Are you to return a message for me?"

The ingvald growled, shaking his head back and forth. "No message back. No choice."

"Then you'll return to the brood?"

It nodded, pawing at Talon's skin as he dangled the morsel out of its reach.

Jagged scars ran in two uneven downward lines on the creature's chest, signaling his sister's brand, binding the creature to her. He could have easily overridden the bond, but other solutions were more appealing than practicing that form of the Art.

Talon appeased the ingvald and moved his hand close enough for it to snatch the bug from his fingers. The beetle's carapace was no match for the savage teeth.

"Thank you for your message." Talon tried not to cringe at the sound of the bug being consumed next to his ear.

The ingvald slurped, licking its claws as Talon scratched the creature's chin. It purred, grinding like two stones, lifting its head for further affection.

Talon didn't bother with his Art. It wouldn't have worked against the little creature. Instead, he encouraged it down into his arms like a house cat, teasing little scratches around its neck while he cautiously positioned his hand. With a jerk, he twisted the creature's head before it had time to react. The crunch made Talon's gut writhe, tortured with the image of Amarie's body falling to the ground at Alana's feet. The limp ingvald collapsed to the ground as a chill traveled up his spine, and he swallowed the bile in his throat.

Talon nudged the body into the bushes of the garden. He could already feel the solid shape beginning to fade, the powers that held the corrupted together falling apart. The body would be gone by morning, but he couldn't risk Amarie seeing it.

Looking at the house, his heart stopped as he saw Amarie standing near the garden staring at him. She was wearing one of his shirts but hadn't bothered with breeches. "Everything all right?"

Did she see?

Talon urged himself to breathe. He smiled and nodded. "Everything's fine." He crossed the garden to her and kissed her head. "I'm sorry I woke you. You need your sleep."

"I'll catch up on it tomorrow night." Amarie studied him, her jaw clenched, but looked away without voicing her thoughts.

Talon took her hand and urged her back towards the house. "I'll make us some tea."

Amarie nodded, following. Once inside, she disappeared into the bedroom while Talon set to work in their kitchen.

A battle of wills ensued inside him, in a struggle that would leave no one victorious. No matter what path he chose, it ended in pain. Alana remained a constant threat, and the ingvald proved she'd always be able to find him.

I can't stay with Amarie.

The idea of missing the birth of her child and abandoning her to raise it alone made his eyes burn. But he was as much a risk to her as Kin had been.

Breaking her heart is better than Uriel getting her.

All the happy dreams of holding Amarie, teaching the child to walk and being together as a family, vanished. They'd died with a silent scream within him the moment the ingvald's eyes met his.

Talon stared at the teapot, waiting for it to cool before pouring in the herbal mixture Kalstacia concocted for Amarie. He gnawed on his lip, barely noticing when he bit too hard and tasted blood.

Fully dressed in looser breeches and a tunic, Amarie reemerged and crossed to the table. She often mentioned how big her belly felt, even though it hadn't grown much. Talon found her beautiful and even more tantalizing, which she hardly understood.

They made eye contact, and her shoulders slouched. "You still seem troubled." She leaned on the back of a chair. "Is that dream still bothering you?"

"Yes." Talon arranged the pot and a pair of ceramic mugs on the table before her. "I might have overheated the water, so I'd give it a little bit." He sat down, and she reluctantly joined him. "I can't stop thinking about the danger of staying here." He swallowed, avoiding her gaze as he approached the topic he loathed to consider. "And what danger I might pose to you and the baby."

The color drained from Amarie's face as he mirrored the sentiment she'd heard from Kin before. "What are you proposing?" Her whisper barely reached his ears.

His gut twisted, and he wondered if Kin felt the same way when he told her she wasn't safe with him. "We should leave Eralas. We can't risk the council putting things together, and with the possibility of Alana finding me—"

"All right." Amarie interrupted him. "We don't have to stay here, but where do you think we should go?"

"Well, I think you should go to Olsa, and I—"

"Wait, what?" Amarie's spine straightened. "Are you suggesting we separate?"

Talon's heart sank, a horrible silence vibrating between them while he tried to think of what to say. Finally, he nodded. "We need to. Because—"

Amarie gasped and stood up, knocking her chair over behind her. "By the gods." She pressed a hand to her chest. "You're seriously doing this to me, too?" Backing up, she stumbled on the chair, but righted herself as he jumped up. He caught her wrist, but she yanked it free. "No. Don't touch me."

"Amarie, listen," Talon begged. He tried to organize his thoughts, but they jumbled together. "I'm a danger. If Alana and Uriel find you, and if the baby is a girl—"

"You're leaving me, too. What happened to all your promises?" Amarie shook her head. "I can't lose you. Not like this. I'm not afraid of the council. I'm not afraid of your fucking sister. Tell me where she is, and I'll kill her myself." Her eyes flashed with the tones of beryl.

"Don't say that." Talon's shoulders drooped in defeat. He hated the next thought that came to his mind, the only one he could think of to calm Amarie and settle the argument. "We'll only be apart for a few weeks. Long enough for me to find a way to keep Alana off my trail. Then I'll find you."

Amarie cringed and whispered, "Liar." She stepped back again.

Talon forced himself not to pursue her. "No, I'm not lying to you.

I promised I never would." The deceit slid too easily from his tongue. "We would leave the island separately, you go south, and I, north. But only for a few weeks, a month at most. Then we'll be together again. I'll be at your side when the baby is born, just like I promised."

Amarie clutched her belly, tears falling down her cheeks. "I don't believe you." She closed her eyes and let her head fall forward.

"Niané." Talon dared a step forward. When she didn't recoil, he wrapped his arms around her before she could change her mind. He pulled her close to his chest, burying his face in her hair. Everything ached. "I've said many times I'll do what's necessary to protect you, but leaving you... That would destroy me."

Doubt radiated from her shaking body, but it didn't form into words. She breathed in at his bare chest, a hand gripping around his torso. "I love you."

"And I love you. In ways you'll never understand."

"Tell me where to go, and I'll wait for you there," she mumbled into his skin. "I'll go, if you swear you'll meet me."

He closed his eyes to dam the welling hot tears. "Derryton." He chose the first city he could think of to the south. It'd be far from Nema's Throne and Alana. "It's on the southern edge of Olsa and—"

"I know where it is." Leaning back from him, she tightened her grip on his waist as she met his gaze. "Swear it."

Something in Talon cracked, and he doubted his ability to say the words. But he locked away his emotions with a practiced breath, forcing his face to remain serious. "I swear it. I'll meet you there."

The way she closed her eyes at his promise made his gut churn. She didn't look relieved, but heartbroken.

Does she know?

Fear regained its footing inside him. He pushed it away and lied. Again. "A month, at most."

Chapter 14

During the first several days at his family estate, Kin wandered the halls of his home, memories of his mother following him in each room.

Her laughter echoed within him, bringing him to a place of purgatory in his grief. Denial haunted him each morning, before the grogginess wore off and reminded him of the loss the world had suffered.

The loss he blamed himself for, even if Alana had been the one to stop her pulse.

His father's anger, which Kin had prepared for, resounded hollowly beneath his numbed senses.

The ceremony to mark Lindora's journey into Nymaera's Afterlife was simple. Just how she would have wanted it. After the ritual of pouring sacred water over her freshly covered grave, Hartlen gave a brief, forced apology to Kin, then excused himself. In the weeks that followed, Kin hardly saw his father, even for meals.

Mercifully, Alana stayed away from Kin during his mourning. She seemed content to manage him from a distance, occasionally sending ingvalds and demanding an update on his progress towards the Berylian Key. Each response he sent insisted he needed to stay home for one more week.

Kin saw to his mother's duties, Alana and Uriel be damned if they questioned his time spent at the estate. The quiet routines wouldn't last. He could only delay so long.

After a month, the agony of the loss faded to a dull ache in Kin's heart. Vengeance replaced it, and his dreams depicted different ways he imagined obtaining it.

Every time he reached into the void of his soul which contained the Art, Uriel's presence slithered into his veins. An incurable infection continually beckoning him to return. He couldn't exist without it, but Lasseth had pointed him towards possible salvation.

Rahn'ka.

Kin had spent many nights dwelling on the information Lasseth provided about the mysterious Art users. Lasseth had believed there to be only one, but memory provided Kin an alternate truth.

The Rahn'ka could tear a person's soul from their body.

It sounded impossible, considering the expenditure of energy typically only sampled small parts of a soul. A Shade's power, even as it drained the essence of those around, couldn't boast the same ability. But he'd seen it before, felt it.

Disbelief and shame had led Kin to avoid trying to understand what had happened to him in that Lazuli alley. Telling Uriel about the devastating defeat became unnecessary when he caught up to Bellamy again shortly after, no longer protected by who Kin suspected to be a Rahn'ka.

But why had a Rahn'ka been interested in Bellamy?

Months before meeting Amarie in Capul, he'd arrived in the Helgathian city, seeking another wayward Shade after tracking the young man to the last place he'd accessed his power.

When he found Bellamy, the defected Shade hadn't been alone. Two men and a massive valley wolf were with him. The black beast detected him first, ruining his stealthy approach through the mouth of the alleyway.

"Run!" Bellamy had shouted.

The only movement was from the dark-skinned man as he drew a dagger. "Shades have such perfect timing." The man took hold of the wolf's ruff. "I don't much feel like running, how about you?"

They know what I am?

The fairer man leaned over Bellamy, and his face looked oddly familiar beneath the thick brown beard. "Nope." He turned to face where Kin stalked within the shadow.

The wolf's handler held a split dagger, grip flexing on the hilt. The other, even bulkier with muscle than his companion but shorter, turned to face Kin's shadows. He parted his feet to take on a fighting stance, but withdrew no weapon.

Cocky bastard.

Kin surged forward, his shadows crawling across the cobblestone. A flash of light emanated from the cocky one's boot as it touched the ground, and Kin's entire being vibrated as he struck an invisible wall. His shadows curled up, coating the shield manifested in front of him.

Taking his human form, Kin gave them the opportunity to back down. All he wanted was Bellamy. He ignored their interactions with each other, glaring at his target, inwardly debating how long it would take for the men to give up.

I just want to get my task done and move on.

The wolf handler slumped on a crate, drawing Kin's attention.

The cocky man stood straighter, rolling his shoulders as if rejuvenated despite the drain on maintaining his shield. The next thing Kin knew, the Art user had seized hold of him.

Agony ripped through his body, each sinew of his flesh clinging desperately to his soul as it pulled away from him. It manifested as a pale shape, hovering like a ghost. His eyes burned with tears of pain, blurring the alleyway.

The man clutched Kin's soul in his hand, despite standing yards away, the muscles of his arm quivering at the strain.

In that horrible moment, Kin wished for death. His essence crackled, the bond to Uriel stretched to its limit, unwilling to release the soul it infected. When the man let go, the blue-white light he'd yanked from within Kin slammed back into place, and his vision went black.

He'd been ignorant. Arrogant. Luckily, when he woke, the two men and their wolf were gone, and Bellamy hadn't had the nerve to slit his throat.

While nursing his wounded pride and pounding headache, Kin learned why his attacker had looked familiar. A wanted poster hung plastered to the entryway of the tavern he retreated to.

Damien Lanoret.

His drawn portrait featured a clean-shaven face and a different hair color, but his eyes were unmistakable. Damien's desertion of the Helgathian military prompted a hefty reward for his head, but it didn't seem enough for the power he wielded.

Kin snapped back to reality at the chime of the estate's dinner bell.

He took up the packed satchel from the base of his bed and threw it over his shoulder, tapping the hilt of a new sword at his hip. As an afterthought, he picked up a brown cloak, his old black one stashed in a trunk.

A piece of pale parchment sat on his desk, a simple letter to his father stating he needed to leave. He didn't waste his time explaining anything beyond that, only that he hoped he might someday forgive his son.

Slipping from the estate to the stables, he kept a wary eye on the sky and rooftops for lingering ingvalds. A suspicious murder of crows gathered in the vineyard at the front of the estate, lining the gates.

Kin took the back trails instead, following the stream with the tawny mare the stable boy tacked for him, always watching the sky. He pulled the brown hood over his head and returned to the roads only after he could no longer see the estate behind him.

He gradually found new comfort in the monotonous sound of pounding hooves, even if traveling by horseback made the journey southeast more tedious.

Let's hope that this Damien didn't get himself captured or killed by Helgath yet.

The man's presence in Lazuli explained the altered hair color, likely trying to avoid the authorities within the country responsible for his bounty.

But why even risk returning?

During his aimless travels, he prodded for information about the Helgathian deserter. He hardly believed the tales told until several people corroborated them. Damien had made friends with the right people, throwing the entirety of Helgath into a political stalemate among its ruling houses.

Even with the knowledge, he resorted to tracking known sightings, since Damien's current location seemed a widespread mystery. Kin's dedication to travel by horseback waned in Quar when he needed to choose between crossing through the Gilgas Desert during the peak of summer or backtracking to a pass in the Belgast Mountains of Olsa. The temptation to transform into a raven nearly won. It would have sped his journey exponentially, and he missed the feeling of the wind rustling his feathers.

Kin denied himself. If he found Damien and his assumptions were correct, Kin would be permanently forgoing his access to the Art. He needed to grow accustomed to life without it, even if that meant adding two weeks to his journey.

Wanting to make up whatever time he could, Kin veered off the main trade road to cut through the forest along the mountains. By the time he realized how much slower weaving through the trees was, he'd invested too long to turn back.

Night approached, the sun setting behind the trees after a long day's travel through the woods.

His horse's ears swiveled around, her legs stiffening as she rocked back.

"Whoa, what's wrong?"

A howl shook through the trees, and the horse reared.

Kin tightened his grip on the reins, keeping his seat. He couldn't stop the horse from spinning around, trying to go back the way they came. He hurried to dismount, tugging on her bridle to force her to stop.

"Take it easy, girl."

He felt far more stable on the ground, able to use his strength to control the frightened horse. After calming her, he secured the reins to a low branch, thin enough for her to break if danger approached.

"I'll be right back."

Another howl rumbled, and Kin turned towards the origin. He walked ahead, examining the large bush at the base of a steep cliffside. Using his sword, he pushed aside several boughs to see beyond.

Cliffs dove into a narrow gorge, housing the dim shape of pillars, cream-colored in the dying daylight. The man-made structures stood on either side of the narrow fissure.

What am I doing?

Kin took a step into the brush. Weaving through the broken branches, he turned the hilt of his sword in his palm, finding what comfort he could in it as a lower wolf cry erupted.

I can handle fighting a wolf if it comes to that.

The carved stone monoliths along the sides of the fissure suggested ruins, too much of a coincidence for the ancient structure to be near where Damien might linger. The Rahn'ka deserter had been seen in the nearby city of Jacoby, though Kin had decided against visiting because it'd been over a year since the report.

Though, even in Lazuli, he had a wolf with him.

An odd sensation in his chest kept his feet moving through the bush-covered entry. The natural hallway of rock to the right opened into a circular canyon, dense with vine-choked pillars. In the center, the rocks swirled towards a stone column. He eyed the darkened cave beyond, but the towering ruins beside him lured him closer first. A grand arch beckoned him into a collapsing hall, thick with shadow. He contemplated the value of using his power to pierce the darkness, but the risk of alerting Uriel to his location kept it a bay.

Kin followed a descending stairwell, blinking at a flickering light in the distance.

Strange.

He rounded a corner, approaching a pair of torches on either end of a hallway. At the end, light flickered off a metal door, emblazoned with intricate vine patterns. He stopped to listen, but heard nothing other than the wind behind him.

A scuffle and crunch from the other side of the door made him jump. His grip tightened on the hilt of his sword.

A man chuckled within, encouraging Kin's hand to close on the handle. He tested the knob, and it clicked open with a twist. His pounding heart skipped a beat as the sound echoed down the hall, and the noise inside stopped.

Nowhere to go but forward.

Kin bounced his weapon, then shoved the door open. It resisted the movement, a heavy pressure wanting to keep it closed. Pushing with his shoulder, he used his sword for leverage against the cold surface. He blinked at the roaring fire ahead, a spit propped over it, roasting an indistinguishable hunk of meat. A smear of blood on the dirt-covered ground trailed into the darkness beyond. A high roof kept the moon and starlight at bay, except for a round opening at the center, where the smoke from the fire escaped.

A man crouched beside the pit, too proper looking for the environment around him. A rough black beard stubbled his rich umber skin, and the light of the fire made his eyes a bright amber. His head angled towards Kin, and he rose to his feet.

The wolf handler who fought beside Damien.

Kin sidestepped to free his weapon, letting go of the door. It slammed shut behind him. He steadied his heart with a deep breath, the smoke burning his lungs.

"I know you," the wolf handler said, eerily silent on his feet as he stepped forward.

Kin's stomach curdled at the tone, the hairs on his neck standing up. He reached back for the door handle, instinct telling him to flee. Where the knob should have been, was flat, and his fingers found no escape.

Fuck.

A big shadow moved on the other side of the fire, entering the light in a sensuous motion. Clawed paws of mottled black fur skimmed the dirt as the wolf lowered its head. Wet blood glistened on its maw, and it growled.

"Easy, boy." The man's voice rumbled in his chest. "I doubt *Shades* taste very good."

Kin swallowed and stepped left with his back against the wall. Knuckles white, he lifted his sword.

The wolf, with shoulders as high as Kin's hips, prowled forward in agonizing slow motion, amber eyes locked on him. It was the greater threat, forcing Kin to watch the man in his peripheral vision.

"Is Bellamy dead?" The man spun a dirty hunting knife.

Kin hurried to change his tactic and loosened his grip on his sword. He let it hang down as he lifted his palms. "I'm no threat to you. I surrender."

The wolf loped in front of Kin, encouraging him to flatten against the wall. After lifting its nose to sniff near his stomach, it circled towards the man, disappearing into the shadows. The beast's claws tapped in the darkness as it paced somewhere next to him.

"You didn't answer my question." The man growled, taking another step closer, only ten feet away now.

Kin resisted readying his sword again. "Last I saw of him, he was alive. But it's been over a year, so for his sake, I hope he's dead." The memory of delivering Bellamy to their master tasted sour. "But I swear I'm no threat."

The man's expression didn't change, other than a sidelong glance into the shadows where his furred beast lurked. "Shades are always a threat."

The wolf lunged from the darkness, leaping for Kin's throat.

Kin threw himself from the wall, grateful he'd left his cloak behind with his horse, otherwise the beast would have caught it. His boots slid across the dirt, and the man's arm closed around his neck. Just in time, Kin wedged his hand up between, grasping the man's forearm.

With surprising strength, the man squeezed, forcing Kin's knuckles into his own throat and he choked for a breath. The pressure felt like his neck neared snapping, and the edges of his vision darkened when the man threw him to the side.

Kin hit the ground, rolling as the wolf chased him across the floor. Teeth gnashed next to his face, and pain sprung from his arm as the animal's jaws clamped down on his bicep. His left hand empty, his sword on the ground, he threw a wild punch at the wolf. It connected, but the animal didn't release, clamping down harder, claws scrabbling in the dirt.

Hot blood soaked Kin's arm and he screamed. The power within him clambered to be released. It growled louder than the wolf, begging him to use the chitinous armor his new rank granted. It would have broken the creature's hold, protected and healed his wounds, but Kin used the pain to strengthen his resolve.

The wolf loosened his grip and stilled but held steady as the man crouched near Kin's head. "Where are your shadows?" he snarled, and steel glinted in the firelight.

"Death is preferable, if I must choose." Kin stopped fighting, and it took all his will to resist the temptation of the Art within him.

"Something we agree on." The man drew the blade to Kin's throat.

He lifted his chin in acceptance.

"Stop!" A new voice echoed through the room, and a figure rushed from the darkness behind Kin's attacker.

The knife paused, and Kin's eyes widened as the wolf handler calmly contemplated the order. "No." The muscles in his bicep tensed, and the cold steel grazed Kin's skin before the wolf handler's eyes rolled back into his head.

The knife clattered to the ground, and his limp body followed it.

In similar form, the wolf flopped onto the dirt, sending a cloud up into the air.

Kin blinked away the dust as a face lowered, upside down, over his.

"You..." Damien narrowed his eyes. "I should've let him kill you."

Kin groaned, and closed his eyes, letting his head fall back against the ground. He heaved a breath, rubbing his injured throat. "Thank you." His fingers came away sticky and he cringed.

"Get up." Damien nudged Kin's shoulder with his boot. "Hands out. You reach for any shadows and I'll put you back on the ground."

Kin's shirt sleeve clung to his arm, drenched with crimson from the wolf bite. He struggled to sit up, but managed, closing his good hand around the injury to slow the bleeding. "I'm here to talk. I've been looking for you."

"Well, you can forget that," Damien growled. "I'm not going to go willingly." Stepping to the side, he picked up Kin's sword. He spun it in his grip, testing the weight.

Kin grimaced. "I'm not here on behalf of Uriel."

Damien looked at him. The firelight shone gold in his short hair. "You say his name a little too casually for being his slave." He walked to the downed wolf handler, tugging on his shirt to roll him onto his back. Frowning, he took the hunting knife and tucked it into his belt.

Kin eyed his attacker, who looked peacefully asleep. "Isn't he your friend? You were together in Lazuli."

"Not sure you're in much of a position to be asking questions." Damien slid Kin's sword into his belt. On the left side of his neck, just visible beyond the collar of his light-brown tunic, a script was tattooed in a dark-blue ink. It disappeared under his shirt but reappeared on his forearm.

"You're a Rahn'ka, aren't you?"

Damien's entire body tensed, the casual demeanor vanishing with a single word. His eyes darkened as he met Kin's. "Where did you—"

"Please," Kin managed, forcing his feet beneath him. "I swear I only want to talk. If you sense me reaching for the Art, kill me."

Damien's rip corded muscles looked ready to pop before he finally relaxed. The air around them was suddenly easier to breathe. "Fine." He eyed Kin's injury then the dormant forms of the wolf and man. "But not here."

Not going to argue that.

Kin nodded.

Damien crossed to the door, exposing his back. The gesture was simple but encouraged Kin to heave a sigh of relief. With a brief whisper of Damien's power, and a flexed arm, the handle-less door flung open.

They climbed the stairs in silence, and Kin paused to lean against the wall to catch his breath. His head swam, and he tried to grab the stone, but found no grip. His vision blurring, he shook his head. "Just need a minute." The night noises garbled in his ears, and the sensation of falling overtook him. Then blackness.

When Kin woke, his pain intensified, and the sun stabbed his eyes. His head rang with the morning song of a sparrow, tilting its head at him. It sat on the crumbled edge of a hole in the ceiling, watching him.

The room smelled of night jasmine and rosemary, and Kin lifted his hand to his forehead. His muscles protested as if they hadn't moved in days. The sleeve of his blood-soaked tunic had been cut away, exposing flawless skin.

What?

Kin lifted his arm, touching the flesh to search for the bite wounds from the wolf, but only small round scars remained. He sat up, too quickly, and braced himself from behind when his head spun. His hand sank into a straw mattress.

"Welcome back." Damien's voice thundered and Kin winced.

"What happened?" Kin rubbed the back of his neck. His fingers slid to his throat, remembering the knife wound, but nothing remained of that, either.

"You fell down the stairs after passing out. Blood loss, I'm guessing. And don't think I wasn't tempted to leave you there."

Kin eyed Damien, who sat on a short stool in the corner of a small room. He'd been fiddling with Kin's sword and turned to prop it into the corner.

"Instead, you healed me. Why?" Kin pulled himself to the edge of the bed. He arched his back in a satisfying stretch.

"Curiosity, mostly." Damien shrugged. "Never met a Shade dumb enough to say Uriel's name aloud, or who'd choose death over using his power." He scratched the back of his head. "So... talk. He motioned with both palms up. "I'm listening."

"I'm not entirely sure where to start." Kin ran a hand through his hair.

Damien remained stone faced at the comment. "Let's start with your name then, and how you got here. Or should I just call you Shade?"

"I'd rather you stick with Kin." Continuing, he told the Rahn'ka the truth about his life with how he fell into service. He hadn't expected it to come out so easily considering he'd never told anyone but Talon the entirety. It was strangely liberating to refer to himself as a Shade and forced servitor of Uriel. He didn't hide his regret, admitting his faults.

Damien emanated power as Kin spoke. The sensation of his Art tickled at Kin's, another torturous reminder of what he desperately wanted to access. It'd been three weeks since he'd used the power more than necessary to remain sane.

"Uriel." Damien said the name with a casual reverence as if he truly understood its power. "So, you don't follow him blindly anymore?"

"Not anymore, but I did. Like a foolish child." Kin averted his gaze to the cracked ground.

"What changed?"

"Have you ever loved someone?" A vision of Amarie flashed in his mind.

Damien paused, a smirk touching his face as he rocked back on the stool. "Love, huh?"

"Pretty sure that tone means you're familiar with it." Kin glanced up, catching the glimmer of sunlight on a simple silver band on Damien's right hand before he closed his other hand over it.

Damien frowned, and sighed as he uncovered the wedding band. "I am. But if you claim love is responsible, then the infection has spared at least part of your soul. And now you'd like me to cleanse the rest of it? What makes you think I can?"

"No need to play coy." Kin gave a sideways smile. "We both know that you have access to an Art unlike anything else in Pantracia. I was told that another of your power separated a Shade before."

"Where did you hear that?"

"I'll tell you if it really matters, but the man who knew her is dead now, too. She killed herself rather than be captured, years ago. I don't know exactly when."

"Why should I put myself in the same danger?" Damien tilted his head. "For a man who tried to kill me last time we crossed paths."

"You were merely in the wrong place at the wrong time." Kin sighed. "It had nothing to do with you, but the man you protected. He'd strayed from his service, and my task was to return him so he might see the error of his ways."

"Oh, I'm aware of the purpose." Damien's tone saddened. "I'd hoped Bellamy would kill you himself."

"He should have." Kin cringed. "I had no choice but to continue pursuing him, and he knew it. I think he gave up in the end."

Damien bit his lip. "Damn it. He deserved so much more."

"Your friend asked about him, too. And he was with you in the alley that night."

The telling tension returned but vanished quickly. "He cares for the same reason I do. Bellamy saved someone we love." He spun his wedding band absently. "I don't look forward to telling her Bellamy's fate."

"Two men loving the same woman? Sounds complicated."

Damien grinned, and shook his head. "Oh, her favorite word. It's actually less complicated than it sounds."

Kin grimaced, swallowing the headache developing in his forehead.

Damien cleared his throat and sat up straighter. "All that aside, I'm not particularly inclined to help you. I can feel the twisted power inside you, how it's rotted your soul. It's hungry to consume more. Devour you like a rabid wolf. It's already starving. Have you looked at yourself recently?"

Kin had been trying to ignore the changes. He'd convinced himself his sunken, dark-set eyes came from the stress of losing his mother. The blue lines of his veins shone through his paling skin. He ignored his failing strength because he could still hold his sword.

"When you don't feed the connection to Uriel, it feeds on you." Damien pointed at him.

"I won't allow it to control me." Kin leaned forward. "I don't know what he senses when I do. But if I don't use the power at least a little every few days, my head feels like a grygurr axe is splitting it in half. And I feel cold constantly."

"All that suffering. You're stubborn, but why do I get the feeling you're not fully ready to let it go?"

Kin silenced the curse on his tongue. "It's complicated."

Damien quirked an eyebrow with a hint of a smile. "Humor me."

"I'm afraid I still need it. Not for me, but for her. My position under Uriel helps me protect her."

"The woman you love." Damien nodded. "And Uriel is after her because of her influence on you?"

Kin debated how much he wanted to reveal. But he needed to convince Damien to help him. "She's more than a woman. And I'm not being a clichéd lover. She controls immense power. Uriel pursued Amarie long before I met her." He winced, realizing he'd said her name aloud.

Kin wondered if she was safe in Eralas. Talon certainly remained at her side. While Kin knew nothing for certain, if Amarie moved on and cared for someone else, it changed nothing for him. He'd always love and protect her.

Damien leaned forward. He paused, contemplating, before he spoke. "While I'm intrigued by your plight, I'm not sure how to help you with it. I'm busy looking for answers to other problems, and I might not be able to do anything for a while."

"Then I'll wait." He'd wait as long as it was necessary to keep Uriel from Amarie. "Uriel wants me to find the Berylian Key, but I can't, that task would destroy so much."

Damien choked on air, his eyes widening. "The what?"

Fuck.

Kin's brow tightened and the room spun before he squeezed his eyes shut. "I shouldn't have said that."

"You said Berylian Key. You know what it is?"

Kin pushed himself back on the bed and leaned against the cool stone wall beside it. "It isn't that important."

"You just said finding it would destroy so much. And you mean Amarie. Why would..." Damien paused. "Amarie has it, doesn't she?"

"I didn't say that," Kin tried to backpedal. "I didn't say my task had anything to do with Amarie. Why—"

"You didn't need to say it." Damien stood. "This is a lot to consider, and I need time to process." He turned towards the door, and Kin stood to follow.

The sudden shift left him off balance, and he fell onto the bed.

"Stay here," Damien instructed. "We both know I could force you if necessary."

"My horse..."

"I've already taken care of her. She's safe inside the sanctum, too."

Kin managed a nod, swallowing his rising nausea. It'd been too long since he'd reached for his power, yet the temptation oddly quieted.

He's already doing something.

Making the power harder to grasp did nothing to the symptoms of his weakened body. When he opened his eyes, Damien was already gone.

Chapter 15

Autumn, 2611 R.T.

Amarie awoke to darkness, an excruciating tightness wrapping around her midsection. Toppling to her side on the cool ground, she gasped and clutched her pregnant belly. "Talon," she pleaded, even though he wasn't with her. He'd never met her in Derryton as promised, so she'd continued west alone.

Crying out, she rolled onto her back, vaguely aware of hooves shuffling nearby.

Viento huffed near her ear as her pain dimmed, only to return in another agonizing wave, threatening the control of her hiding aura.

It's too soon.

Hooves, again, resounded louder in her ears. Boots.

"Talon." She tried to call out again, her voice nothing more than a hoarse whisper.

Hands touched her forehead and painfully prodded her abdomen. His presence lacked Talon's energy, and she opened her eyes. A man crouched next to her, and she tried to coax her eyes into focusing on his face.

Deylan leaned over her, his brown eyes wide. "I've got you."

She breathed a sigh of relief, trying to understand why her brother was there. Another wave of pain crashed through her middle, and she yelled, rolling onto her side.

This is my fault.

She'd ridden too hard from Derryton and not rested nearly enough. Emotions got the better of her, and she'd ignored what her body needed.

With another agonizing convulsion beneath where Deylan's hand pressed to her abdomen, everything went black.

Amarie's mind felt hazy when she gradually roused. Her midsection no longer ached, and she checked her belly. It was still gently rounded, and after a moment of relaxing, she felt the wriggles of the child within.

Closing her burning eyes, she rolled onto her side, the mattress beneath her providing much needed support for her protruding stomach. Raising a hand, she touched the pillow under her head and opened her eyes.

Warm morning sunlight cascaded across the small room, furnished with a simple table, a desk, and two armchairs, one occupied. With his head tilted back, Deylan slept only a few feet away from her, and she smiled.

After their father's death, Amarie failed to locate her brother. She feared the worst, and seeing him alive lifted her darkened spirits. The secretive faction sworn to protect the power of the Berylian Key had limitations about interfering. In the back of her mind, she wondered if he'd be reprimanded.

Looking at his face, his features reminded her of the father she'd barely known. Gratitude mixed with overwhelming disappointment. It wasn't Talon at her side. Her heart ached with the loss of his embrace. The loss of his love.

Her eyes flicked to where her pack rested on the table, and the journal resting next to it. She'd written in it daily since leaving Eralas, using it to talk to Talon. Sometimes, uninspired, an entry would be brief. *Where are you? Why didn't you meet me?* Her doubt occasionally calmed, and she wondered if he'd been hurt, or worse. But then her mind would replay how he'd held her at the docks at their departure. Hugging her too tightly, kissing her too long.

He never intended to join me in Olsa.

Amarie sighed, shifting to get comfortable, and the wooden bed frame squeaked.

Deylan woke with a swift inhale, kicking his feet out in front of him before a smile touched his lips. "How are you feeling?" His deep baritone voice reminded her of Kin's. He rubbed his hands over his face, sitting up straight as he cleared his throat.

She nodded, a hand still on her belly as she sat up.

Deylan leapt to his feet, helping her.

"I feel fine. Where am I?"

"My mother's house. My daughter and wife live here, too."

"Where? How far from where you found me?"

He smiled. "Not far. We're west of Jacoby in my home village."

The idea of family warmed Amarie's heart. "I couldn't find you in Rylorn."

Deylan's expression sobered, and he settled back into the chair as she turned to hang her feet off the side of the bed. He shook his head. "By the time I got there, I couldn't find you either. But I was relieved to hear you were all right."

"I wish I could've gotten the same news of you."

Deylan fell silent before motioning with his chin to her belly. "Congratulations." He smiled. "You had some early contractions, but the baby is fine. The faction is abuzz with the news of the potential Key's blood being part auer."

Amarie dropped her gaze to the floor, and Deylan tilted his head.

"Is it not Talon's?" He dipped his chin to catch her gaze.

Shaking her head, she chewed on her bottom lip.

"Shit." Deylan heaved a breath. His hand closed on her knee.

"Kin doesn't know. He can't. If the one he serves ever learned..." Sighing, she cringed. "My child has the blood of a Shade."

Deylan glanced at the window and then back at her. "He wasn't so bad, you know."

"Did you meet him?" Her heart sped.

"He saved my life in Rylorn."

Amarie's brow furrowed, and she gaped at him. "What are you talking about? Kin was in Rylorn?" Questions whirled through her mind, but she stilled her tongue to wait for answers.

Deylan inhaled deeply before nodding. "Kin warned us when

Helgath figured out the truth about our fake Key. We were stubborn, but he's the reason I wasn't arrested too. The reason I even caught up to you and Talon while he went after Dad." Deylan kept talking, while Amarie was too stunned to speak. "Kin helped me bury him, too."

Amarie squeezed her eyes shut.

"Where's Talon?"

She opened her eyes and muttered, "Probably at a tavern in Ziona having an ale with Kin."

Deylan frowned. "He left you, pregnant, on your own? Auer bastard."

Nausea that she hadn't felt in months crept into her stomach. "Yes. Even after promising not to. After telling me he wanted to be a father to my child. After calling me his niané..." She swallowed. "He still left."

Deylan grumbled something incoherent and then cleared his throat. "My mother is a midwife. She gave you some herbs to stop the contractions. She guessed you're still several weeks away yet, but you'll be on bedrest, I'm afraid. You can stay here, with family, for as long as you want. That includes after you have the baby."

She nodded slowly, and the tension in Deylan's face faded. "Will you stay too?" She wasn't surprised when he shook his head.

"I can't. I need to return to the faction. I'm in enough trouble already, but you'll be in good hands here."

He left her to rest, and Cassia, his mother, came to check on her that evening. Her face cheerfully wrinkled, she spoke in a tone that somehow encouraged Amarie to relax. The tea she made tasted like Kalstacia's, and Cassia didn't question when Amarie rejected it, preparing a broth instead.

After giving her a day to acclimate, Deylan brought the rest of his family to meet her.

"And what's your name?" Amarie looked down at the little girl, with rosy cheeks and rich brown hair, peering over the edge of the bed.

"Ilia," she whispered, grinning as she ducked out of Amarie's line of sight to hide behind her mother's skirt.

"She'll lose her shyness in a day, and then you won't be able to get rid of her." Deylan chuckled, receiving a sideways glance from his wife, Roslyn.

Ilia tugged on her mother's apron and pointed at Amarie's rounded belly. "Is there really a baby in there?"

"Yes, child," Cassia crouched next to her granddaughter and pinched the end of her nose.

Ilia squirmed and giggled, burying her face into the layers of her mother's dress.

Roslyn tugged on the fabric to free it from her daughter's hands. "Why don't we let Amarie rest, now?" She looked warily at Amarie. "It's a pleasure to meet you."

Amarie nodded, even though Roslyn's tone lacked sincerity. "You, as well." She forced a smile.

Ushering the six-year-old out of the room, Roslyn left with a glance over her shoulder at her husband, a difficult look to interpret.

Deylan gave her a single nod.

"I'll be back shortly with lunch." Cassia paused at the door.

"Thank you." Amarie waited until the woman left her alone with Deylan. "Your wife doesn't like me."

"She will. She's just nervous about new people, especially when our daughter takes a shining to them." Deylan crossed the room to her bag. "Do you need anything?"

"My journal and graphite?" Amarie motioned to the book he'd removed from her pack the day before.

Picking it up, he returned to her. "I didn't read it, by the way, I was just—"

"It's all right." Amarie took the book. "There's nothing interesting in it, anyway."

Alone again, Amarie took a deep breath and flipped her journal open to the last entry.

You're not coming, are you?

The heavy-set handwriting imprinted the parchment.

I knew it. I could see it in your face and hear it in your voice. You lied to me. Why? You could have told me the truth. I waited for you in Derryton for almost a month, like an idiot. I even left a note with the innkeeper should you arrive late. Where did you go, instead? Are you back home in Eralas? You're no better than Kin. No, you're worse. At least he had the guts to tell me the truth.

Amarie swallowed, turning the page, and pressed the graphite to the paper for a new entry.

I almost died. The baby almost died. Would that have been a curse or a blessing? Who would the Berylian Key have brought back? Me, I suppose. Though I could ask Deylan, he might know.

She paused, her graphite hovering above the page, and heat built behind her eyes.

I loved you, but you know that. I need to stop writing to you. You'll never see this. It's a shame, because you would have made a wonderful father. We could have had a life. The family neither of us ever had. Instead, this baby will grow up without one. I hate what you've done, how you've left me. Abandoned me. Just like everyone else. Goodbye, Talon. I won't waste another page on this futile endeavor.

Lowering her hand, Amarie stared at the page. Steeling her resolve, she shut the book and tossed it aside.

Confined to her bed for most of the passing days, each seemed slower than the previous. After spending one day with Ilia, idly drawing on scraps of paper, Cassia suggested a new, passive hobby to fill her time. She graciously provided Amarie with supplies, even though painting had never been an interest before.

Sitting at her window, Amarie painted the view of grassland and the sky. Once she grew bored with the same setting, she painted from memory. She painted Viento, and the araleinya flower. When the sun disappeared behind the rain clouds of autumn, she switched to using charcoal. Her imagination gravitated towards swirling darkness and lashing shadows, the depictions invading her serene landscapes. Sometimes, a face emerged, and she would capture the likeness of Kin or Talon. She sketched Kin with obsidian eyes, slowly evolving into her imagination of Uriel. Shadowed tentacles and chitinous plates.

At the end of each day, she tucked her drawings in a thin fabric sleeve, hiding her damned thoughts from her visitors. The child kicked, as if in protest, each time.

After three weeks, Amarie no longer painted scenery. She dripped black paint over a once-bright depiction of a valley, muddling the image.

A chill wafted in from her window, and she stood from the stool next to her easel to close it. Her lower back ached, and she grunted as she slid the window closed. Stretching, she rubbed her arms, willing the goosebumps away.

Glaring at her pack, placed inconsiderately on the ground, she awkwardly stooped to lift it to the table. Rifling through, she searched for her cloak, neglected since arriving in Eralas. Finding it, she pulled, sending something spinning from within it to the floor with a thump.

Her gaze landed on the package, wrapped delicately with twine. Her breathing quickened, but she couldn't move.

I didn't put that there.

Dread filled her stomach.

Sighing, she bent over again, cringing as she plucked the nondescript bundle from the floor, turning it over. On the side that'd landed on the floor was a single calligraphed word.

Yinn'ai.

Aueric and written in Talon's hand. The term used for an unborn baby girl.

It can still be a boy.

She closed her eyes.

I was right. He planned to leave.

The confirmation hit her like a brick to the stomach, and she gritted her jaw. Putting the package down on the table, she eyed her cloak.

Did he leave something for me, too?

The desperate notion filled her with shame, but she reached into her pack anyway, searching for anything meant for her.

Her fingers closed around an unfamiliar bundle, half the size of her palm, at the bottom of her pack. Reluctantly, she withdrew it. Talon had correctly assumed she wouldn't get so deep into the pack until long after his failure to meet in Derryton. If only he'd put as much effort into helping her understand as he did in plotting his desertion.

She collapsed into an armchair, staring at the fine twine tied in the same fashion as the larger package. Part of her didn't want to open it, but her curiosity got the best of her, and she pulled the tie, throwing the wrapping aside.

A wooden box inside clicked open in her palm. Within, a piece of paper lay folded beneath a silver chain. On the metal hung an opal pendant, carved into the shape of the open araleinya flower. Inlaid sapphires ran amid lines of silver to illuminate the delicate stamen of the bloom. It was the size of her thumbnail, with intricate Aueric craftsmanship.

Sliding the chain to the side, she slipped the paper out from under it. She snapped the box shut and placed it on the corner of her desk. Her eyes burned. Swallowing back her emotions, she opened the note.

> *My Araleinya,*
> *I'm so sorry for the lies. I don't expect you to forgive*
> *me, or ever understand why I had to. Alana found*
> *me in Eralas, and I couldn't risk her finding you,*

too. It shatters my heart to leave you like this. You are rarer than this bloom, but I've been a hypocrite. Kin promised me he would do anything necessary to keep you safe. I never suspected I'd find myself in the same situation. I came to love you, cherish you, beyond reason. I wanted to raise your child with you and help you find the joy you deserve. But you're both safer without me. You will forever be my niané, but I cannot be yours.

Always, Talon.

Hot tears raced down her cheeks as she read and reread the note, her heart wrenching in her chest. Anger flooded her, attempting to drown the agony as she crumpled the parchment into her fist. With a flash of intent, the paper burst into flames, disintegrating to ash.

Grief tumbled through her body, prying a sob from her throat. She stood and reached for the necklace box, but pain shocked through her swollen belly.

Crying out, she buckled forward, clutching the side of the desk.

Cassia arrived in time for the next body-rocking contraction.

Chapter 16

Another ingvald came instead of Alana.

Despite Talon's early arrival for their rendezvous in Nema's Throne, his sister hadn't shown up.

The beady-eyed creature crashed through the window of his second-floor room at the inn, smearing little trails of blood from where glass cut its husk-like body.

It shook like a soaked tabby cat, purring as it preened it's wings.

"Speak." Talon prodded it with his foot and it spun to hiss at him. He kicked it a little harder.

With bulging eyes, it growled. "Treama. Three months. Warmer." It resumed licking its wounds with its forked tongue.

Of course, Alana had told the creature to offer the consolation prize of warmer weather as opposed to giving a reason for the change.

"Fine." Talon plucked the ingvald up by the ear, flinging it out the window. Pulling his notebook from his pocket, he studied the dates, calculating the time required for travel. He traced the weeks down the page, and his finger slowed as it passed over an old note.

Baby due.

A lump formed in his throat as he glared at the words scrawled in his own excited hand. He'd written it while Amarie slept, her subtly grown stomach framed by their sheets. Leaning down, he'd kissed her skin, feeling the child within give a nudge in return.

Talon blinked away the heat in his eyes and forced himself to return to counting weeks. To his dismay, it brought him right back to the same week. And he looked at the words again.

They're all right. They're safer without me.

He clapped the notebook shut and tucked it away.

Broken glass crunched beneath his boots as he picked up his single pack and went to retrieve Lynthenai from the inn's stable.

Chapter 17

Darkness surrounded Kin, embracing him like a nurturing mother as he huddled with his head in his hands. His body shuddered, cold sweat running down his temples. It dripped off his stubbled chin, expanding the darkened stain in the dirt floor. Using the heel of his boot, he smeared the mud away.

Days bled together, making time unfathomable within his windowless room somewhere deep in the ruins. The sanctum, Damien called it. Consciousness blurred with dreams, making the distinction of reality difficult to find. He dreamt of his mother, warm and accepting, but then horribly cruel. Of Amarie, accepting her into his arms, only to have her slit his throat. He woke, always with a start, questioning it all. He couldn't recall the last conversation with either, muddled with feverish dreams.

Stagnant air weighed heavily in his lungs, not satisfying them no matter how much he breathed.

He scratched the smooth spiderweb scars thick across his forearm where his tattoo used to be. The bone-white skin stretched unnaturally, the geometric symbols swallowed beneath the mutilation. His skin pulsed in his vision, a vein in his wrist pounding in sync with the war drum in his head.

This is how I die.

"You're not dying," Damien grumbled, sliding a plate of food onto the little stone table next to the bed.

Kin sat on the floor, not entirely sure when he'd left his mattress, a knee tucked up against his chest. He looked up, and the flame of a candle sparked to life, searing Kin's eyes. He winced, burying his face among his folded arms.

Damien pushed the candle farther back, allowing the shadow of the table to pass over Kin. "Besides, I'd just bring you back."

Kin laughed, but his tongue stuck to the roof of his mouth.

The sound of the dirt grinding beneath metal tore into his ears, and he dared a glance to see Damien providing a tin cup of water. He scrambled for it, afraid the cup would vanish like the dreams, and drank. The water burned as it hit his throat, even though it was cool on his lips. He sputtered to slow its descent, and relief followed.

"You should let me die." Kin shook the cup, trying to encourage the last drops into his mouth. "It'd be easier than this." He abandoned the cup, clapping it down to the ground. He leaned his head back, neck bending uncomfortably over the edge of his bed. The discomfort of the stretch briefly distracted from the rest of his body.

"Gods, you act like I've been denying you water. There's a pitcher on the table." Damien snatched the cup, his shape moving amid the light piercing Kin's eyelids. "Death might break the connection but would defeat the purpose of the journey. If I brought you back, you wouldn't feel all this suffering. Without suffering, there's no redemption. You must prove your desire to be free of Uriel. Otherwise, what would stop you from taking the power again when you miss it?"

"You talk like you can actually bring someone back from the dead." Kin opened his eyes the barest amount and sighed in relief when the light didn't hurt as much.

Damien stood, leaning against the desk with his hands at his sides. "Your doubt is expected, but it's not as complicated as you'd think." He gave a wry smile. His hair was cropped short, mirroring the wanted posters in Lazuli when they first met, but the beard made him look older.

"Nothing has that power." Kin paused as he remembered Amarie's broken body in his hands. Flashes of her corpse, then the terrified look on her face as she scurried away from him. "At least, I used to believe that."

Damien held out the drinking cup again, waiting patiently as Kin leaned to take it. "I believe it's safe to say we've both seen far more than we once thought possible." Pausing, he poured his own drink from the dented pitcher. "What happened to Amarie?"

Kin shifted, disconcerted by Damien's perception. The man had continuously asked questions about Kin's deepest thoughts, as if able to read his mind. "It doesn't matter."

The silence between them thickened, the tap of Damien's finger against his tin cup echoing in Kin's head.

He grimaced and turned away, another flash of Amarie's glazed eyes staring lifelessly at him.

"She died, didn't she?" Damien's brows furrowed. "But she came back?"

"Has anyone ever told you that you're remarkably frustrating?" Kin growled, gripping his pounding head.

"You'd be surprised how often." Damien smirked.

The wolf howled from somewhere in the sanctum. It vibrated against the stone walls, drawing Damien's attention towards the metal door to Kin's room.

He pushed away from the table, already crossing the room as hurried knocks thundered on the door. Jerking it open a crack, a hushed voice whispered from the other side.

Doesn't anybody understand that I have a bloody headache?

"I'll be back later." Damien slipped out of the room before Kin could answer. He slammed the door, and Kin's body shook with the noise.

"Asshole," he muttered, resting his forehead on his arms.

Kin gasped awake again, jolted from the image of Amarie strangling him. He wheezed, clutching his throat. His forearm knocked someone's hand away, and he opened his eyes.

The Rahn'ka knelt next to his low bed, while Kin laid on his back. "Interesting. I didn't expect that to be a symptom."

Kin cringed and rolled onto his side, facing the wall. "I'm not an experiment. The nightmares are nothing new."

"I didn't mean the nightmares, those are definitely normal."

Thank Nymaera.

"I was referring to your heart. It stopped."

Kin lifted a hand to his chest, pushing his ribs as if he could feel the muscle beneath. "Told you I was dying."

Damien chuckled and moved away. His feet shuffled against the ground, and he pulled something off the table. "Guess I have to stay and babysit now." He batted at Kin's feet to make space and sat on the end of the bed.

Kin ventured a glance through the dimly lit room.

Cross-legged, Damien sat with a massive tome in his lap. The yellowed pages cracked as he lifted the cover and opened it near the middle.

"A little light reading?" Kin mumbled, resisting the urge to kick the book shut with his boot.

"We can call it that. You might make all this research easier on me if you'd tell me more about the Berylian Key and how it relates to your friend."

Kin grimaced. "I'll pass."

"Then I'll talk." Damien turned another page, and Kin rolled his eyes. "If you witnessed Amarie return from death, and she is also linked to the Key, then I must assume the events are related. So, either the Key brought her back, or..." Pausing, he huffed. "Unless she doesn't have the Key at all."

"Just stop," Kin interrupted before he could continue. "She doesn't have the Key."

"Of course she doesn't. I've been daft. She doesn't *have* it, she *is* it, isn't she?" Damien turned, wide-eyed, to Kin. "That's why she couldn't die. That's why Uriel wants her. Gods, does Uriel know the Key is a person?" He slammed the book shut and stood up in a fluid motion.

Kin groaned, trying to form words, but instead rolled onto his stomach to bury his face in his pillow. "I never said that."

"But it's true. You're far worse at hiding your thoughts in your current state. Amarie *is* the Berylian Key. Kin, this is remarkably important. Where is she?" Damien dropped the book onto the table.

"Like I'd tell you if I knew." Kin's pillow muffled his words.

Damien sighed. "Would you be more cooperative if I told you there might be a way to sever her from the power?"

Everything in Kin stiffened, and the ache of his body vanished into sudden whirling thoughts of Amarie. Freeing her from the power, and the danger.

If we were both free...

Kin pushed himself up, facing Damien. He ignored the blinding pain caused by the light, searching Damien's face. "How?"

Damien gave the barest smile beneath his beard. "Just have to provide a different vessel for the power. It used to be in an object, so there's no reason it couldn't be again. Time it right... and it should be simple enough."

"You make it sound like you're just planning a trip to the tavern down the street."

"For me, that's all it is. If I follow the steps in the right order, it would work. Her soul would need to leave her body, and while it's gone, I entrap the power. Then bring her back."

"Wait," Kin whispered, his stomach turning over. "You're talking about killing her."

"Only temporarily."

Kin let out a long breath. "And that's a trip to the tavern for you? I don't think I want to know what you'd consider complicated."

A fist thundered on the door, making Kin jump.

"Damien!" a man's voice yelled.

Looking at Kin, Damien sighed. "This. *This* is complicated." He rushed from the room.

Kin rocked to the edge of the bed, forcing his legs to hold him as he stood. The room rotated around him, but he steadied his stance with the table. He eyed the tome Damien had left behind, touching the dried leather binding. Scrawled on the front were symbols Kin didn't recognize. He opened it, discovering more of the same drawings, and closed it in defeat. The remounting pain in his head informed him he wouldn't have been able to read, anyway.

Damien didn't return, leaving Kin to dream-filled sleep. The distant howls mounted that night, leading to Kin's imagined death coming at the maws of a hungry pack.

"You look like shit." Damien came through the door.

It felt like months had passed, but Kin couldn't be sure, and he hadn't heard the wolf again. He sat with a bucket wedged between his feet, waiting to see if his breakfast would remain in his stomach. His back thick with sweat, he'd abandoned wearing a shirt despite the chill of the surrounding stone.

Without preamble, Damien withdrew a dagger from his belt and flipped it to offer the hilt to Kin.

He eyed it suspiciously, squinting through the darkened room. At least Damien had the kindness not to light a candle.

"Where in all the hells have you been?" Kin growled. "You said my heart stopped, then you just vanish?"

"I kept an eye on you." Damien bobbed the hilt at him. "Besides, it's only been a week."

"So, you've reconsidered and are now providing me with the means to kill myself? I hadn't considered you that generous."

Damien scowled. "It's not for you." He abandoned the attempt to give the blade, dropping it onto the table instead.

The sound rattled through Kin's bones, and he slapped his hands over his ears. A wave of nausea washed through his gut, forcing him to choose between the bucket and blocking the sound of Damien's footsteps. The wave of sickness escalated, and he fumbled for the bucket just in time.

"Gods." Damien groaned. "Still no better, then?"

Kin spat to cleanse the acidic taste from his mouth, setting the bucket down. "What does it look like?" His body convulsed, a winter chill vibrating through him. Goosebumps rose along his skin and he shivered as he jerked a blanket from his bed over himself.

Damien's freezing hand touched his forehead. "You're molten."

"It's like I'm naked in an Isalican frost field." Kin's teeth rattled.

"Some good news, though." Damien settled onto the bed next to Kin. "I resolved my other situation, so I'll be focused on you now. At least mostly."

Kin gave him a sideways glance. "I feel so blessed. Maybe we can go down to the local tavern and have an ale."

Damien shook his head, scratching the back of his neck. "At least your sense of humor is still intact, it seems. I think I found a solution to your problem."

"You'll have to be a bit more specific."

"Amarie. Separating the Berylian Key. The text I have access to is a little vague, but I'm pretty sure this will work."

Kin lifted his eyebrows, looking from Damien to the dagger. He couldn't make out the details in the dark room, other than the long straight blade and dark stone handle. He shuddered, pulling the scratchy wool blanket tighter around his shoulders. "Pretty sure?"

"Well, I'm *certain* the dagger will kill her, provided it strikes the right place. It's just a matter of whether it can contain the power of the Key. Worst case, it snaps back into her and brings her back to life either way, right?"

Kin gaped, unsure how the Rahn'ka could make the matter sound so simple. He opened his mouth to question him, but his body ignited with invisible fire licking his skin and he flung the blanket off. Sweat ran down his muscles, tickling like insects crawling over him. He sucked in a breath, trying to stabilize his pounding heart.

"I don't know you're in the condition to talk about this right now. I didn't think the withdrawal symptoms would be this bad. Bellamy's didn't seem this severe."

"Bellamy served for less than a year before he lost the stomach for it." Kin scratched his forearm, digging his nails into the scars. "I've been infected for eleven."

"We'll talk about this later, then." Damien stood, taking the dagger. "If you keep getting worse, I don't know how much longer you'll last. You might die, and I don't think you'd want me to bring you back."

Kin shook his head. "Not if it'll risk a relapse."

"I know we discussed it before, but I feel the need to remind you... I can't completely kill your connection, only bury it. If you wanted to, even after all this, you could become a Shade again." Damien turned from the doorway. His hazel eyes shone with something Kin suspected to be regret. Pity.

"I won't." Kin gritted his jaw. "I refuse to be Uriel's servant or his pawn."

"I'll try to come up with something else to help you," Damien whispered, closing the door quietly as he left.

Chapter 18

Winter, 2611 R.T.

Staring at her daughter's ice-blue eyes, Amarie's heart beat out of time with her head. The few months since her birth blurred together, lost in a haze of sleep deprivation and tumultuous emotion. Even the agony of labor dissolved to a vague memory.

The village's wet nurse offered to care for Ahria to let Amarie sleep, but she refused. She slept next to her baby, letting her nurse while she rested.

Amarie's belly slowly shrank, even though she hardly left her room. She tried to go for walks each day, but some were harder than others. Often, she wrapped her arms around her infant and wept. Tears for the father Ahria would never have, and tears because of the mother she'd been cursed with.

"Beautiful girl." Amarie sat on the back porch in a rocking chair while her daughter gripped a handful of the blanket covering them both.

She'd hoped for a boy. A boy would've been spared the burden of the Key, but the gods hadn't offered such mercy. Instead, they graced her with a girl who had her father's eyes. It only seemed fitting to give her the name she and Kin had jokingly discussed in Delkest. The one piece of her past she allowed into her future.

Ahria fussed, and Amarie resumed rocking the chair, hushing her with a soft tone as tears welled in her eyes. Lifting the baby, she held her to her chest, breathing the sweet scent of her hair.

"I'm sorry." She listened to Ahria's steady breathing as the baby drifted into sleep. "You deserve better."

Soft footsteps resounded behind her, the hinges of the door squeaking. She cringed, wishing for solitude.

"She's perfect."

Amarie looked up at Deylan. She smiled despite herself and shook her head. "She would be, if she didn't one day have to be the Key."

Deylan crouched next to her, putting a hand on her knee. "I hear she came early despite my mother's medicines. How are you recovering?"

Amarie nodded, unsure why a lump formed in her throat. "I'm fine. She's sleeping a little longer each time, and nursing her is easier now."

Deylan sighed. "I'm happy to hear that but tell me more about *you*. I understand you haven't been yourself."

"I'm doing my best," Amarie choked out, closing her eyes.

Her brother's arms wrapped around her in a gentle hug, carefully avoiding the slumbering Ahria. "No one is doubting that." Releasing her, he looked her in the eyes. "I want to make sure you're taking care of yourself too, letting people help you. Parenthood isn't easy, and there's a community here ready to be useful to you."

Amarie looked at the floor, her eyes glazing over as she considered what everyone in the town expected of her. Her shoulders weighed heavy. "They're strangers."

"They don't have to be." Deylan squeezed her knee. "We're worried about you."

"We?" Amarie looked at him again.

Deylan tilted his head. "Mom and Roslyn may have mentioned it to me. Talk to me, little sis. What's going on?"

Amarie glanced at the sleeping baby before sighing. "I'm not good for her." Her voice cracked, and she took a breath before continuing. "She deserves better than the cursed life she gets. Better than having me as her mother."

Deylan furrowed his brow, his gaze briefly leaving her before returning. He waited patiently.

"I love her so much, I can hardly breathe. But I keep thinking..."

Tears welled and fell, her voice breaking again as she spoke through the sobs. "She'd be so much safer without *me*, guiding all the shadows to her like a beacon. They don't know her, but they know me. And if I'm with her, they're going to find her."

"They all think you're dead. They won't find you because they're not looking. You're safe here."

Amarie looked away from Deylan to a pile of crates behind the neighboring house several yards away. Shadows twitched within the wood, and she squeezed her eyes closed for a moment.

You're imagining things.

"I'm not safe," Amarie whispered. "And if I'm not, she's not. If I don't die, then she never needs to learn the curse of her blood."

"Amarie." Deylan touched her shoulder. "Listen to yourself. You love this little girl, and the best thing for her is to be with her mother."

She glared at Deylan. "The problem is that I *am* listening to myself. It's only by my weakness that I can't let her go. It's selfish to keep her with me."

"No, what Talon did was selfish. Would you still feel this way if he was here?"

Amarie cringed. "Talon isn't here. So it doesn't matter. Even if he was, nothing would be different. In fact, she'd be in even more danger. Maybe he was right to leave me."

"Next thing you'll say is that Kin was, too," Deylan grumbled.

"He was. I've made some poor decisions in my life, but Deylan, I don't think this one is. Truly. I should be as far from her as possible to give her the best chance. It doesn't mean I don't want her. Hell, it doesn't even mean that Kin didn't want her. It just means that she can have a better life than running from our shadows."

Ahria whimpered and stirred in her mother's arms.

Sighing, Amarie rubbed the baby's back. "She deserves a normal life. A life brimming with family and love. I can't give that to her, but maybe someone else can. Don't you understand?"

Deylan met her gaze and pursed his lips. He heaved a sigh before dropping his head. "I understand why you feel the way you do. I just wish there was something I could do to convince you that you deserve the same chances."

"I had those chances." Amarie's tone darkened. "I misused them."

"And I have half a mind to go let two of those chances know what I think about them. Then maybe stick them a few times with my sword for good measure."

Amarie smirked sideways at her brother. "And one more time for me, all right?"

"You got it, little sis." He teasingly pinched her cheek. "But maybe you should come inside and get some rest while Ahria's asleep. I can take her for a bit."

Amarie nodded reluctantly, even though handing over her child made her nauseous. "I'm glad you're back."

I should get used to being without her, anyway.

Deylan prepared to leave again the following day, and his departure sparked an argument with his wife. Amarie tried not to listen as she stood in her room, looking out her window while holding Ahria. Being married to a man within the faction would be difficult, and she suddenly empathized with her mother. Though they weren't wed, she and Kalpheus loved each other all the same.

The image of Kin's face flashed in her mind, and she frowned. Chewing on her bottom lip, she placed the sleeping baby in her bassinet before opening the drawer where she kept some of her charcoal drawings. Her skills had improved over the months, and she withdrew the last one she made of Kin.

She'd left his irises bright, but his eyes were sunken. The rough depiction of a scruffy beard graced his chin. Her finger traced the scar she'd drawn over his temple and down his cheek.

"Did my mother feel this way about Kalpheus?" She furrowed her brow and tucked the drawing away.

Was your reunion in the Afterlife a happy one?

She wondered what it would be like to see Kin again. Gazing at Ahria, she clenched her jaw. Imagining the Shade's embrace sent waves of dread through her, mounting into immeasurable fear.

"I'll never tell him about you." Amarie swallowed her emotions and peered down at the little girl. "And maybe no one will ever tell you about me."

Today, she would talk to Cassia about finding adoptive parents for Ahria. A family, hopefully with siblings. Her throat tightened, but she steadied herself with a slow exhale.

This is for the best, my precious girl.

The next day, Cassia introduced her to a young family in the village who'd been struggling to conceive a second child. A sharp pang pierced her gut when she handed Ahria to the blonde-haired mother, her toddler's dirty fingers pulling on her apron to get a better look at the baby. They were eager to accept her as their own, and plans fell into place for them to adopt her. Even knowing she'd be cared for and loved, Amarie couldn't bring herself to leave. She cherished each day, knowing the next would be their last together. And each day she'd convince herself that she needed just one more.

Following her routine, after dropping Ahria at the Mordov household for the afternoon, Amarie confined herself to her room with her drawings.

Pushing the thick piece of charcoal over the parchment, she created a dark bloody pool. The viscous liquid spread across the parchment, encompassing all she imagined her death would be. She stared at the grainy smudges and ground her jaw. She tore the page from the easel, crumpling it into a ball. Chucking it in the corner of the room, it joined the ever-growing pile of her discarded wicked thoughts.

No longer able to prolong her self-torture, she kicked the easel's base, and it clattered to the ground. She threw the little box of charcoal Cassia had given her on top of it, spinning to pull her pack from underneath the bed.

She jerked open drawers, flinging clothing and items into the pack without any thought.

Her grasp landed on the small wooden box she'd stashed away, hoping not to think about it again. Swallowing, she opened it and stared at the araleinya necklace Talon had hidden in her pack. Breathing hard, she couldn't bring herself to wear it or destroy it, but her heart skipped a beat at another potential purpose for the jewelry.

Lifting it out of the box, she closed her fist around it, shutting her eyes to find the weave Talon had taught her months prior. A location enchantment meant for tracking objects. Her Art wasn't advanced enough for her to spell Ahria herself, but she could do it to the trinket.

Drawing her power to the surface, the semi-precious stones warmed in her palm as she wove essence within them. Exhaling, she opened her grip and eyed the pendant that looked the same. Yet, she could feel it deeper in her soul.

Trapping it back in the wooden box, she tucked it in her pack with the sealed package labeled Yinn'ai and swung it over her shoulder. Viento's stall housed the rest of her belongings, stashed in case a hasty escape became necessary.

Scrawling a sloppy goodbye message on a stray piece of parchment for Cassia and Roslyn, Amarie left her room. Everyone would be downstairs, but she avoided them and exited out the back. She pulled her cloak tighter, her breath creating clouds of winter frost.

Crossing the town to the Mordov house, she stopped at the front door. Within, Ahria laughed and squealed, playing with her new older brother. Her heart wrenched, and she choked back a sob. Placing the package and wooden box on the front doormat, she sidestepped to peer in the fogged window.

Her daughter sat in her adoptive mother's lap, shrieking with delight while her brother shook a noisy toy in front of her.

Amarie shook the thoughts of staying one more day from her head and cringed as she stepped away from the window.

Ahria is happy. And most importantly, she's safe.

Lifting a hand, she rapped on the door. Without waiting for someone to answer, she jogged from the home to the stable.

Her hands shook as she tacked Viento, tears blurring her vision and wetting her cheeks. The moisture chilled instantly in the winter air, and she swiped it aside. Talon had taught her to control the blue flames of her misery, but they still danced in her veins.

Hooves and hearts pounded as she raced east from the small town. Jacoby was only a day's ride away, and if she reached that far, she'd be able to keep going. Maintaining her hiding aura felt futile as she rode into the empty grass plains already heavy with snow. Screaming her agony, she abandoned it, internally daring Uriel to come find her.

Chapter 19

Talon reached Treama a month before his sister's supposed arrival and performed his old routine. Finding an inn near the city's docks, he rented a corner room on the top floor.

Despite never being much of a conversationalist, he recognized his exaggerated reclusiveness as days passed without event.

I need a distraction. And I won't find it trapped alone in a room.

After almost a week of taking his meals on trays, Talon forced himself into the public. Beside the inn, the raucous sounds of merriment permeated in a constant state from a tavern. The foggy windows glowed with warm orange firelight, banishing the cold brought by the wind whipping from the wharf.

Talon braced himself for the usual stares as he crossed the threshold, unwilling to hide his heritage. Warmed by his Aueric blood, he lacked a coat, unlike the locals.

The Thorn's Edge bustled with business, positioned on an ideal fork in the main road from the ports. City guards, hair let loose and armor partially removed, populated the front tables with a demand for more ale. Not unusual for any city, but in Ziona, all the guards were women. Stoutly built and muscled, they kept their swords at their sides.

A pair of women ran the main bar, one with a head of auburn hair tied in a messy pair of low buns. Her partner, darker in complexion, tucked loosened braids behind her ears, mussed during the day of work. Exhaustion dulled her eyes far more than her red-headed partner who filled a tray of mugs for a waiting serving boy.

Talon didn't have time to take in more of the active room before a large woman with a stained apron approached him.

"Greetings, stranger." The woman tilted her hips, accentuating curves beneath her breeches. Wrinkles aged the corners of her lips, lines from a happy life. "What can I do you for?"

"Looking for a meal." Talon gestured with his head towards the bar. "Just me."

"Well, my girls Talia and Idris will see to you, then. I'm Yedra, and you can give me a shout if you need anything."

"Thank you." Talon slipped onto one of the bar stools.

The red-headed bartender beamed, scrubbing the wooden surface in front of him. "I'm Idris. What can I getcha? Ale's running low for the night, so I'd hurry and order if you'd like one."

"Wine would be better." Talon smiled. "And some bread if you could?"

After giving him a quick nod and a smile, she slipped back towards her partner, nudging her in the side with a whisper in her ear.

Talia blushed and beat Idris with the rag in her hands. They giggled together, and Idris moved away. The smile vanished from Talia, and she turned away to see to another patron at the end of the bar.

Idris returned with a glass of red wine, sliding it across the bar.

"What's so funny?" Talon kept his tone gentle.

Idris's pale cheeks grew rosy. "Just teasing her. Trying to cheer her up a bit. Poor thing's husband died this summer, and she hasn't been the same since."

Talon's brow furrowed, and he glanced down the bar to the woman, who looked younger than Amarie, and already a widow.

"Don't sell a whole lot of wine." Idris pulled his attention back. "So hopefully that one works for ya. If not, let one of us know and we'll getcha something else."

Talon gave her a subtle nod, lifting the glass to his lips. It tasted watery and lacked body, but it was drinkable. He settled into his old habit of people watching, even though it felt strange now. He observed Talia most, considering the hardships she'd already encountered so young. She reminded him of Amarie, her eyes haunted by suffering he'd never be able to understand.

Talon tore a piece of bread as a pair of drunken guardswomen sidled up to the bar beside him.

"Their king is a tyrant," one said to the other. "And last I heard, he hasn't aged a day in the last ten years."

"Guess they're stuck with him for a while, then." The blonde guard scoffed. "Damn unnatural for men to live so long..." Her voice trailed off as she looked at Talon with a sneer.

Talon avoided the glare, keeping his eyes forward. In his peripheral, he saw the guard tense beneath her armor.

"Don't see your kind 'round here much." A drunken timbre tainted the second guard's voice.

Talon set his glass down. "I'm just passing through. Not looking for trouble."

"Ain't no trouble." The blonde gritted her teeth. "Unless you stick around longer than you're welcome." She met Talon's eyes, but he didn't blink.

"And that pretty auer face of yours won't be encouraging any extensions." The second balled a fist and placed it firmly on the bar top.

"I'll do my best with the generous welcome you've already granted me, then," Talon muttered, turning away. He picked up his drink but froze when a hand closed on his forearm.

"Mouthy, ain't you? Maybe your welcome is ending now."

"That's enough, Freida. He's a paying customer and it isn't your place to decide his welcome. I'd hate to go to Commander Kidesh about you... again."

When Freida released his arm, Talon broke eye contact with her. Behind the bar, Talia stood with her hands on her hips, a dirty bar towel still clenched in one. Her honey-brown eyes glared at the guards, and despite her shorter stature, she radiated authority.

"Talia, he—"

"I won't have any of what you're selling." Talia cut Freida off. "You and Eda are always starting up trouble when there isn't any. I have half a mind to call Yedra over here to kick the pair of you out."

"No need for that." Eda lifted her palms off the bar in surrender. "Come on." She tugged at her companion's sleeve.

Freida growled and turned to Talia, pointing a finger at her. "Best remember your place. I don't much care if you shirked your duty for a dead man and his child, but I won't be talked down to by a barkeep."

Eda tugged on her friend again and Talia's eyes widened.

"I think you better listen to your friend." Talon turned on his stool to face them. "No need for this to escalate any further."

Freida glared at him, her fury averted from Talia.

"Problem, ladies?" Yedra's jovial voice cut through the tension, and Freida's eyes moved from Talon.

Freida rolled her shoulders, squaring her feet. "No, ma'am. Just a little misunderstanding."

"Good to hear it." Yedra eyed them. "But I think it best you two head back to the barracks for the evening."

Eda tugged again, and this time Freida obeyed and stepped back. She scowled at Talon before spinning and walking out the front door. It slammed shut, silencing the dining hall briefly before the conversation resumed.

"You all right, girl?" Yedra stepped to the counter.

Talia nodded quickly, blowing at a loose strand of her brown hair on her forehead. "They're drunks. I don't pay attention to them."

Yedra nodded, then returned to walk the floor of the dining hall.

Talon eyed his glass thoughtfully as Talia heaved a breath and took her dirty towel to the bar beside him.

"I appreciate your intervention." He gave her a smile.

Talia looked up from the bar top, surprise rimming her tired eyes. "Usually foreign men get a bit touchy when a woman defends them."

"Foolish men, maybe."

She smiled back and gestured her chin towards his nearly empty glass. "Can I get you some more?"

Talon shook his head. "I'll save sampling more of your selection for another day."

"Planning on being in town for a while, then? Regardless of the shameful welcome?"

"About a month. I'm not easily put off by rude behavior. I'm rather accustomed to it. I more regret how they treated you."

Talia shrugged, tucking her towel into her apron. "Nothing I haven't heard before. I've made peace with my decisions."

"But that doesn't make it easy to be reminded." Talon's tone softened. "I am sorry for your loss. I can't imagine your hardships." He felt a pang in his chest as he imagined Amarie in front of him instead.

Will she end up working a job like Talia to support a fatherless child?

"Thank you. Ultimately, I'm lucky. I have my son to remind me of his father, and to keep me moving forward."

Talon pursed his lips and focused on the grain of the bar top. Unlike Talia, Amarie wouldn't remember him when she looked at her child.

She'll think of Kin.

"You all right, mister?" Talia ducked her head to catch his gaze. "Didn't mean to upset you."

"I'm fine." Talon swallowed the lump in his throat. "I... knew a woman like you. You just remind me of her."

Talia offered a smile. "You sure I can't get you something else?"

Talon sighed and shook his head. "Another night."

Returning to the Thorn's Edge became a nightly routine, as did his conversations with Talia. He confided in her about his love for Amarie, and eventual abandonment.

Talia didn't question his reasons when he purposely left out details, only listened. She told him about her husband, and the horrible pain involved in watching his slow death from Cerquel's plague. They'd both lost, in different ways, and found comfort in each other's mourning.

A month later, the expected knock of breakfast's delivery sounded on the door to his room.

Talon rose from his single bed and pushed in the chair of the small desk to allow the door to open. Iron hinges creaked as he cracked the door to see Alana's emerald eyes.

"Hello, brother."

Talon frowned and pulled the door open. "Let's get this over with. What do you want?" He stepped to the bed to let her in.

She sealed the door behind her, disapprovingly eyeing the small room. Spinning the chair free from the desk, she settled into it. Her dark green dress slit halfway up her thigh on both sides, revealing black breeches beneath. She ran her fingers through her hair, twisting strands around her obsidian-painted nails.

Talon recognized her usual anxious behavior and narrowed his eyes. Seeing her for the first time since discovering her treachery steeped his grief with rage.

"Have I done something to deserve such rudeness from my own blood?" Alana leaned towards him. "Come, set it aside as we always have. We've been through too much together for you to look at me as if I'm a bowl of rotted fruit."

"Rot is all I see when I look at you." Talon growled. "Why did you summon me? I refuse to be treated like one of your corrupted."

Working her jaw, Alana fell silent for a moment. "I need your help with something. I've made a mistake." She spat the words through gritted teeth.

Talon straightened and resisted the urge to start listing her wrongdoings aloud. "What mistake?"

Alana's nails grated over her leather breeches. She pressed her lips together in another uncharacteristic bout of hesitation while staring at something invisible, drifting in the air above his bed. "I need your assistance finding Kinronsilis." She cut each syllable of the Shade's name short. "I was keeping an eye on him, but he's evaded me."

Talon barked a laugh. "You... lost Kin? He gave you the slip and you honestly ask me for help?"

Alana glared at him, her green eyes paling. "We both know that you and Kin had a different kind of connection. It's imperative I find him."

"Imperative to whom? You? Your master? Certainly not me."

Alana eyes narrowed to slits. "Imperative to me. For me. Now stop playing around the subject and assist as you always have. I know you can find him."

"I absolutely will not." Talon crossed his arms. "You put no value in family. You only tear them apart."

Alana sighed, shaking her head. She daintily crossed a leg over the other and leaned back into the chair. "I can guess your inference. I only killed Lindora because—"

"What?" Rage surged through him, elevating his volume. "You killed Kin's mother?" He stalked forward, forcing Alana to lift her chin to look at him. Visions of the matronly woman flooded Talon's mind. She'd been a genuine lady, and one Talon appreciated the candidness of. Lindora would kiss his cheek whenever he arrived, and the sweet lily scent of her greying hair reminded him of his own mother. Lindora became the closest thing to a mother he'd had since becoming a rejanai.

Alana shrugged in the perforating silence, a little hum of disinterest on her lips. "An already short life simply made a little shorter. But with purpose." She twisted her hair around her finger. "It'd been intended to encourage Kin to remember his tasks, and he gave me little choice in the end."

"Like our parents then?" Talon's anger took control. "Like the choice you made to kill our mother and father? Is their blood less important than mine?"

Alana's casual movements froze. "Yes," she hissed. "Their betrayal demanded my direct response. It was a simple choice."

"Simple?" Talon failed to block the emotional sob in his throat.

"Yes. Simple. Our *own* father revealed us to the council. He needed consequences for the betrayal of his children. Kin's defiance calls for similar action."

"If it's so simple, why don't you kill Kin? You have no qualms against murder. You *are* the fiend the council believes you to be."

Alana shot to her feet, stepping to Talon. He lifted his arm and her clawed nails dug into his wrist as she twisted it aside. "I am no fiend," she whispered dangerously. "A juvenile mind like yours cannot understand the complexity of the master's will." She twisted his wrist, spinning his entire body with it. He cried out as she shoved his hand against his lower back, straining his shoulder. "You've been speaking to the council. How?"

Instinct spurred him to reach for the power of his Art, and it answered, springing to life in his trapped hand.

Alana growled, recoiling at the sudden scorch, shaking her hand. Before Talon could morph the energy into something substantial, Alana's power rose. The light in the room dimmed, the window shadowing over to block the sun.

"Tell me, brother. What have you done?"

"Other than discover the lies you've spoken to your siblings?" Talon's body shook. "You've kept enough secrets to allow me this one. I still have friends in our homeland, ones who confirmed suspicions I already had."

Alana's lips formed a thin line. "You forget all I've done for us. All I did for you."

"The rudimentary training you provided me before we became rejanai? Or are you speaking of all the messes you left for me to clean up behind you?"

"Insolence," Alana spat. "I merely showed you the path, you're the one who took it into darkness."

"I'm no longer the terrified child you manipulated into taking blame for your evils." Talon took a step towards her. He reached deeper for his power, and it surfaced. His skin burned as the entirety of his pool prepared to lash out at his sister. He held it steady, daring her to make the first move. "This is over. You are no longer my sister."

Her eyes flashed, lips curling into a snarl, but her attack didn't come as Talon expected, her power fading with her exhale. "Brother." A forced softness mellowed her tone. "You can't leave like this. I need your help, and now you deny me?"

"Not just this plea to find Kin. All future requests. Whatever may happen to him, he'll get what he deserves. Just as you will, dae'fuirei." Talon offered no mercy as he named her the worst corruption the Aueric language could describe. "Goodbye. Shall we never meet again." He shoved past the woman who'd once been his sister.

Alana stumbled back against the chair.

Snatching his pack from the desk, he crossed through the door in a smooth motion. The door slammed shut behind him. She could keep the room. He needed to cleanse himself of all he had been. As he walked down the narrow hallway, wood and metal crashed behind the closed door, accompanied by Alana's furious roar.

Rumor of Alana's visit to Treama, followed by her sudden departure, spread through tavern gossip. Included in the stories, Talon refrained from public houses for a time, relocating to an inn further from the waterfront. He sent the previous innkeeper a bag of iron marks after hearing the room he'd rented had been destroyed by the mysterious auer woman. Plenty to pay for the damages.

After a week, deep winter locked all ships in the docks, leaving Talon stranded. He could take the land routes, but the idea of traversing the snow soured his already somber mood. Instead, he indulged himself in returning to the Thorn's Edge.

"Idris!" Yedra's eyes darted up and down the bar as Talon took his usual seat. "Where'd Talia go?"

Talia's head of messy-braided hair popped up from behind the bar. Her eyes looked more tired than usual, and bloodshot. "Right here, ma'am."

"Well quit ducking down like that every two seconds and maybe you won't fall so far behind, girl! You're holding onto this job outta the—"

"Mum." Idris gave Yedra a pointed look, and the matronly woman sighed.

"Everything all right?" Talon glanced at Talia, who averted her eyes back below the bar.

"Surely." Yedra nodded. "Ain't nothing to worry your pretty little head about, anyway. But I best go check on the other customers." She turned from him, crossing towards a table of city guards, who seemed equally uncomfortable about the confrontation at the bar.

Talia's side of the bar was practically empty, while every stool on Idris's was occupied.

Furrowing his brow, Talon leaned over the bar as Talia knelt. When she came back up, her face mere inches from Talon's, she jumped with a gasp. Her hand closed on a worn chain around her neck, grasping the pair of wedding rings she and her late husband wore.

"Startled me." Talia laughed at herself. The stress lines, which had begun to fade, had returned with dark circles beneath her eyes.

"Sorry." Talon sat up straighter. "What's wrong?"

Talia's eyes widened at the sound of scuffling at her feet. It resolved into a resounding thunk, quickly followed by a wail. She disappeared behind the bar again, hushing. "Oh, Conny."

Idris slid in to hide Talia from the rest of the bar, noisily pushing some mugs together. "Usual today?"

Talon narrowed his eyes. "Is that—"

"Talia!" Yedra approached the bar, and Talia jumped again.

The girl partially stood, still stooping below the bar.

The wails reduced to murmured sobs.

Yedra sighed as she put her hands on her hips. She looked sad despite her previous annoyance. "Is that boy of yours back there again?"

Talia groaned, but nodded. "I'm sorry, ma'am. There's no one to watch him anymore, and I need this job..."

"Behind a tavern bar ain't no place for a baby, and it's keeping you from doing your work." Yedra frowned. "Plus, he's disturbing the customers. You head home and take care of that boy."

Talia sighed as she lifted a child onto her hip.

The toddler had a dusting of black hair and tears falling down his bronze cheeks. He gripped his mother's blouse, burying his face into her shoulder as his little body heaved with sobs.

Talia's shoulders slumped, rubbing a hand on her son's back. "But I need the pay from—"

"Don't make this any harder." Yedra pursed her lips. "I know it ain't easy and I really am sorry, but I gotta think about my business. Until you find someone new to watch him, better to head home."

"I'll watch him," Talon blurted before he fully thought it through.

Both Talia and Yedra's gazes turned to him, washed with surprise.

"Oh, I couldn't ask you—"

"You don't need to. I'm offering." He held up a hand before Talia could protest further. "I'll sit right here at the bar, so you can keep an eye, if that's all right with Yedra. I'm sure I'll be able to keep him entertained."

Yedra glanced at Talia and shrugged. "Makes no nevermind to me. As long as he ain't back there."

Talia hesitated still and watched as her employer turned and walked away. She eyed Talon, and the boy wriggled to be free. He turned in her hands, bleary eyes looking at Talon with curiosity.

Talon smiled at him. "His name is Conny?"

"Conrad." Talia stepped around the end of the bar. "Conny's just a nickname." She eyed Talon one last time before lifting her child towards him.

Talon took the toddler carefully, and Conrad didn't protest as Talon settled him against his side. Taking his napkin from the counter, he dried the baby's tears.

Conrad fidgeted, pushing away the cloth with chubby hands.

"Bump doesn't look too bad." Talon inspected the mark on the child's forehead.

Talia smirked, and her tension ebbed away. She began cleaning now that her hands were free.

Talon turned his attention to the boy and whispered little

observations to him, pointing out things behind the counter. A new distraction became necessary when Conrad grew restless, and Talon wove a bit of energy into an ice shard, twisting it to refract light from the window.

The evening wore on, the tavern gradually emptying.

Talia cleared the mugs from the bar. "You're awful good with kids. But you and Amarie never had any, right?"

A pang shot through Talon and he struggled not to flinch. "No. I don't believe children are part of my destiny."

"Shame." Talia scrubbed the surface next to him. "You have the touch. Look, I owe you. How about you let me pay for your meal—"

"Paying for my meal defeats the purpose." Talon bounced Conrad on his knee. "You said you needed the money, and I'm in a position to help."

"Hell of a man." Idris smirked at the other end of the bar, proving her eavesdropping skills. "Say Talon, you around tomorrow? Talia's got another shift—"

"Hush." Talia frowned. "Ignore her. You've done enough already."

"I can watch him tomorrow." Talon had considered it in the quiet moments of the tavern, in which Talia was too busy to pay him any attention. Holding the child in his arms felt oddly comforting amid his raging guilt for Amarie.

This can be part of my penance.

 Chapter 20

Kin's muscles burned, the winter air chilling the sweat dripping down his back. Lifting himself into another pull-up on a thick horizontal root between ruin structures, his arms shook. After so many months of self-inflicted imprisonment, pushing the limits of his body invigorated him. He'd never felt so uninhibited, no longer drawing power from the shadows. His body finally felt like his own.

Still not permitted to leave the sanctum, on Damien's advice, he remained active within. If he left the ruins, Damien feared his symptoms would return. The uncertainty encouraged him to take advantage and enjoy his current state of wellbeing. A headache lingered at his temples, but he hardly noticed.

Dropping to the ground, Kin stretched his hands and smoothed his long hair back. It fell over his ears now, nearly to his shoulders.

Amarie would hate it.

He smirked at the memory of her cutting his hair.

"Should we cut it off, then?"

Kin whirled around to face Damien. "Would you stop that? It's the most... unnerving thing to get used to."

"I can't help it." Damien laughed. "For what it's worth, it drives my wife crazy too. Would you like to take a walk today? It might be a good opportunity before it snows again."

Kin tugged his shirt on, followed by his cloak. Snow covered the land, a foot deep in untouched areas. Paths were clear, and the idea of seeing scenery other than the decaying buildings made him eager to go.

Nodding, Kin approached Damien. "Do you even have to ask? Let's go. Can't wait forever to test your work."

As they walked side by side from the ruins, Damien pulled the familiar dagger from his belt. The obsidian blade was serrated near the handle, smoothing out at the tip. As Kin accepted the guard-less hilt from the Rahn'ka, he tilted it in the afternoon light, admiring the silver-etched inscriptions along the length of the weapon. He recognized the language from the tome Damien had been reading.

Drawing in a deep breath, Kin held it for a moment. His shoulders weighed heavily with the dagger's implications. "So, I would use this to kill her?" The words tasted bitter.

She'll be happy when she learns about the plan.

Damien nodded. "And the power of the Key will enter the dagger. Once it does, I'll bring Amarie back, and she will only be a woman."

"She'll never only be a woman." Kin passed the weapon back to Damien. "This will work?"

"Yes. It'll work. But she must agree first. This is no small feat, and I can't in good conscience do this without her consent."

"Of course." He opened his mouth to speak more, but his insides twisted. Crossing the boundary of the ruins into the woods, a weight struck his chest and his scarred-over tattoo burned. His mind clouded as the veil of his consciousness allowed something in, but he wrestled it back into place. He balled his hand into a fist, stabilizing his breathing.

Damien eyed him. "You feel it."

Kin grimaced. "It's not so bad. I feared how strong it might be, but..." As they kept walking, the feeling grew more intense, but it did nothing to falter his resistance. "I can handle it."

"Good."

Damien led him farther from the ruins, and the trees thinned until they became sparse. Snow-covered grasslands stretched for miles, with only a few disruptions to the flat terrain in sight. Reaching halfway up his calves, the snow slowed their pace, but with no destination, Kin didn't mind.

Kin's breath clouded in front of his mouth, a piece of his hair tickling his jaw. "Maybe we should cut it."

Damien didn't answer, and Kin looked at him. His eyes were distant, staring off to the western side of the plains.

"What's wrong?"

Damien shook his head. "I don't know. I feel... something. And it's moving."

"Towards us?" Panic rose in Kin's chest.

"Not directly, it's at least a mile away, heading east. I've never felt something like this before."

While Kin's shoulders relaxed, he tried to imagine what sensation Damien could possibly have never felt. The concept was daunting.

Damien stepped forward, squinting across the terrain.

Kin lifted a hand to shield his eyes from the sun as he followed the Rahn'ka's gaze.

A figure, far in the distance, rode a black horse. They moved at an alarming pace, unhindered by the snow. He'd never seen anyone ride so fast. Aimed to pass the two men a mile ahead of them, the horse and rider kicked up a cloud of water vapor in their wake.

Kin's senses tingled, daring him to acknowledge another's Art. A second later, it slammed against the barricaded connection to Uriel, and he stumbled forward. He gasped, the familiarity colliding with his soul. A migraine erupted as he lunged forward. He tripped, landing on his hands and knees in the snow. The cold stabbed through his body.

"Amarie!" He watched with blurry vision as Viento carried the woman he loved just out of his reach. She'd never hear him so far away, not over the sound of her horse's hooves.

Why is her hiding aura gone? And why is she not in Eralas? And alone?

Pain shot through his head, nausea bubbling in his stomach, and he gripped his midsection. The slumbering beast within him awoke with a vengeance, gnawing at the barrier Damien had established.

"Kin!" Damien's hand clapped down on his shoulder.

Heat flooded his body, springing sweat on his brow. He gritted his teeth, sucking in the cry of agony. He focused his bleary eyes long enough to watch Amarie disappear to the east.

"She's headed towards Jacoby." Kin choked out the words. "I have to catch up to her. Something's wrong."

"You need to get back within the sanctum. Can you even stand?"

Kin clenched fists full of melting snow, urging all he could into his muscles. Forcing himself up, a new wave of nausea rushed through him, and he immediately doubled back over, head spinning as his stomach ejected its contents.

"Shit," Damien muttered, looping an arm under Kin's shoulder. "We need to get you back. Whatever is happening is because of the Berylian Key. You can't go near her."

Kin spat, squeezing his eyes closed. Grief joined the physical pain, but he shook his head. "Something's wrong."

"I'll say. We need to discuss alternative options for you."

Kin didn't remember the walk back to the sanctum, nor when Damien threw a blanket over him while he shivered on his bed. Somehow, his clothing dried and warmed, but his mind failed to clear. In a merciful embrace, sleep took him.

He awoke to a wet cloth on his forehead and the sound of water being poured. Blinking, he tried to focus as somber blue light radiated from the surrounding walls.

"You need to drink this," Damien said, crossing to hand him a tin cup.

Kin struggled to sit up, propping himself against the wall. A faint heat pulsed from it, bringing comfort. The headache he'd been ignoring mounted into a migraine, and his body felt heavy.

Damien lifted a stool, quietly placing it on the ground beside Kin.

The tea smelled awful, but Kin drank it anyway and it burned his tongue. "What happened? I feel like I did months ago."

"I'm not entirely sure. Something in the way her power interacted with yours brought your symptoms back. It seems my back-up plan might be your only option now."

"Why do I get the impression that I won't like it?" Kin cringed. "She's in Jacoby right now. *Right there.* Something's wrong. Talon should be with her."

"It won't be good for either of you to see each other right now. If this is what her power did from a distance, imagine if you were standing next to her."

Kin heaved a sigh, closing his eyes to the heat rising in them.

"I think it's best if you go with me to Eralas."

Opening his eyes, Kin studied Damien's frown. His stomach curdled. "Eralas? I can't..."

"I can get you there, regardless of your history with Uriel. Besides, I think I've buried the connection enough to allow you past their warding. The only answer for you to fight this is there."

Kin huffed. "That's where Amarie is supposed to be." He couldn't help but wonder if something had happened to Talon. The guilt for asking his friend to return to his homeland rocked his stomach.

Did the auer find him?

Shaking his head, Kin swallowed. "What does Eralas hold for me that Olsa doesn't?"

"Peace. Slumber."

Kin's brow furrowed, looking at Damien's serious face. "I can sleep here."

"Not like the auer can make you." Damien scratched the back of his head. "Amaranthine Slumber is an auer practice that I believe will help you. They put you in a permanent state of sleep, to be ended when they please."

"It sounded great until the end part there. You think this will help me?"

"Logically, yes. You would sleep through your body's withdrawals until it learns to adapt. Then I wake you up and deal with the minor side effects. I think... a year would be sufficient."

"A year?" Kin couldn't help but be skeptical.

Damien nodded. "It's been months already, so I think a year is a good place to start."

"What about Amarie? The plan."

"You've said yourself that Amarie is strong. She'll be all right for a year. You're in no shape now, anyway. It'll have to wait. I'll give you the dagger to hold on to, so it's safe."

Kin frowned, swallowing another bout of sickness. His body trembled, and he clasped the useless blanket tighter on his shoulders. "And that'll work?"

Damien nodded, putting his hand on Kin's shoulder. "It has to."

"You said killing me and bringing me back would work... Wouldn't that be—"

"I thought so when I mentioned it, but with the state of your soul, I can't guarantee it will work. It should be a last resort at best."

Kin's stomach sank. "All right. Slumber, then."

Chapter 21

Viento's hooves thundered against the frozen ground, pounding a trail through the snow. The air clouded behind them as Amarie shared her energy with her horse. They raced over the plains, bound for Jacoby. The wind stung her face, demanding she slow her pace, but she couldn't. If she slowed, she'd turn around and return to Ahria.

Squeezing her eyes closed, Amarie gripped a handful of Viento's mane and begged for strength beyond what her power could give her.

When she reached the outskirts of the city, she debated continuing without stopping. Letting Viento walk, his heaving breath created clouds of frosted air while she glanced at her nearly empty saddle bags. Other than her camp supplies and weapons, she had nothing.

Sighing, Amarie cursed her lack of preparedness.

Viento will benefit from a stable tonight, anyway.

Best to stock up, since winter left hunting scarce and foraging next to impossible. One more night in a bed wouldn't hurt either, but a night of uninterrupted sleep sounded far from relaxing.

After booking a room for herself and stabling Viento nearby, she made her way to a noisy tavern down the block.

The busy streets turned the snow to slush, sloshing under cartwheels and her boots. Pulling her hood over her head as more thick flakes fell, Amarie gritted her teeth. The morning's promising blue sky had lured her into a false sense of good weather.

Feeling light with no weapons other than her dagger, Amarie pushed the door to the tavern open. The crowded room offered no empty tables, but she found a vacant stool at the bar. Leaving her hood up, she slapped an iron mark on the bar top.

It earned her a quick mug of ale, and the attention of the busy barmaid. "Anything to eat, hun? Our special tonight is seared venison with herbed potatoes, or we've a few pheasant pot pies left."

"The venison is good." Amarie dragged her mug towards her as the woman relayed the order to the kitchen. She took a swig, her hood falling back as she did.

"You're a popular one tonight with the looks you're getting." The man to her left turned to her, and she glared at him.

"Leave me alone," she muttered, and he shrugged before turning away. Rolling her lips together, she glanced behind her.

Several pairs of eyes quickly looked away, and she huffed a dissatisfied sigh. One pair, however, remained on her. Dark grey eyes, belonging to a middle-aged man. He stared at her, and all the hairs on the back of her neck stood straight.

Her heart thudded faster, and she turned back to the bar, downing the rest of her drink.

He's a Shade. And he knows exactly who I am.

Adrenaline flooded her veins, and she reached for her Art. Everything she'd recently lost was Uriel's fault. He took Kin from her, Talon, and now Ahria. Using her power to surge the Shade would do little, but it would get his master's personal attention. It would grant her the opportunity to kill him once and for all. And she could reclaim the things in her life she'd lost.

Would I reclaim Kin or Talon?

The thought caused a bubble of anxiety, and she swallowed it without trying to answer.

The barmaid placed a steaming plate of food in front of her, oblivious to the silent exchange of energy between the Art users in the room.

Holding her power ready, Amarie spun to face her nemesis. When his gaze lifted to meet hers again, she lurched off her seat, only to be stopped by a woman stepping in her way. Her view of the man obstructed, Amarie scowled as the woman touched her elbow.

"He's not what you think," she whispered.

"Excuse me?" Amarie met the shorter woman's gaze and recoiled, bumping into her stool. One green iris, one yellow. "You."

Flashes of the woman passing her in the dormitory hallways in Eralas came to her mind. Just before she'd made a deal with the elders to save Talon's life.

The woman placed a hand on the shoulder of the man sitting next to Amarie and whispered something in his ear. He nodded, vacating his seat for her, and she sat down facing the bar. "You remember me."

Amarie looked at the Shade and watched him embrace an elderly woman while a child raced to cling to his leg. Her back straightened. She looked down and rubbed her neck. "How did you know...?" She sat and looked at the woman who'd stopped her.

"That you thought he was your enemy? Your energy was boiling. I'm sure every practitioner within a block of here knew it. But he's a local with just enough power to make him noticeable to people like us." A mug of ale landed in front of her, and she sipped while motioning for another for Amarie.

"You know who I am." Amarie's gut swam with a mixture of anxiousness and excitement.

The woman nodded once. "I was there when you shared your power with the council. The council swore all witnesses to secrecy, but there's no rule against talking *to* you." She motioned with her chin to Amarie's meal. "You should eat. The food is good here. I'm Mira."

"Amarie." She stabbed a potato with her fork. "This can't be a coincidence. What do you want from me?"

"I recognized you the moment you came into town. Your timing couldn't be better." Mira sighed. "I was hoping you'd help me."

Amarie shook her head. "I'm not interested. Just because you're auer doesn't mean I have to help you. And helping strangers hasn't gotten me far in the past."

"Is that why you're flaunting your power, now? To dissuade anyone from approaching you?"

Amarie took a bite of venison, ignoring the question.

"You might want to reconsider being so blatant this close to Helgath..." Mira drank her ale.

"I'm not afraid of Helgath."

Mira fell silent, and Amarie's shoulders relaxed as she ate her meal in peace. The woman said nothing to her for a while, drinking and chatting with other people at the bar.

"Do you know everyone here?" Amarie gritted her teeth.

"Yep," Mira chirped, tilting her head. "Is that a problem?"

"No. Why would it be?"

"How about you tell me?"

Amarie rolled her eyes and rose from her seat, pushing her empty plate away. Without another word, she headed for the door. Snow fell in massive clumps, but she needed the fresh air.

The bells on the door chimed as someone followed her out. She didn't need to turn around to see who it was. "Persistent, aren't you?"

"Yep. Is that a problem, too?" Mira came up beside her. When Amarie didn't stop trudging through the snow, her smile faded. "Please, I really need your help."

"Why?"

"There's someone who keeps showing up, and he's got this strange power. Every time I get close to him, he just vanishes into shadows. I don't think I'm—"

Amarie stopped and faced Mira. "What did you say about shadows?"

Mira slid to a stop in the snow, nearly colliding with Amarie. "I know it sounds ridiculous. Like the old myths." She shook her head as snow collected in her dark-brown braids. "But it's true, I swear."

Amarie's heart picked up its pace again. "Does he have a tattoo?"

Mira pointed to her forearm. "Here. How did you—"

"Why would a Shade be following you?" Amarie blinked away the flakes sticking to her lashes.

"I don't know. Maybe because I have the Art? I don't know what to do, where to go—"

"Eralas. Go back to Eralas, they can't follow there."

Mira's eyes widened, and her mouth kept moving, but Amarie didn't hear her. She stared at the woman's two-tone eyes, imagining them turning black like Trist's had. If a Shade pursued Mira, then Amarie had a chance to lure it from the shadows and use it to taunt Uriel into revealing himself.

As she refocused on the conversation flying past her, Mira was still talking. "...and then what would I do? I wouldn't be able to—"

"I'll take you."

She won't get hurt.

Amarie buried the hint of guilt rising in her. "Can you leave first thing tomorrow?"

Mira led a grey mare into the stable Amarie had instructed. The bags hanging from her saddle bulged, a bow tied to the top of her packs. Two braids secured her hair at the sides of her head, over her ears. The rest joined in a ponytail, swaying as she joined Amarie. "Before we go, you should hide your power. If you can."

Amarie met her gaze, tilting her head at seeing two matching green eyes. "All right." It took a breath of focus to wrap her energy beneath her aura, and she smirked. "Better?"

Mira heaved a short sigh and nodded. "Figured we didn't need any *extra* attention."

Morning sun cast a blinding glare off the snow as they rode from the stable, Amarie's bags as heavy as Mira's.

They headed southeast, planning to follow the border of Helgath and cross at Quar, making their way to the southern coast. The beach would take them to Lazuli, where they would alter course northwest, aiming for the point closest to Eralas. A small port town, Hoult, often sent minor vessels to and from Ny'Thalus, giving Amarie an easy escape into Eralas should her plans go awry. The journey would take weeks.

After successfully entering Quar, they found a place for a hot meal and a drink. Although located in a rather dingy part of town, Brigg's Hollow tavern provided them a spot away from prying military eyes. With a stable nearby, and empty rooms, it was the best option.

The door dragged on the floor as Mira heaved against it.

Amarie pulled her scarf down from over her face, walking to the table closest to the fire. The midday crowd had left the place mostly vacant, and she slid a chair out to sit down. Pulling off her gloves, she laid them on the brickwork next to the blazing flames to let them dry.

Mira followed suit, rubbing her hands on her arms. "I can't wait for spring." She scooted closer to the fire. "New season, new year, new beginnings. Do you like spring?"

A barmaid brought them hot mugs of mulled wine.

Amarie took a sip and then shrugged. "I don't think a new year can give me a fresh start. Never has before."

"You make it sound like you've done horrible things." Mira lifted the steaming mug to her lips. "Can't be all bad. You're helping me."

"I've made a lot of mistakes. But most of the time, I was trying to do the right thing, like a damn idiot."

Mira gave a dry laugh. "I know how that goes. Those are the things that always come back to bite us in the ass."

Amarie smirked. "Really? What have you done?"

Mira grinned and shook her head. "I might have some posters with my face on it in this country. I've also made mistakes that other people paid the price for." She turned her mug on the table and her smile faded. "Doing the *right* thing wasn't high on my priority list most of the time."

"Well, you won't get any judgment from me." Amarie tapped her mug on the table in a motion for a refill. "But you will get more wine."

As the sun dipped low in the winter sky, serious conversation devolved to humor, with discussions about each man who entered the tavern. Amarie encouraged Mira to talk to a particularly handsome soldier, but she declined, pushing Amarie to instead.

"I hardly need more rebels in my life." Mira laughed, nursing her mug. "I've got plenty, thank you."

Amarie raised an eyebrow. "Rebels, huh? Getting involved in the mess of Helgathian politics?"

"I'd rather move to Feyor." Mira sighed. "But we don't always get to choose our path."

Amarie nodded, finishing her mug. "Don't I know it. I still think you should talk to him, even if it's just for one night. You seem tense."

"Right, because you're the picture of relaxation." Mira clicked each of her silver rings on the table as she drummed her fingers, and they both laughed.

Mira glanced at the soldier across the tavern, then at Amarie. "He keeps looking at you. Rebels are great distractions, I would know."

Amarie lifted her gaze, meeting the eyes of the red-haired stranger. He smiled at her, and she wondered if Mira was right. Someone different from the men who'd broken her heart.

The door ground open as another soldier entered the tavern. He paused just inside, eyeing the man who'd smiled at her. Expressions soured between them, and several other un-uniformed men in the tavern looked up.

Tension filled the air, and Amarie looked at Mira. "What's going on?"

Mira kept focused on the people in the tavern. "Just wait..."

"He's here!" The newcomer turned over his shoulder, shouting out the open door. Boots thumped on the porch outside.

The red-headed soldier remained seated but straightened his back. "Come to join me for a drink then, Sergeant?" He raised his mug in invitation.

"Don't be stupid, Jett." The sergeant scowled. "We all know what you've been playing at."

A pair of soldiers entered, holding the door open.

The casual observers in the room stood. The one closest to the door, a blonde, muscular woman, spoke. "You're not welcome here."

The Sergeant pushed her aside, and everyone sprang into action, chairs striking the ground as they fell backwards.

Mira darted from her seat, and Amarie followed, unsure which side they were on.

When Mira grabbed the guard who'd shoved the woman, Amarie bit her lip. "I guess we're rebels today." She ducked when a man swung at someone next to her.

It'd been a long time since she'd gotten involved in a tavern brawl, but the action felt good. Adrenaline fueled her, fighting alongside Jett, Mira, and the others.

Jett jerked the burgundy scarf of one of the attacking soldiers, flinging him on top of his table. His half-filled ale clattered to the ground. With a thud, his fist connected with the soldier's jaw, and he prepared for another strike.

An enemy soldier approached behind him, next to Amarie, and locked his forearm around Jett's neck, pulling him off his comrade.

Amarie leapt, yanking a chair from the ground and crashing it over the soldier's back, reducing him to a heap on the floor as Jett spun around. He grinned at her before rejoining the chaos, and a swirl of nerves collected in her stomach.

Someone gripped Amarie's shoulders and slammed her into the tavern wall, knocking the air from her lungs.

Jett's mouth claimed hers, gasping for a breath as he pressed her hard against the wall inside her room.

She wrapped her legs around his waist, nails gliding along the back of his shirt, the events of the tavern brawl blurring into the sweet taste of him on her tongue.

They'd slipped out the back with the barmaid's help, and Mira had insisted on turning in for the night, leaving Jett and Amarie alone.

His coarse hands ran up her sides, banishing thoughts of anything else. He smelled like ale and sweat, and his muscled arms carried her to her bed.

Her fingers tangled in the curls of his red hair, his stubble rough on her neck as he kissed her.

Amarie's heart pounded when she loosened her hiding aura, and he didn't react. He continued to eagerly kiss her skin, shedding the final layers of clothing between them.

When morning sunlight touched Amarie's eyelids, she stirred, squinting at her surroundings. She turned her head slowly to the side, catching sight of the naked, slumbering man beside her.

Jett's hand rested on her bare hip, and she carefully removed it. Rising from the bed, she tiptoed to her clothes, pulling them on. Glancing back at the man in her bed, she cringed and exited the room, boots in hand. Racing to Mira's door, she didn't bother knocking before entering, closing and latching the door behind her.

Mira, already dressed, looked at her and a grin spread across her face. "Have a good night?" She wiggled her eyebrows.

Amarie frowned. "That was a stupid thing to do."

"But was it *good*?"

Shaking her head, Amarie pulled her boots on. "It doesn't matter, it was wrong."

"Why? You both clearly wanted it." She lifted a steaming cup of tea from the table beside her and offered it out to Amarie.

Amarie sighed, considering Mira's point. "Yes, but... I still want someone else more."

"Kin or Talon?" Mira met her gaze, tilting her head.

Amarie flinched, taking the tea. She'd confided in Mira on their journey, filling her in on the most basic details of her tangled love life without mentioning her child. "Does it matter?"

"Yup. Who would it be, if you could choose?"

"Kin." Amarie wondered at her certainty as she said his name, staring at the steaming mug. "I think it's always been Kin, and I was too blind... or stubborn to see it."

"Or hurt." Mira gestured to the cup. "Drink up."

Amarie nodded, lifting an eyebrow at the tea. "I'd like to leave soon, before Jett wakes up and comes looking for me. I need to make a stop at an apothecary."

The last thing I need is another unexpected child.

Mira shook her head. "That's what the tea is for."

Chapter 22

Spring, 2612 R.T.

Conrad's favorite toy quickly became the little boat Talon fashioned out of a branch found on one of their walks. In the months of minding him, they occasionally ventured from the tavern, and Talon taught the boy about the world around him.

The wonder of the child, the unyielding curiosity, lightened the burdens of his grief. Amarie's baby would certainly heal her, just as Conrad had him.

Conrad pushed his little boat around the tabletop, avoiding the obstacles Talon had created with several cracked mugs he'd volunteered to fix. Wedging little bits of oak into the broken parts, he used the Art to seal it back together.

"Boat!" Conrad crashed it into Talon's chest. "Boom!"

Talon laughed and encouraged the toy back onto the table. "Easy, Captain. Best to keep that thing in the water."

Conrad giggled, running around the other side of the table as the door to the Thorn's Edge chimed.

Talon looked up, and his chest seized when his eyes met Deylan's.

Amarie's brother glowered, chest heaving as if he'd run there. He wore a heavy woolen cloak to block out the early spring chill, the point of his sword protruding from behind.

"We're not quite open yet, but breakfast—"

Deylan stopped Talia with a wave. "I'm not here for food." He spoke in a monotone while maintaining eye contact with Talon.

Talia frowned and followed his gaze. She furrowed her brow, hurrying from behind the bar to pick up her son. His boat hit the ground, and Conrad cried out, but Talia stepped aside with him.

"It's all right." Talon closed his eyes a moment to fight the anxiety rising in his chest. "He's a friend of mine." He stood and stepped towards Deylan. "Is something wrong?"

"Outside. Now." Deylan turned and stalked from the tavern.

Talia took a step towards Talon, and he patted her shoulder.

"I'll be right back."

"Do you want me to fetch some guards? I can sneak out the—"

"No, that's not necessary." Talon squeezed her shoulder. "I don't think he'd try to hurt me."

Talia nodded, gripping Conrad tighter as Talon exited the tavern's front door.

Deylan led him around the side of the building and into the alleyway, lined with crates and barrels.

"What's happened?" Talon approached Deylan from behind. "Is Amarie all right?"

Deylan spun around, fist raised. It slammed into Talon's jaw with impressive force, whipping his head to the side and causing him to stumble. "You selfish bastard," he growled, his fist still clenched and knuckles white. "You were supposed to protect her, not leave her alone to fend for herself. And pregnant!"

Talon touched his jaw, opening it gradually. "I had to." He heaved a breath, straightening to meet Deylan's glare. "You don't understand the danger—"

"I found her nearly dead, and you dare try to justify it?"

Talon's heart stopped, and he stepped forward. "But she's alive? Just tell me she's alive, and the baby is safe."

Deylan narrowed his eyes. "She's alive. Her baby came early, but she's fine, too. No thanks to you."

"A girl." Talon dropped his gaze to the ground, swallowing the sudden fear that accompanied the news.

"I'm surprised you care, what with your new family." Deylan motioned to the tavern.

Talon lifted his head, his eyes burning. "Of course I care. I love that baby girl more than you could imagine. She's the reason I had to leave. To protect her and her mother from Uriel."

Deylan's eyes darkened. "And who was to protect her from you?"

"Me? I—"

"You broke her, just as she'd begun to finally heal. She was a beautiful mother for the time she allowed herself to be happy, but she thinks she doesn't deserve it, that she's not enough. Without you there to reassure her, she..." He shook his head, swallowing. "Another family adopted Ahria."

Talon flinched, his entire body sagging at the news. "She left? That wasn't supposed to happen."

"No, it wasn't. She thinks she's the danger. I wonder where she got that *concept*... It looks like she's headed for Eralas."

"How..." Talon shook his head at his ignorance. Of course Deylan knew, because the faction did. "Does the faction have plans for Ahria then? What's their opinion on the matter?"

"The faction is dedicated to the Key, and Ahria is the new host in the event of my sister's death. So, they are less concerned that Amarie hasn't been strict about using her hiding aura in Helgath. But if she puts the Key's power in danger, the faction will act."

"Act? Act how?"

Deylan looked down, gritting his jaw. "They'll kill her, Talon. Rather than let Uriel or Helgath obtain the Key."

Breathing became impossible. "Because the power would pass to Ahria, and then the faction would claim the baby, wouldn't they?"

Deylan nodded.

Talon winced. "And Amarie is alone, running around, basically begging Uriel to send Shades after her. Do you think she's trying to draw attention away from Ahria?"

"Probably. But she's not traveling alone."

"Who's with her?" Talon furrowed his brow. His heart leapt at a possibility. "Kin?"

"No. It's a woman. We don't know much about her. We don't even know where Kin is."

"Well that problem is going around then." Talon tried to find comfort in the fact that Amarie had found a new companion, but his gut didn't trust it. "She'll be safe in Eralas. It's better for all involved if I stay away."

Deylan sighed and rolled his eyes. "You idiot. She's looking for you. When she realizes you're not there, she has no reason to stay there, if she even makes it there at all."

"I don't know if I'm still being watched." Talon fought the instinct to run to Amarie, convince her to return to Ahria with him. It wasn't too late for them to be a family.

"By who?"

"My sister. The entire reason I'm a threat to Amarie. She's loyal to Uriel in a way far more demented than Kin."

"Alana." Deylan nodded. "She's in Feyor."

"Her eyes are not restricted to those in her head. What's she doing in Feyor?"

"We have no idea. Her movements around Pantracia have been erratic over the past few months. Like she's looking for something."

"Kinronsilis." Talon shook his head. "It doesn't matter. I don't know what you think I can do. Amarie probably hates me, and I might just push her away from Eralas faster."

Deylan shrugged, his shoulders slumping. "I've never seen her so reckless. She took to painting while she lived with my mother, and the pictures started off normal, but... They became dark. Depictions of shadow monsters, of herself dead, of you and Kin and some of Uriel. At least, how she imagines him, I'm guessing. Look..." He produced a small book from within his cloak. "I probably shouldn't have taken this, but I found it under her bed. The first page is addressed to you." He offered the book to Talon. "If after reading this, you still don't believe you can help, then I'll go to her myself and pray I'm enough."

Once Talon took the book, Deylan walked past him, disappearing into the street.

Talon ran his finger over the leather cover, his stomach rolling while imagining what was inside. He felt the chill of the air for the first time, goosebumps erupting on his exposed arms. Swallowing, he opened the cover, tracing his name written in Amarie's loose hand. He stepped back, leaning against the crate as he contemplated the first page. The blur in his eyes made it impossible to read, and he glanced in the direction Deylan had gone.

Inside. Get a drink and then read it.

Despite his thought, Talon turned through each page, allowing himself only short phrases on each.

> *I miss you.*
>
> *I love you.*
>
> *I can't wait to see you.*
>
> *It feels wrong to be without you.*
>
> *Where'd you go? Why didn't you come?*
>
> *You left me.*
>
> *I can't stop thinking about you.*

Talon closed his eyes, hot tears stinging his skin as he flipped to the last page. Amarie's neat handwriting had devolved into large swooping letters, unevenly filling the page. The graphite smudged, leaving grey fingerprints between words.

> *...you would have made a wonderful father.*

Her words raked against Talon's heart, as he thought of his time with Conrad. His betrayal suddenly felt so much worse.

> *We could have had a life. The family neither of us*
> *ever had.*

Her kindness was more than he deserved, even if interspersed with painful realities. The child would grow up without him, would never know a father like he'd hoped to be. He'd abandoned them both without allowing himself to conceptualize the consequences.

> *I hate what you've done, how you've left me.*
>
> *Abandoned me. Just like everyone else.*

Talon forced in a breath, his knees buckling. He fell back against the crate, gripping its corner for support. His knuckles white, he choked back a sob.

"Talon?"

He jerked his head up, spotting the fur-lined hood around Talia's face. She frowned, holding it in place from the wind tearing through the seaport. He saw Amarie in her for a moment, but then it disappeared before he could allow himself the delusion.

Talia walked towards him and touched his arm. Her hand burned against his chilled skin. "I know you're an auer, but you'll still catch a fever if you stay out here like this."

Talon put his hand over hers and shook his head. "I'm sorry, but I have to leave."

"Leave?" Talia's eyes widened. "What's wrong? Your friend—"

"He just told me things I needed to hear. But Amarie—"

Talia turned her hand in his and gave it a squeeze, her lips turning into a smile. "You don't need to explain. We both knew you wouldn't stay in Treama forever."

"Conrad—"

"Will be fine. I can take a day to figure something out. You've done enough for me already." She pulled Talon to his feet, surprising strength in her small frame. "But you better stay in touch. I look forward to meeting Amarie someday."

Talon smiled, but it fell away. "You deserve a life far grander than this one."

"I'm happy being a barkeep." Talia waved a hand. "Gods know I have plenty of trouble just keeping that place in order, imagine me having to manage more..." She laughed. Taking a step back, she eyed Talon for a moment, then stepped into him and wrapped her arms around his waist.

Talon welcomed the hug, returning it.

"Be safe," Talia whispered.

Talon nodded, stepping back. "You too." Turning, he jogged after Deylan.

Chapter 23

Traveling along Helgath's southern coast held few complications, but abundant memories. The last time Amarie had been on a beach was in Capul, and she didn't appreciate the constant reminder of Kin in the back of her mind. Guilt plagued her for what happened in Quar, even though she reasoned she had every right to do whatever she wanted. Jett had been a worthy distraction, even if temporarily.

Amarie didn't notice any signs of a Shade following them, eyeing every black-winged creature with suspicion. She grew closer to Mira, but the friendship failed to heal her damaged heart. They took part in more tavern brawls, but none ended with the same steamy finish the first had. Instead, Amarie steered clear of men, and Mira stopped encouraging.

Halfway between Lazuli and Hoult, she began letting down her hiding aura at night while Mira slept, hoping to keep the Shade's attention.

The plains on the northeast coast of Helgath offered poor land for farming, leaving most of the area uninhabited. So close to Eralas, the military avoided building outposts in fear of aggravating their usually friendly neighbors. The rugged ground donned layers of lichen, with old monoliths and hardened paths. Stonework hinted at the existence of a previous city, lost long before humans claimed the rolling hills. Remnants of what could have once been walls formed the continuous rocky hills of the countryside. The plains stretched all the way to the sea, dropping in massive, uneven cliffs.

Wind raged across the land, creating constant noise in Amarie's ears. The cloudless sky shone with bright morning sun, reflecting in glittering rays off the ocean. She dismounted Viento, leaving him to graze while she approached the edge of the cliff and looked down at the waves crashing against the rocks below.

Mira touched her elbow. "Where's this port town you mentioned?"

"Hoult. A mile north or so." Amarie swayed in the breeze before stepping away from the edge.

Mira sighed. "Let's go, then. I feel exposed out here."

Amarie looked back at the ocean, peering at the outline of Eralas's black cliffs in the distance. The shadow of Ny'Thalus hung over the choppy waves, cast by the oversized beech tree forming the docks. The sight flooded Amarie with memories of when she'd seen it with Talon at her side. Cringing, she let her hiding aura down. She was running out of time to meet Mira's Shade.

Mira sucked in a breath. "What are you doing?"

"Breathing. It's stifling beneath my aura, and no one is around, anyway."

Mira shook her head, stomping back towards the horses. "It's not a good idea."

Amarie ignored her, turning back to the horizon. She breathed in the salt air, trying to still her roiling emotions. They tumbled like a rip current, pulling her further into the dark ocean.

A raspy caw echoed behind them, and Amarie spun to face it. A vulture circled above a crooked ancient monolith protruding from the ground to the south. It looped lazily, gradually descending.

"Can we please go?" Mira called.

The bird landed atop the pillar, its head swinging to look at Mira before its beady eyes locked on Amarie. In a blink, the creature melted, shifting into pools of darkness. They gathered where its claws had been, slipping down the backside of the stone.

Amarie's eyes widened. She'd suspected Mira lied about the Shade following her, but now it proved true. "Mira!" She drew the dagger from her thigh.

Mira spun, her horse letting out a sharp whinny as the auer tore her bow from the saddle. "Shit." She nocked an arrow while her eyes traced the shadow's rapid movement.

The Shade rushed forward like a serpent through the grass, tendrils lashing at the ground and propelling it forward.

Amarie smirked, sucking in a deep breath of her power. It rushed into her veins with little effort. Fire sparked to life, spreading out from her feet. It swirled against itself, creating a barrier.

The Shade reared back, embers gobbled up by the shadows as they swelled to form the body of the man controlling them. His back rose from the darkness, uncurling as he lifted his shoulders and stretched his pale neck. The black at his feet boiled like tar, his hand running through pitch-colored hair.

Mira's bow twanged as she loosed an arrow, but Amarie met it with a blast of fire, deterring the strike. The ash caught in the wind, spreading across the plain.

"What are you doing?" Mira gaped at her.

The Shade lifted a thin eyebrow at Amarie, tilting his head. "Yes, girl, what *are* you doing?"

Amarie growled and stomped through her flames. They licked up around her boots, but she didn't feel the heat.

Lashes of shadow shot forward to penetrate the fire, but when they struck the blaze, they recoiled with a sizzle.

She stopped three feet from the Shade. "I have a gift for you. Care to be Uriel's most beloved servant?"

The Shade took a wary step back, cringing at the mention of his master's name. "How—"

Mira shouted something, but Amarie couldn't make out the words over the roaring inferno.

Amarie lunged, the fire dying as she grasped the Shade's arm. Closing her fingers around his bicep, she gritted her teeth and flooded him with her power.

The Shade moved to grapple her, but stopped when the rush of energy struck him. His body trembled, eyes closing as his head languidly swayed back. "Mmmm." He hummed, but the tone had changed. It sounded like another voice mingled with it. His eyes opened, overtaken by a gold-flecked void. "Now what is this?"

"Hello, Uriel." Amarie's heart pounded in her ears. "How kind of you to join us."

The Shade's head rocked back, an unnatural laugh barking from his mouth. "Amarie... Back from the dead." The strange melded voice buzzed through the air. The Shade's free hand whipped across his body, snatching her wrist in a vice grip. "And now you're mine."

"Come get me, asshole." Lifting her dagger, Amarie swiped it across the Shade's throat. Crimson sprayed into the air, covering them as the body crumpled to the ground.

"Amarie!" Mira turned and ran to get the horses while Amarie stared at the dead body. "Are you insane?"

Amarie met her halfway, mounting Viento. "I need to get to the port before he shows up, then at least I'll have an escape."

Mira swung onto her horse's back. "Are you kidding me? We can't use—"

"Uriel stole everything from me!" Her shout made Viento shifted anxiously under her. "I will *kill* him if it's the last thing I do. Feel free to take a different path." Digging her heels into Viento's flanks, she took off at a gallop across the terrain. There was no telling how long it would take Uriel to manifest physically, but imagining a shadow beast pursuing her left no time to waste. Soon, another set of hooves joined her, and she frowned at Mira's choice.

They arrived in Hoult, their horses panting. A heaviness filled Amarie's stomach. Only one ship occupied the docks, and she didn't recognize its flag. No one walked the streets, eerie silence hanging like a thick fog over the buildings.

Viento snorted, sidestepping as they entered the village square.

"Where is everyone?" Mira's tone held a fearful edge. "I thought you said they run ships to Eralas often."

"They do. At least they did. I don't know." Amarie slid off Viento's back and slung the reins in front of Mira, who narrowed her eyes. Sliding her new sword out of the sheath strapped to her saddle, Amarie eyed Mira. "You need to go. This is my mess, not yours. Please take Viento and get somewhere safe."

"I can help you."

Amarie shook her head, taking a step back. "If I need to let my power loose, you can't be nearby. Please go. Now."

Mira hesitated, but spun her mare around, kicking up a cloud of dust as she raced from the town with Viento.

As the haze in the air settled, Amarie sighed. "Now what, genius?" She paused, looking around the deserted town. Something to her left shifted, and she lifted her weapon.

"Now we get you out of here." A man emerged from inside a home she'd thought was empty.

"Who are you?" Amarie took a cautious step back. She stared at his eyes, searching for hints of black or gold.

"I work with your brother. They do too." He motioned with his bearded chin.

Amarie whirled around as a man and woman emerged in a similar fashion, each with a copper sword at their side. She looked back at the first man and took a shaky breath.

The faction?

"What was my father's name?"

"Kalpheus. Good man. Can we go now?"

Amarie glanced in the direction Mira had gone, but the woman was nowhere in sight. "I'm not going with you."

"I'm afraid I'm not at liberty to give you a choice." The man took a step towards her.

Amarie ground her teeth, realizing their awareness of her daughter.

They'll kill me.

She didn't fight as the man closed his arm around her bicep and led her to the dock.

Amarie rolled her shoulders, shirking the man's grip as they walked. "How did you beat me here?"

"We've been tailing you since Jacoby."

"I watched for someone following me, I would've seen you."

"We took shifts in different towns, so you'd never see the same face twice. We got lucky that the next trade off was to happen here. Gave Rissa time to get everyone out." He gestured towards the woman walking behind them.

"Where's Deylan?" Panic for her brother filled her.

"Don't know." He shrugged. "Last I heard, he was getting on a ship in Ziona, headed this direction. But he's going to miss out on all this fun."

They stepped onto the dock, their boots echoing on the wood.

The faction leader halted and turned to her, glowering like a father might. "What were you thinking?"

Amarie swallowed, heat rising in her cheeks. "I want to kill him. I don't want to hide anymore, and if he's dead, I wouldn't have to."

The man shook his head. "I doubt a creature like this one will simply *die*."

Amarie sighed as they walked again, approaching the massive three-masted galleon, which dominated the whole dock. Narrowing her gaze at the crow's nest, above the secured pale blue sails, Amarie squinted.

A watchman, his body limp, slouched over the side of it.

She stopped and stared.

Stillness plagued the air as her escort halted. The only sound was the surf, constant in its pulse against the shore. No cry of gulls, or distant goat bawls from the livestock pens. Instead, the steady drum of a pair of boots on the ship's deck.

A single figure appeared at the top of the gangplank, the sun highlighting his windswept brown hair. He gave a confident smile, eyes shadowed as he descended towards the dock.

The three escorting her drew their copper swords, all eyes locked on the man.

Amarie's heart thundered in her chest, and her power thrummed in her veins.

Uriel slowed, sucking in a breath that lifted his broad shoulders and chin. A finely trimmed beard covered his jaw, and his smile broadened. "Delicious." He sensually touched his lips and chuckled. "How foolish of me not to see the truth before. And how tricky of you to let me keep believing this power wasn't simply you."

The man next to Amarie lifted his sword, but instead of aiming for Uriel as she expected, he swung straight for her throat. Her eyes widened as the copper blade on her other side followed suit, aimed for her. She caught the first blade in her bare hand and screamed as it cut into her palm.

The pressure behind the attack relented, and the faction leader's scream joined hers. Rissa and the other man's began a moment later. Metal thunked to the dock, and Amarie stumbled several steps back from the boiling shadow seeping from her would-be protectors. Tar melted from their eyes, leaving hollow sockets. Black veins curled up their necks onto their faces. They collapsed, one after the other, toppling to the ground amid bone-rattling wails.

Blood pooled in her palm as she tried to comprehend what had happened. Amarie covered her mouth with her hand, smearing the sticky warmth on her face.

The pools of shadow flowed from the faction's bodies, writhing together across the dock. They collected into a solid growing mass. Uriel stepped from it, transported from his previous position.

Meeting his eyes, she forced her fear away.

I will end his reign.

Beneath the swirls of obsidian and gold, human eyes shone a tumultuous sea blue.

"Amarie." Uriel tilted his head as he stepped closer, while she stepped back to maintain the distance between them. "I should thank you for giving yourself to me so willingly."

"I'm not surrendering to you."

"No?" Uriel's smile persisted. "But it'd be so much easier for you if you did. So much less painful." His power pressed against hers, biting into the waves of energy like acid.

"Easier for you, you mean." Amarie let her energy respond, and it lashed back, tasting bitter shadow.

"Tell me, my dear, does Kinronsilis know you still breathe?" Uriel purred, keeping his pace steady.

"I'm sorry, who?" Amarie cocked her head in mocking, lifting her sword tip towards him.

For the first time, Uriel's grin faltered, and he frowned. "Don't play coy. He was quite insistent you were dead, even through all his screams while I persuaded him to talk."

Amarie's eyebrows rose. "I guess you're not as persuasive as you think." Her gut rolled, imagining Kin in pain.

Dying.

Is he still alive?

She clenched her jaw, forcing herself to focus.

Gods, please let him be alive.

Uriel eyed her sword and stepped to the side, closer to her. Extending his hand towards her cheek, he sighed as she batted it away with her blade, the sun glinting off his gold signet ring.

"I assure you, I can be quite persuasive. Let's just say it depends on you." He took a step back, the length of his shadow expanding around him. "But I *will* have you."

Amarie shook her head. "I'll enjoy watching you fail."

She lunged, channeling energy through her sword. Fire erupted beneath her feet, filling her steps. Swinging at him, her blade connected with his responding vine of shadow.

The tendril curled around his arm, hardening into a stony surface. A jagged edge formed past his knuckles, and he parried her with the manifested blade. Each subsequent blow, he blocked, always prepared before she could find a weakness.

She changed tactics, quenching the rising fire. Focusing on her blade, she pulled destructive energy from her ocean of power and bruise-colored smoke engulfed the steel.

A tentacle struck it, and hissed, shuddering.

Uriel retreated into the empty village square.

Amarie followed, breathing as Talon instructed her to control the Art. It swirled in her bloody palm, collecting into the same destructive smoke. Her already sore muscles screamed as she thrust her arm forward, launching the attack at Uriel. In tandem, she shifted her weight and swung her sword, cutting through tentacle after tentacle. The air filled with the scent of burning decay. The farther Uriel retreated, the bolder Amarie became. She roared, swinging her sword for his neck.

His hand shot up and caught the blade.

She yanked to get it back, but he held strong.

Smiling at her, he tutted his tongue. "You try my patience." Wrenching her sword from her grip, the tendrils consumed it. It fell away in flecks of ash.

Amarie drew back and heaved for breath, empty-handed. Gazing at Uriel, she narrowed her eyes. Not a hair was out of place and not a drop of sweat glistened on his brow. His expensive clothing bore no dirt, not even a wrinkle.

He's toying with me.

Doubt clouded her mind, and he grinned.

Opening his mouth to speak, Uriel's shoulder jolted forward with a blow from behind. He closed his mouth, eyeing a shining shaft protruding from his upper back. Smoke hissed from the arrow's entry point. Uriel turned as another struck, and he stumbled forward.

Orders to attack rang through the streets.

Amarie ducked, holding her hands over the back of her head as arrows sank into the ground beside her. Her arm burned, a long cut bleeding from a graze. The pain felt beyond physical, the weaves of her energy near the wound pierced. The edges charred like a flaming piece of parchment.

Uriel bellowed, spinning to face where the attack originated, yanking the first arrow free. Trails of blood ran down his back, but globules of shadow crept to plug the wound as quickly as it appeared.

Amarie fled, forcing her tired legs to run at a crouch towards the nearest building. She threw herself against the door, arrows thunking into the wood next to her head. Collapsing to the ground, she kicked the door shut behind her.

In the darkness, she gasped, anxiously touching the tear on her arm. The arrow had sheared through her clothing, and the gash stung. Gritting her teeth, she withdrew her dagger and cut a strip of fabric from the bottom of her shirt while assessing her surroundings.

Dim light penetrated the musty window at the front of the general wares shop. She inched the curtain aside as she used her teeth to secure the bandage around her arm.

Flashes struck like lightning. A man and a woman with whips lashed at a large mound of onyx seething at the center of the town square. Another whip crackled as lightning bolts left glowing crevices on the undulating shadow's surface. The next strike came, but the whip never returned, the ebony infection grabbing hold of the tip, sucking it into the mound. Uriel's power ran up the whip's length like oil seeping up a wick. It struck the wielder in the chest, propelling him backwards in a fit of screams. Bones snapped, the tendrils pounding his body against the ground with a crunch.

Another volley of arrows soared from the roof directly across from where Amarie hid. The shafts protruded like porcupine quills from the mound. With a contraction, the arrows sank into the blob, sputtering with smoke. Uriel's writhing mass quivered, flexing an instant before arrows exploded from its surface.

The faction shouted, diving to the ground to take cover. One of the archers fell from the rooftop, an arrow in his neck.

Uriel's human form manifested, the excess ink around him dripping to the ground. The tailored vest showed no sign of blood or tears and his face shone with rage. Reaching, he spread his fingers towards the archers on the roof struggling to regain their footing.

A wave of sickness filled Amarie's gut as the men on the roof collapsed without obvious reason. Their bodies withered, drying as if left in the desert sun for years within the space of a few breaths. Their flesh stuck to the roof tiles, quivers rolling to the ground.

Uriel's chin rose, his head tilting back as if relishing in the flavor of a fine wine. He didn't face the whip coming at him again, but raised his arm to block it.

The lightning wrapped around his arm, but a thin transparent layer of black glass protected him. It sparked, white-hot electricity fragmenting out, reflecting in the darkness of his eyes as he turned to his attacker.

Uriel suddenly vanished, molting into shadow.

The woman released the whip faster than her compatriot had, hurrying for the sword at her side. Before she could withdraw it, her face flushed. She choked, hands clawing at her neck. They grasped nothing, scratching her skin as ebon veins erupted towards her eyes. Falling to her knees, Uriel's shadows boiled out of every orifice of her face. She died, gagging.

Uriel emerged from the pool of black engulfing her body. He glanced down at her corpse, running his hand casually through his hair. Turning, he faced the building Amarie hid in.

She hastily dropped the curtain, trying to steady her breathing.

"Amarie..." Uriel called out in an elongated, sing-song tone.

Looking at the dagger in her bloody hand, Amarie debated skewering her own heart. When she didn't resurrect, would Uriel know what it meant? Would he learn of Ahria, sentencing her daughter to a life of suffering?

Closing her eyes, she pushed the option aside. Her child would not suffer for her mistake. She opened her eyes to the sound of cracking. The walls around her ruptured, the stone crumbling. Wood splintered as shadow tore it from its foundation.

Dust coated her and the air, the sun unable to pierce the haze stretching from Uriel's body. His hand closed in her hair, and he pulled her free of the debris with a single jerk. She slammed to the ground, all breath expelled from her lungs as Uriel planted his knee on her chest, pinning her.

"I'm tired of this game." Uriel's hand gripped her jaw, forcing her to face him. The corrosive power burned her skin, delving into her soul. "You *will* accept your fate."

"You clearly don't know me." Amarie grabbed at his hand in her hair. Something mechanical rhythmically clicked near her ear, but she ignored it. "You think you're powerful, but you can't even manage your little Shadelings."

Click.

Uriel growled, lowering his face to hers. "You know where Kin is, don't you?" His grip tightened on her jaw. "Tell me where he is."

Click.

Amarie's eyes widened.

He's lost Kin.

Against her better judgment, she laughed. "Whenever you think you lost him, you lost him much sooner."

Click.

"He knew what I was for months while you were still chasing useless shards like an imbecile."

He lifted her head, slamming it onto the ground and she gasped.

Click.

"I'm patient, girl, but don't test me."

Click.

Amarie stared at him. "Fuck you."

Click.

She spat a mouthful of blood in his face.

Click.

Uriel grimaced. "Hard way, then."

Click. Click.

Releasing her hair, he pressed his knee into her sternum.

Click. Click. Click.

The clicking rose to a deafening buzz.

Then it abruptly stopped.

In a boom, the surrounding air pulsed, each thread of the fabric resonating. It tightened, drawing the contained energy to a dead halt. A bubble of pale gold activated, rapidly growing to surround the village square.

Uriel looked up, his brow furrowed as the air around them cleared.

Amarie drove her dagger into his abdomen. It connected with a squelch, sinking deep.

The blow forced Uriel back, loosening the pressure on her chest enough for her to roll away, abandoning her weapon in his gut. She staggered to her feet, pulling at her power, but found it difficult within the pulsing device.

Uriel cried out, touching the hilt of the dagger. He remained kneeling on the ground, the shadows around him trembling.

Taking advantage of his distraction, Amarie retreated. Her back touched the faction's constructed barrier, and it tingled on her skin. The Art-formed shield should have prohibited her from passing, but the Berylian Key's power nullified the field, forcing it to give way. It snapped back into place after she pressed through.

Uriel stood, back hunched around his injury as shadow tentacles curled up his legs. They wrapped around his hips, rising towards the blade. Grasping the hilt, they yanked it free. It clanked to the ground, only a thin layer of blood on the steel proving she'd done any damage.

Shadows dripped from his body, crawling across the ground to the golden barrier. They struck the bottom with a sizzle and recoiled.

Uriel narrowed his eyes at the shield and stooped to pick up Amarie's dagger. The ground beneath him had turned a rotted grey, the grass between cobblestones withered. His corruption extended far beyond the barrier, his power destroying all life before its erection.

He bounced the dagger in his palm, testing the weight as he walked to the edge of the barrier.

The sphere shimmered, pulsing minutely slower with each breath. But it contained him, leaving Amarie her last opportunity.

Exhaling, she embraced every last drop of her power. She opened the floodgates while Uriel nonchalantly poked the barrier wall with the tip of her dagger.

Without warning, he drew his arm back and flung the blade at her. It passed, unhindered, through the golden wall, aimed low on her body.

Her power already on the surface, she redirected the attack with a swat of her hand. Sparks of blue exploded as her dagger struck an invisible force inches from her skin, sending it flying.

Uriel tilted his head, a sinister smile coming to his lips as he backed towards the center of the sphere. "Show me," he taunted. "Let me see what the Berylian Key can do."

Drawing on everything she contained had never been purposeful before, and her willingness allowed her to focus on the sensations while it overtook her. Her feet left the ground as the energy pulled her upward, ripping debris around her body. Bits of wood circled around her like a tornado, stones and barrels of abandoned goods. Currents of the Art shocked through her, building into a storm between her palms.

Her vision tainted with shades of beryl, she stared at Uriel. Time slowed, her ears deaf to anything other than her steady breathing.

The shadows at Uriel's feet boiled, moving in slow motion as they twisted into tendrils cocooning up around him. His hands lifted, beckoning the gloom into a knot above his head, spreading to encompass him in darkness. It swelled to fill the barrier, vines of obsidian lashing at the thinning translucent golden walls.

With a dying hum, the shield vanished.

Uriel's shadow exploded, the cloud of night polluting the air and obscuring the sun.

The light of the Berylian Key brightened around Amarie, illuminating all she needed.

Crying out, she thrust her hands forward, releasing the energy. It surged at the melanoid beast with deadly design. Her power arced forward, radiant, lancing mercilessly through the pile of tar. It carved a wide path through the village square, tearing apart the street and ground beneath into a jagged ravine. Striking the blackness, it gouged a crater in the surface, reflecting to the ground. Gigantic cracks split the fluid outer shadow, turning it to stone. It thundered at the impact, quivering as the Berylian Key's power forced its way into the weaknesses, jarring them apart.

A man's voice cried out, mingled with a primordial roar. The onyx shattered, breaking into hunks of ash. The human form remained, stripped of the blanket of shadows, and power surged into him. His back arched in torment, and Amarie did not relent.

Uriel fell, clawing at the ground as his body convulsed. The ground beneath him corroded, falling apart to join the cyclone of Amarie's power. He dropped lower into the growing crater, and ocean water rushed in as the shoreline disappeared.

Uriel struggled to kneel, his fists planted against the crumbling ground. The saltwater rushing towards him turned to steam as it neared the beam of power holding him down. The trembles of his body slowed, then dissipated as he lifted his head in defiance. The void of his eyes met Amarie's, a wicked smile playing on his lips.

His clothing rippled around him, wrapping tight as an inky stain spread across the fabric. He hunched forward, and spikes erupted from his spine. Shadows pooled beneath him, the blackened form of his body growing as his face mutated into a maw of razor teeth. He rose to four legs, armored with shiny chitinous plates.

As shadow unfurled the details of his body, a wicked tail of woven tendrils lashed behind him. A massive serpentine neck lifted out of the steam, and clawed feet sank as the ground turned to solid ashy stone. Parts of his enormous body pushed past the maelstrom, disappearing into the saltwater. Canine features boasted hollows for ears, and spheres filled with shadow for eyes.

Uriel's clawed hand lashed through the air, swatting Amarie's floating form from the sky. Tumbling through the mist, she collided with the ground. Something cracked as she hit, and she rolled several yards before coming to a stop.

Sunlight blinded her as it penetrated her eyelids, and she blinked rapidly to get her vision to adjust to the abrupt change. A bank of darkness loomed over the crater where the little fishing village had been, the shadows of Uriel's growing form stirring within as water rushed to swallow the remnants of the village.

She rolled onto her stomach, and pain shot through her side.

Whimpering, she tucked her right arm against her and tried to stand. Her exhausted body couldn't support her weight, and she collapsed.

Thunder rumbled towards her, shaking the ground. She cringed, trying to force herself up to face the threat. Sweat dripped from her brow as her eyes focused on two large shapes. Horses. She shook her head, blinking again.

"Amarie!" Mira shouted. "We need to get out of here."

Amarie hadn't seen the woman dismount, but arms lifted her. Leaning on Mira, Amarie groped for Viento's saddle. "I told you to get away from here."

"I don't take orders well." Mira pushed Amarie onto her horse before mounting her grey mare.

The grass around them shriveled and the ground shook, making the horses balk.

Uriel lumbered over the mouth of the crater, water dripping from the tangle of shadows.

"Do you have a plan?" Amarie swallowed.

Mira nodded. "All you have to do is keep up."

Glancing back at the monstrosity as Uriel's muzzle opened in a snarl of anger, Amarie nudged her horse. "That, I can do."

The horses took off across the plains, heading straight for the shore. The plant life around them decayed, crumbling to dust as they raced to get ahead of the rot.

Mira stayed the course, unflinchingly pointed at the ocean rather than away from Uriel. Waves crested over the rocky beach, and Amarie saw no escape.

The Art burst from Mira. The water crackled, freezing. The uneven waves ruptured into little flurries of snow, blanketing the flattened surface of pale-blue ice.

Amarie held her breath as Mira's horse reached the first stretch of frozen ocean. Hooves struck the ground with a hollow echo, finding traction within the dense snow. Looking ahead, the silhouette of Ny'Thalus brought hope.

The ice and snow expanded as Amarie rode, remaining solid until

Viento galloped over it. She dared a glance back and watched as the ocean slammed against the glacier, tearing apart the path.

Darkness engulfed the Helgathian coastline, rising in gigantic clouds of sinuous shadows stretching in twisted arcs. They flowed towards the collapsing bridge.

The canine form, as tall as the cliff side, rushed across the water. He didn't hesitate, despite the failing bridge. Shadow gathered beneath his paws to support his weight above the sea. The creature boiled like storm clouds, teeth gnashing at the air, bounding around the melting icebergs.

Readjusting to face forward, Amarie mustered what little energy she had left and expelled it into those around her. Mira, her horse, and Viento. She fueled them, and their pace increased until Amarie thought they might take to the air.

The limbs of Ny'Thalus beckoned to them, stretched across the ocean's surface like waiting arms.

A thunderous boom rocked the ice, sending cracks past them. The structure trembled but held. The sound of Uriel's rage mingled with the crash, vibrating the air.

Birds nested around Ny'Thalus squawked, a cloud of beating wings erupting from branches and cliff sides. They turned inland, fleeing the beast on the sea.

Screams came from every direction, and auer rushed for cover. They scrambled away from the docks, flooding the single long ramp towards the forest. The sun above Eralas fell behind a blanket of shadow, plunging the coastline into darkness.

Hooves met the wooden docks, ice crashing into ships and splintering their hulls. Amarie followed Mira onto land and then looked back again.

Uriel's beast form slammed into the protective wards of Eralas, spreading onyx tendrils high and wide, encompassing the shield. A luminescent green line hovered ten yards above the ocean's surface, encircling the entire island.

Uriel's canine maw bit and chewed on the transparent surface, his eyes wild. He roared, beating his body against the wards. The air vibrated, but nothing gave way.

What have I done?

Amarie gripped her reins tighter, but her surroundings blurred. Before she could slow Viento, her vision went black.

Chapter 24

As shadow engulfed his homeland, Talon's stomach dropped out. The banister of the ship was the only thing holding him on his feet.

Deylan paced next to him, hands tangled in his chestnut hair. He held his mysterious communication device in front of him, staring at the face of letters and arrows. "No one is answering!" He started dialing his message in again.

Talon swallowed the bile in his mouth. The commotion was dizzying as the captain shouted commands to his men to turn them about.

The low hum of the auer barrier reverberated against Talon's senses. The dim hoop of pale green showed just how close the ship had gotten to reaching Eralas before the wards activated, barring all new entrants. If the captain was foolish enough to try, the ship would have shattered against it like hitting a stone wall.

Talon blinked through the sun at the fishing village he'd watched get swallowed by a ball of pulsing beryl light.

The shadow creature thrashed against the auer wards prohibiting him from reaching his prey.

Amarie's alive. She made it to Eralas. That was Viento you saw.

No matter how much he repeated it, he doubted her survival against Uriel.

"How could anyone survive that?" Talon whispered. "Deylan, just look at it."

Deylan joined him at the railing of the ship, the strange compass-like object still in hand. He stared at the Helgathian coast, shaking his head. "I don't know. Are you sure that was her? How was she riding over the ocean?" Looking down again, he pushed his finger to the device. Pressing on a small circle, he turned it one direction until a needle touched the letter he wanted, then reversed the direction until it got to the next letter. A cumbersome method of writing, but with no limitations for distance, it proved effective for the faction.

"I want to believe it was her. Gods, Amarie. What did you do?" Talon had feared she was trying to get Uriel's attention, and she'd succeeded. The creature's roars echoed like distant thunder. Talon had been afraid of Uriel before, but now...

"Someone's responding!" Amarie's brother stood still as the message came in, the dials whirring around on their own. His eyes tracked the movement, widening as he comprehended the information.

Talon bit his tongue, respecting the focus required to decipher the rapid message.

Deylan's hand rose and covered his mouth, his chest heaving. "The faction tried to kill her." He paused. "Failed. Uriel protected her." He paused again, stone still. "We lost everyone there."

"The faction underestimated Uriel." Talon couldn't muster an emotion other than indifference. "Perhaps we all did."

"My sister certainly did." Deylan watched the still-spinning dials. "I have to report in person. But it looks like Ahria is unaffected, which means—"

"Amarie is alive." Talon's entire body numbed, his hands shaking. Even the relief of the news did little to calm his anxiety. "Ahria. If Uriel ever found her..."

"He won't."

"Eralas's borders will be sealed for months, at least." Talon looked at his homeland, shrouded by shadows. "I can't imagine Helgath will be very welcoming right now, either."

Another thundering howl rolled across the sea.

Deylan's vision jerked down again, as the device spurred into action once more. His eyes narrowed. "They're ordering Amarie be cuffed and detained at the next sighting. For evaluation and possible termination..." His voice trailed off, disbelief clouding his eyes as he looked at Talon.

"I can tell you now, the auer won't let that happen." Talon shook his head. "And they're the ones who have her now."

"Why won't they?"

Talon blinked, looking up at him. "She didn't tell you?"

Deylan frowned. "Tell me what?"

Talon groaned and rubbed the back of his neck. "She made an alliance with the auer. They know what she is, and she promised to aid them should they ever call on her."

Deylan closed his eyes briefly, and then let out a dry laugh. "That will work to her advantage now. But why would she do that?"

"For me. To convince the council to revoke my banishment."

Deylan's jaw flexed.

"I know," Talon interjected before he could speak. "I don't deserve her love. I had to leave, but I should've done it differently."

"If you had, perhaps the faction wouldn't have suffered such devastating losses today."

"Amarie would have tired of fleeing Uriel at some point, regardless. Kin saw to that."

Deylan shrugged. "I suppose. Shit. If I see her, I'm supposed to detain her. How am I supposed to do that?"

"You won't see her then." Talon raised an eyebrow. "Because we both know I'd stop you if you tried. I'll be your scapegoat."

Deylan gave him a sideways look and sighed. "I'll keep that in mind."

"What about Ahria? What will the faction do with her?"

"Watch her. Until they need her, she'll remain where she is."

Talon heaved a breath, looking at Deylan. "Where is she?"

Amarie's brother stiffened, hesitating. "She's safe."

"I won't kidnap her. You can tell me where she is."

"And if Alana follows you there?"

"She won't. Now that I've seen this." Talon gestured with his head back to shore. "I'll make sure Alana can never find me again, and I'll kill her myself if she does."

Deylan exhaled slowly. "Ahria is in a village west of Jacoby, in Olsa. She was adopted by the Mordov family."

"Thank you."

Disembarking in the small port city on the northern tip of Helgath's east coast took longer than usual. Three other ships arrived first, diverted because of the unknown force wreaking havoc in the major shipping lane. Unequipped for the number of large ships, most anchored and sent dinghies to shore. A tall galleon from the Helgathian armada dominated the whole fishing dock, gold and crimson flags proudly proclaiming their arrival.

Large chunks of ice floated in the strait, making their way to the ocean as they melted. Crew grumbled at the new required post at the front of the ship, encouraging the miniature icebergs around the hulls with long poles.

"Hope your paperwork is in order." The captain tipped his hat as Talon and Deylan descended the rope ladder to the rowboat that would take them ashore. "Military will be up in arms."

Talon eyed Deylan, and the man nodded, keeping his voice low. "We'll be fine. I'll take the lead." He leaned close to Talon to whisper his plan.

The captain hadn't been wrong about the runaround they received when they arrived on land. The dockmaster had been relieved of his duty by the arriving naval force, and they took Deylan and Talon aside for questioning.

Offering his paperwork, Deylan huffed a sigh. "Good afternoon, Private. I empathize with your plight here at the docks, but we can't afford much more of a delay."

The taller of the two men snatched the papers, lifting them close to his face. His eyes widened, and his shorter, rounder companion plucked them from his hands.

"Sir." The clean shaven private struck his chest with a fist in salute. "Apologies, but I'm sure you understand procedure."

"Of course. This is my advisor." Deylan motioned to Talon. "Our journey to Eralas was interrupted, but we plan to resume it as soon as possible."

"What was the purpose for your travels?" The second soldier offered the papers back.

Deylan shook his head and took his paperwork. "Confidential."

The two soldiers exchanged a look, but the tall one shrugged. "Thank you for your patience, Colonel Fellton. You're good to go."

"I need to see the site."

The private gritted his jaw. "Access is being restricted, sir. While we await the Chief Vizier's arrival and assessment of the—"

Deylan huffed. "With all due respect, Private, I outrank you. I need to visit the site, and my advisor will accompany me. You have my word that we won't disturb anything."

Talon gave the private a stern look, hoping to provide enough intimidation to dissuade further question.

"Very good, sir." The private pressed his fist against his chest and averted his gaze. "Horses are available at the southwest edge of the village."

Deylan returned the salute and exited the barricaded area with Talon following closely behind.

"That's some impressive paperwork you have there," Talon whispered. "Courtesy of the faction, I suppose?"

Deylan nodded. "It has its perks. Depending on what's needed. You should see my collection of identities."

After obtaining two horses, Talon mounted a soot-colored gelding, missing Lynthenai. Unable to obtain passage on a ship designed for proper equestrian transportation, he'd left her in Astar, a trade port on Ziona's coast. He paid an ample amount of silver florins to maintain her stay at a stable outside town until he could return or send for her. But now there was no telling how long it would be.

Making their way south to the fishing village, previously known as Hoult, Talon steeled his senses against the decay. Despite the rugged terrain, life had been there before. A startlingly clear line ran across the ground between life and death. The green grass turned brown and rotted, crumbling to ash the closer they grew to Hoult.

Approaching a military outpost, Deylan dismounted and looped the reins of his skittish horse around a post.

Talon followed suit, letting Deylan lead the way through the makeshift encampment, flashing his papers as needed, until they exited out the other side on foot.

Military personnel scurried about the outpost, trying to keep commoners away while preserving secrecy of the location. With the sun lower on the horizon, shadows were long and dark.

The growing void in Talon's senses tightened the farther they walked. Then, abruptly, his connection to the Art disappeared. Breathing felt laborious as Talon sought for any thread of power still within him.

He caught himself starting to call for Deylan and choked back the word. "Colonel." He stepped closer to the pit.

"What is it?"

"I don't know." Talon furrowed his brow. "Something is blocking me, though. From the Art."

Deylan paused and his gaze trailed to the ground before he nodded slowly. "That's because we've just witnessed the birth of a second Lungaz."

"What?" Talon tried again to reach his power, not wanting to believe. But nothing was there. He felt hollow, less than his full self. It made his stomach roil and a headache pound in his temples.

"I need to get a better look" Deylan stalked off again.

A soldier tried to warn Deylan not to get any closer, but he shrugged off the suggestion, approaching the mile-long crater with wide eyes. "Nymaera's breath." He stopped at the rim of the devastation.

Nothing remained of the village, or even the terrain. A smooth white-ash stone formed a perfect sphere cut into the coastline. The ocean had flooded into the opening, bits of debris floating in a lazy circle around the new bay.

Talon knelt and touched the smooth surface of the stone. It felt cold, and nothing else.

"Lungaz isn't a crater. Which means—"

"That was Amarie. And Lungaz... was Uriel." Talon swallowed the nausea. He'd never been to Lungaz and now knew why every living thing avoided it. The absence, the silence, felt horribly wrong.

Deylan's breath quickened. "I've never seen the power of the Key released like this. No wonder she was afraid to use it."

Talon thought back to the small crater she'd formed before regaining control during their training and marveled at her strength. "Amarie." He shook his head. "What were you thinking?" His gaze rose, and the sun shimmered off something metallic protruding from the crater's rim ten yards away. He stood and walked towards it, eyes pinned on the spot he'd seen the flash.

"Give me your sword." Talon held his hand out towards Deylan without looking back at him.

"Why?" Deylan's blade scraped against its scabbard as he removed it. He placed it in Talon's hand as the auer knelt.

A bit of steel glimmered, partially buried under the hard surface the dirt had transformed into. He could just make out the end of the hilt, traditional auer craftsmanship engraved in the metal.

Talon spun Deylan's sword in his palm, slamming its rounded pommel into the rock to reveal the dagger hidden beneath. The repeated strikes formed little dents in the sword's iron hilt.

Deylan cleared his throat. "You mind not damaging faction property?"

Talon tossed the sword back to him with a shrug.

Deylan caught it and lifted it into the sunlight to study the damage.

"I don't have the Art. Seemed the most elegant solution." Talon brushed away the shards of broken stone and lifted Amarie's dagger from the ground. Dust stuck to the blood still clumped on the blade. "How about a handkerchief?"

Deylan sighed but dropped a bit of cloth into Talon's hand.

Carefully, Talon wiped the blood off the dagger. He made certain to clean away every speck before sliding the blade into his belt and folding the blood-stained handkerchief. He stood, offering the cloth to Deylan. "Better keep this safe."

Deylan took it, narrowing his eyes. "You think it's his, don't you?"

"Better to assume and be wrong than to let it go to waste."

Deylan nodded, tucking the cloth into a small pouch on his belt.

Talon idly touched the dagger at his side, facing the sea. He looked past the ice still floating in the strait and watched the shadow beast circle Eralas.

Concentrating her power into creating a bridge across the strait was beyond what Talon had taught Amarie. And after the expulsion of enough power to create a crater, he wanted to believe she would've finally drained herself.

Her companion created their escape over the ice.

"And you know nothing about the woman she traveled with?"

Deylan shook his head. "Nope. But you can bet the faction wants to find out more about her now."

Talon sighed. "Me too."

Chapter 25

Amarie's shoulder exploded with pain, rocking her from unconsciousness. She gasped, her surroundings a blur of candlelight and garbled noise. Instinct propelled her to sit up, but someone's hand pushed her firmly back down.

"Mira?" Amarie blinked the haze from her eyes as she focused on the auer standing next to her. His features sharpened, and she looked from him to the woman on her other side, recognizing neither of them. "Where's Mira?"

"You should worry about yourself." The man removed his hand from her. He looked across to his companion, and she nodded, spinning on her heels to dart out of the room.

Amarie laid in a small, dark room. A curtain of vines and flowers covered the only possible window, but no daylight streamed through the cracks.

"Is Mira all right?" Amarie tried to remember the moments leading up to her black out.

The man hesitated, eyeing her up and down as if to evaluate if she would try sitting up again. "She's in much better condition than you. And she actually responds to healing. You must stay still. We're not as practiced in mending without the Art." He turned to a table beside him, sorting through piles of cloth and glass bottles.

Amarie nodded, paying attention to the rest of her body. Her ribs ached, along with her right arm and her knees. Even her face hurt. "What's the damage?"

"Besides extensive?" A bemused look danced in his dark purple eyes. "Do you want me to recount all of them? Suffice it to say, you look like you were thrown through a few walls."

Footsteps scuffled through the door out of Amarie's sight, hurrying to her side. Her vibrant green eyes fooled Amarie's heart into sudden fear, thinking at first it was Alana. But Kalstacia's short black hair and thinner features allowed her to relax.

"You're awake." Kalstacia touched Amarie's shoulder. "We'd worried..."

"That I'd never wake or that I'd die?" Amarie smirked, but found comfort in Kalstacia's presence.

"Both were distinct possibilities when our menders discovered that they couldn't do anything for you. That would've been pertinent information to have long before we reached this moment, sister." She gave a small smile before she turned to the other auer and held out her hand. She didn't speak, gesturing for him to hand her a pungent smelling bowl.

He obeyed, lifting it from the table and passing it over Amarie.

Nestling the bowl next to Amarie's hip, Kalstacia wrung out a cloth in it. "This is for your ribs." She lifted the bottom of Amarie's shirt, her corset already removed. Tucking the warm silk against Amarie's lower ribs, she pulled another length from the bowl.

Amarie raised her left arm cautiously, reaching to touch her face. Wincing before she could, she lowered her arm in resignation. "Do I dare look in a mirror?" She gave Kalstacia a half-hearted smile. "I missed you... Is Talon here?"

Kalstacia frowned, her thin eyebrows drawing together. "Talon?" Her hands continued with their work of wrapping the cloth around Amarie's right forearm, which had hurt too much to even try moving. "No. I haven't seen him since you both departed for the mainland. I feared he'd been with you but didn't make the crossing with you and the Mira'wyld."

Amarie's heart sank.

Mira'wyld?

"He wasn't with me. We didn't leave together. He was supposed to meet me in Olsa, but..." Amarie sighed. "I haven't seen him since we were here. I thought maybe he returned." Closing her eyes briefly, she took a steadying breath as her eyes burned.

"Nordandril. Would you please fetch hot water? And some more prelter weed." Kalstacia focused back on Amarie, eyes worried.

The man, still fussing with bandages, looked up in surprise. "Of course, Lady Mender."

Kalstacia let out a sigh, glancing behind her towards the door after his departure. She crossed around to the other side of Amarie and picked up a bandage. "Talon left while you were still with child?"

Amarie nodded, swallowing back her emotions.

"Oh, Amarie." Kalstacia brushed tears from Amarie's temple before pressing a damp cloth to her jaw. It tingled, the medicine taking effect. "No woman should have to bear such a weight alone." She quieted for a moment, pursing her lips. "Does the baby live?"

Nodding again, Amarie sucked in a breath through clenched teeth. "She does. A family in Olsa adopted her," she whispered, not trusting her voice any louder.

The auer gently traversed Amarie's abundant wounds with the cloth, resupplying it with more liquid from a vial from time to time. She remained quiet, chewing on her bottom lip and nodding solemnly. "Then I'll have to see to reprimanding that brother of mine when I see him next. But right now, you need to be thinking about what you will say to the Council of Elders. They'll have been alerted that you're awake and want to meet soon."

Amarie cringed. "The council needs to remain ignorant of the baby." She turned to get a better look at Kalstacia, who nodded in agreement. "But Kalstacia... What do you mean *the* Mira'wyld? Is her name not Mira?"

"I don't know her name." Kalstacia shrugged. "Merely her title. No auer but a Mira'wyld could manipulate the Art like that. And only a single bloodline carries the power. This one is new, born from a rejanai, human pairing. I don't know much, I'm sorry." She secured a bandage around Amarie's exposed shin. "I think you've torn a muscle in your leg. I'll see to getting you a crutch..."

"I'd be dead without her, or worse," Amarie murmured, ignoring the comment about her leg.

"Well, I'm grateful that didn't come to pass."

"Lady Mender?" Nordandril asked from the doorway. "You're required in the east chamber."

Kalstacia met Amarie's gaze and playfully rolled her eyes. "Work is never done. Though I still have you to thank for being so blessed." She gave Amarie's uninjured shoulder a slight squeeze. "You're safe here in the Menders' Guildhalls, don't you even think about going anywhere. I'll be back when I can."

"Before you go, is there a blanket? I'm rather... cold."

Kalstacia looked surprised, but then her gaze softened. "I'm certain Nordandril can find you one." Without her needing to say more, his steps vanished into the hallway behind them.

"And Kalstacia," Amarie whispered. "Is Uriel gone?"

Her smile dropped into a frown that wrinkled her forehead. "It has a name?" Amarie nodded and Kalstacia glanced behind her at the covered window on the far wall and then back to Amarie. "His shadow remains. The whole of Eralas's sky has been consumed. The council is distracted for the time, trying to find a solution. Without the sun, our island will die. But many have faith that this is merely temporary, me included."

Amarie choked back a sob and shut her eyes. "I'm so sorry. I made such a mistake."

Kalstacia brushed away her tears again, stroking her hair back. "You're not the one blanketing the boundary wards. This Uriel is. If the council has allowed a power this strong to grow, even on the mainland, they deserve the scare this is giving them."

Kalstacia tended to Amarie's injuries daily, wrapping and re-wrapping, trying different techniques to aid the healing process.

Restricted to traditional means, Amarie healed slowly. Progress came, little by little, leaving her eager to walk again. Bedrest made her relive her time before giving birth, and those were memories she wanted to forget.

Kalstacia fashioned a crutch for her left leg, since ligaments and muscle had torn, leaving her unable to put any weight on it.

Her right shoulder, which had been dislocated, still couldn't bear weight either, and she felt useless. The scratches and cuts scabbed over, making her face itchy.

The chatter in the Menders' Guild kept Amarie updated on Uriel's continued assault. He never broke through the barrier, abandoning the attack after two days, leaving the blanket of darkness.

Two weeks later, thin beams of light fought through her curtains, waking her from a nap, nestled beneath a pile of blankets.

Joyous cries filled the capital's streets.

The council summoned Amarie the next day, and she welcomed the opportunity to venture outside. Finally beneath the sun, she basked in its warmth, squinting as she hobbled towards the Sanctum of Law with Kalstacia at her side.

"In case you're curious. Being a cripple isn't fun."

Kalstacia laughed. "The city isn't accommodating for it." She let Amarie set the pace as they made their way up the stairs into the sanctum gardens. "How are you feeling though, overall?"

"Like I got my ass handed to me a couple weeks ago." Amarie huffed at the effort of climbing the stairs.

"At least your sense of humor is intact."

"What happened to Mira?"

"Well, she's still on the island. The council has locked down all travel, and the boundary ward remains in place despite the shadow beast's departure. She wouldn't have been allowed to leave. But I haven't heard anything reliable except word of a compound somewhere on the south coast of Eralas."

Amarie nodded, reaching the top of the stairs. "Will you be here when I'm finished in there?"

"Of course."

Sighing, she hobbled forward again. "Wish me luck," she muttered, walking through the doors as the guards opened them.

"Good luck."

Amarie didn't bother stopping at the swirled floor, continuing through the next set of doors alone.

The Council of Elders looked the same as it had a year prior, and she swore some were in the same attire. Erdeaseq, the arch judgment, rose from his high-backed chair at her approach.

Coming to a stop in her circle of roots and vines in front of the steps, Amarie tried to catch her breath. Her power had regenerated, but it did little to heal her injuries.

"Welcome, Amarie." The arch judgment's voice boomed through the empty observation galleries above.

"Arch Judgment. I apologize for the circumstances." Amarie lowered her chin, her hair falling next to her face.

"I should hope." Lo'thec's face reddened. "Your actions have—"

"I doubt she needs to be reprimanded further on the matter. She's clearly aware already." Ietylon scowled, leaning forward in his chair.

"But does she know the danger she threatens our people with? Our homeland?" A female elder shifted in her seat.

Amarie stared at the ground, her hands shaking as tears filled her eyes.

"She's an ignorant child. Holding more power than she could possibly be trusted to wield wisely."

"So, what do you propose, Kreshiida? To destroy the poor child who has not been properly taught?"

"Trusting her training to a rejanai—"

"Enough." The arch judgment's voice vibrated across the wooden floor. Silence descended on the chamber, to the point Amarie swore she could hear grinding teeth. Yet, she didn't look up.

"What do you have to say for yourself, Amarie Xylata?" Ietylon's voice sounded kinder than she deserved.

Amarie stepped out of her circle, limping a few steps closer to the council, looking at Ietylon. "I was foolish. Reckless. I underestimated my enemy, and I accept complete responsibility for what happened. I don't plan to argue with you. You wouldn't have called me here had you not already thought of options for my fate. Do you plan to share them with me?"

The council remained quiet for a moment while the arch judgment resumed his seat. "Your lack of argument will surely leave some of my fellow elder's feeling jilted." He smirked. "I'm certain Olsaeth and Kreshiida were ready to fight with you."

Kreshiida, glaring with her nearly all-black eyes, crossed her arms.

"Before we discuss ramifications..." Ietylon faced Amarie. "We should speak about the creature that pursued you to our lands. You imply you knew it to be your enemy prior to this engagement."

"Yes. He is the master of the Shades. His name is Uriel."

The looks on the elder's faces ranged from anger to confusion, each taking a moment to exchange glances with their neighbor.

The male elder at the end frowned. "Shades are mere myth."

"Just like the Berylian Key, right?" Amarie retorted, and it gained a laugh from several elders.

"Fair enough." The elder's red eyes pierced into Amarie. "This Uriel is a power this council should have been aware of long before now. Perhaps we owe you gratitude for bringing him to our attention."

Several elders growled, and Kreshiida rose to her feet, her body showing her advanced age with a hunch. "You dare—"

"Sit, Elder." The arch judgment stood. "While powerful, his withdrawal makes it clear he must have limits. But his interest in Amarie is disconcerting."

"If I may..." Amarie paused.

The arch judgment tilted his head, a bemused look on his face, but nodded.

Amarie cleared her throat and took a deep breath. "I believe his... size was likely my fault. I tried to kill him, and I didn't think it through. Shades draw their power from their surroundings, destroying life to fuel themselves. Uriel is likely no different, and when I unleashed my power at him, it had the opposite of the intended effect. I believe he absorbed it, granting him the ability to become that beast. The hope this gives me, is that without me, he can't retake the form."

"But it also explains his interest in you." The kinder female elder next to the arch judgment used a gentle tone.

Amarie nodded. "I have no intention of leaving Eralas."

Kreshiida huffed. "And we have no intention of letting you."

The arch judgment shot a glare in her direction. "We have yet to determine the right course of action. This council is divided in their opinion of how best to... *deal* with you."

Amarie met his gaze. "Can I make a request?" Her throat tightened.

The arch judgment narrowed his eyes. "Speak it."

Fear gripped her heart. "I'd like to request Slumber." Her breathing quickened, mirroring the inhalation taken by the council. The hand supporting her weight on the crutch shook. Her mind plagued her constantly, awake or asleep, and she yearned for respite.

"Slumber?" Ietylon's shoulders drooped. "Child, that..."

"I find it an appropriate choice." Kreshiida leaned back.

Ietylon glared. "I disagree. Slumber is the worst of our sentences."

Amarie tilted her head at him. "Please." Her crutch slipped out from beneath her and she stumbled to right herself. "I just want to forget. I don't care when you wake me, but please let me sleep. Give me that mercy. I can't live with these thoughts and these memories anymore, I—" She swallowed, shutting her eyes to hold in her tears.

I can't hurt any more people. If I remain here, in Slumber, Ahria can live a normal life and never be in danger.

"Some would argue that the memory of your wrong-doings is the best teacher. But there may be other benefits to beginning fresh with your training."

"Child." Ietylon ignored Lo'thec's comment, his tone kind. "Do you know what it is you ask for?"

Amarie nodded, briefly casting her gaze downward. "Talon explained it to me, once. I'd like a few days to see to personal affairs, before you carry the procedure out, if you are amenable."

"Of course." The female elder near the center looked to her right, at the arch judgment who hadn't spoken or moved since her request.

"Because it is your request, this council is agreeable." The arch judgment's face was difficult to read. "However, I'd like you to meet privately with Paivesh." He gestured to the woman beside him. "To further enlighten us with what you know of Uriel and his Shades. Then we will grant you the Slumber you seek."

Amarie nodded, her throat dry. "Of course. Thank you."

"Return here when you're ready." Paivesh nodded. "Until then, you may go."

As promised, Kalstacia waited for Amarie outside the sanctum doors, though she stood at the bottom of the stairs.

Amarie pursed her lips, lowering the crutch first, and following with her good leg. Her muscles quivered with the effort, and she gritted her teeth.

Near the bottom, Kalstacia reached for Amarie's elbow, supporting her down the last steps. "How did it go?"

"They granted my request. I have a few days to find a place for Viento, and I'd like to visit the home I shared with Talon."

Kalstacia frowned, her brow wrinkling. "A few days? What request did you make?"

As they walked, Amarie met her gaze. "Slumber."

Kalstacia stopped with wide eyes. "What? Amarie, why—"

"Please try to understand." Amarie struggled to turn back to her and lowered her voice so it wouldn't crack. "I'm not myself anymore. I'm in pain, and it's not the kind that heals. I've hurt so many people, and I've lost so many. I just want to start over. Don't talk me out of it, please. I'd like you to be there with me."

Kalstacia stood perfectly still, examining Amarie's face. She drew in a slow breath and closed her eyes, shaking her head. With another steady inhale, she looked back up and touched Amarie's cheek. "I won't try, because I already know I'd fail. Come with me to my home and let's have some tea together as sisters one more time. Perhaps you can see if Viento might be happy there. Tomorrow, I can arrange a carriage to take you to where you lived with my brother."

Amarie nodded, heat building behind her eyes. "Thank you. For everything."

Chapter 26

Summer, 2612 R.T.

Eralas dismissed and recast the inactivated boundary ward after what felt like years, though it'd been only a month and a half. Deylan left after a few nights, called away by the faction.

Talon rushed through the Ny'Thalus docks, acquiring a horse with as little fuss as possible, and galloped towards the southwest fork of the island's rivers. The old paths towards the banyan tree home returned quickly to him, but the sight of it didn't bring any relief.

The Eralasian forest had reclaimed the structure, foliage growing rampant over the walls and fences he'd labored over. The tree had begun to regrow into its natural shape, narrowing the doorway at the front.

He squeezed through, but already knew Amarie wasn't there.

Inside, everything in the front room was exactly as they'd left it, except for the collection of moss and dirt where some forest creatures had made a nest in the corner of the living room. He continued into the bedroom, finding it in disarray. The clothes they'd left neatly piled on the shelves had been scattered around the room. They still looked clean, so the disruption had been recent. He wanted to believe it to be the handiwork of an animal, but his gut told him differently.

Amarie's pillow lay crooked on the bed, with his next to it. On it, one of his old shirts was crumpled into a ball.

Talon absently touched her offset pillow, lifting it from the bed and pulling it to his chest. He buried his face amid the lingering scent of her hair on the fabric, inhaling. Opening his eyes, he forced himself to loosen his grip and prepared to return it. Where the pillow had been, a folded piece of parchment popped part way open.

Setting her pillow down, he tentatively picked up the paper, unfolding it. Behind the letter, a thicker piece of parchment remained on the bed, but he read the text first.

> *Talon,*
>
> *You may never see this, but it's my last chance to tell you before I enter Slumber. I want you to know that I forgive you. I love you. I'm sorry.*
>
> *Amarie*

Talon couldn't breathe. *Slumber.* He hastily reread the letter, and the lump in his throat grew larger. A sob broke free, and his trembling hands crumpled the edges of the parchment.

How could this happen?

Fear devolved into rage at the council for bringing down so harsh a punishment on Amarie. He forced in a deep breath, looking back to the place where Amarie had slept, his mind torturing him into imagining her laying there again, but this time, unable to wake. His eyes fell on the remaining thicker parchment, carefully folded.

He snatched it up, his body aflame with anger. Unfolding it with more aggression than the paper deserved, Talon blinked at the depiction of himself. In the graphite drawing, he sat in a rocking chair, hair tied neatly behind his head, cradling a baby.

His fury died, quenched by overwhelming regret. The knot in his stomach pulled tight, and he collapsed onto the edge of the bed. Tears erupted from his eyes. Touching the image of the child in his arms, his gaze traced down to the text written below.

She will always be yours.

Something in Talon broke, and his chest heaved. With a bent head, he wept.

"What do you mean she *chose* this?" Talon stared at his sister from the steps of the old family porch.

Kalstacia stood with her arms crossed, lips pursed in a thin line. She looked so much like his mother, stern and disappointed. "I don't know how else I can say it to get it through that thick skull of yours. The pain that girl endured became too much."

"Why didn't you talk her out of it?"

"You know she wouldn't have listened. She's as stubborn as this horse of hers." She gestured behind the house with his chin.

"You have Viento?"

Kalstacia nodded. "I built a stable for him, though he won't let me ride him. I can tell he likes being cooped up about as much as Amarie did. Yet, now she's as cooped up as ever."

Talon collapsed for the second time, falling to the steps and burying his head in his hands. "This is my fault."

"Damn right it is." Kalstacia growled. "Whatever your reasons, I hope they were worth it."

Talon didn't respond, unable to make his voice work. He rubbed his sore eyes.

In the silence, Kalstacia's footsteps approached from behind him. He felt the brush of her skirt against his arm as she lowered herself beside him. Her hand pressing over his shoulders and down his back brought less comfort than he wished for.

"What do I do?" Talon choked. "How do I fix this?"

Kalstacia opened her mouth to answer, but her gaze quickly averted to the entrance to their front yard, where a woman stood.

Long brunette hair, braided against the sides of her head and tied in a ponytail, swayed in the breeze. The stranger waited patiently and, when silence fell, spoke. "I was hoping I could speak with Talon."

Talon straightened, Kalstacia withdrawing her comforting touch as he did. He narrowed his eyes, brushing a stray tear away with the back of his hand. "And you are?"

"I'm the Mira'wyld. Amarie knew me as Mira. I was with her..."

The stiffening of Kalstacia's body made Talon stand. His legs shook, but he kept upright. "You were the one who built the bridge of ice. The reason Amarie escaped him."

Mira nodded. "I wish I could've prevented the whole thing. I didn't know what she was planning." Regret filled her tone, and she looked down.

"Even if you'd known, I doubt there was anything you could've done to stop her." Talon glanced at Kalstacia, who stood and smoothed her dress.

"I'll put some tea on." She dismissed herself into the house at Talon's nod.

"What did you want to talk about?" Talon leaned on the railing.

Mira stepped forward, hands in her back pockets. "I heard about her decision to enter Slumber. I thought I might be able to provide you with some peace with the surely unsettling news."

"Peace?" Talon couldn't stop the incredulous tone. "What peace can you possibly offer?"

Mira smiled. "I've experienced Slumber myself."

Talon narrowed his eyes and considered what she said. "And? What comfort is that to me?"

"People talk of endless nightmares, but there aren't any. It's rather restful and calm. And I regained my memories."

"How?" Talon doubted Amarie would want the memories back.

"While our people are capable, they aren't the only ones. I encourage you to remember that she considered Slumber a gift."

Talon took the deepest breath he'd been able to manage since arriving in Eralas. "Would you like to come in for tea? I'd like to ask you for more details about your time together."

Mira nodded and followed him inside.

Talon returned to the mainland the next week and rode Viento north through Olsa.

The arrival of an auer in the tiny village west of Jacoby became fast news, especially because many recognized the black stallion.

A young girl exploded from the doorway of a house, sprinting towards the horse, yelling. "Amarie!" She paused when she looked up and saw Talon sitting on Viento's back. Frowning, she backpedaled to her front porch. "Granny!"

Swinging from the saddle, Talon gave a reassuring smile. "Sorry, I wish it was Amarie coming back." His chest tightened at the thought of Amarie and the blonde girl playing together, but he swallowed the rising emotion. He turned to Viento and scratched him near his ear.

An older woman appeared in the doorway behind the child and ushered her inside, closing the door while remaining outside. Her grey hair was pinned back in a bun, and flour speckled her apron. "You're Talon."

"She told you about me?" Talon approached the porch but didn't step onto it.

The woman's shoulders slumped. "Hard to miss the likeness. She captured you wonderfully, even though..." She shook her head.

"I come with news," Talon interrupted. "And then, I hope, you might tell me which family Ahria is living with."

The woman's features hardened. "I'm not sure I want to hear what news might cause Amarie to be apart from Viento."

"She's alive." The words tasted dry. Talon fought to remember what Mira had assured him. Slumber held peace, not torment, as the auer wanted their people to believe. "Just... not able to be here."

Sighing, the woman nodded. "I can't promise to tell you where Ahria is, but we should talk more. You can rope Viento here. Then come in for some tea. I'm Cassia."

Talon did as suggested and stepped onto the porch. "I have no intention of removing Ahria from her family. She deserves one. I just want to meet her."

Cassia held the door open for Talon, leading him inside. The furniture was close together, donning warm colors that invited him to feel welcome in the rustic home. The little girl sat out back, next to the sheep's pens, playing in the grass.

Cassia walked straight to the kitchen at the back of the space, an open window welcoming the late summer breeze. "Unfortunately, her adoptive family has already suffered a loss. Ahria's mother joined Nymaera earlier this year after a vicious fever. Lorin is raising the children alone now, with the help of the village when we can." She pulled mugs from the cupboard, preparing tea as she spoke.

Despite Amarie's best efforts, Ahria still didn't have a mother. The pain in his gut led Talon to lean against a dining chair. His knuckles whitened as he fought the anguish.

Cassia eyed him. "I've heard much about you, and some of it doesn't sit well. But I want to give you the benefit of the doubt, as I only heard one side of the story. I can't introduce you to Ahria if your time here will be short."

"Rightfully so. I regret the necessity, but I needed to leave Amarie when I did. I'll tell you all of it, if you're amenable?"

Nodding, Cassia placed two mugs of tea on the small round dining table. "I'd like to hear it."

Talon told her everything, and it felt oddly freeing. He knew so little of Cassia but trusted in her relationship with Deylan. The story's length required a refresh on their tea, twice, and left Cassia looking somber.

"You seem distraught over Amarie's decision. But I have to say that I agree with it. She was withdrawn and so unhappy. I hope it grants her the rest she sought."

"I wish there'd been another way." Talon turned his mug on the table. "It would've been different... If I'd been there."

Cassia nodded. "It might have been different, or maybe not. Dwelling does no good, though, so you must move forward." Standing, she tilted her head. "Ahria needs consistency, not an occasional visitor. What are you hoping for by being here? Amarie told me you would've made a wonderful father."

Talon averted his gaze, studying the grain of the table as if it had answers for him. "I don't know." He sighed. "I needed to come here, even if I've already proven Amarie wrong. I'm unfit, but I wish to correct it."

Cassia placed a hand on Talon's shoulder. "You showed up. Give yourself some credit. A child can't have too much love in her life, and if you truly wish to commit, I'm sure Lorin would appreciate the help. He's struggling to make ends meet as it is, and while he's her father, no one ever said she can't have two."

The thought sent a warm shiver down Talon's spine. He imagined the baby girl in his arms like he had so many times while together with Amarie, and now it was so close to being real. He bit the inside of his lower lip, evaluating the feeling and how right it seemed.

"You don't think Lorin would be opposed to me inserting myself?" Talon looked at her.

Cassia shook her head. "But he can tell you that himself. Would you like to meet her?"

Talon's heart leapt, and he sucked in a sudden breath to keep himself from jumping to his feet. "Please."

Cassia led him across the village, to a home like hers. Knocking gently on the door, she waited a moment before it swung open.

A man with bags under his eyes answered with a smile, greeting Cassia with a hug.

As she stepped back, she motioned to Talon. "Lorin, this is Talon."

Recognition filled the man's face, his smile fading before spreading wider. "Talon. By the Gods, it's a pleasure to meet you."

"I'll admit it's a little odd with everyone knowing me before I meet them." Talon smiled, offering his hand. He forced himself not to immediately look around to find Ahria. "But it's my honor to meet you. A man willing to raise another's child."

Lorin took his hand. "Ahria is a gift. And from what I understand, we're alike in that sense. Please come in."

Cassia lifted a hand. "I'd better get back before my dough is too stiff. Give Ahria a kiss for me." She left and Lorin opened his front door wider.

A low table occupied the center of the room, covered in wooden blocks being stacked by a boy almost the same age as Conrad.

A baby girl stood on wobbly legs, clutching the edge of the

furniture as she reached for a block. Her piercing steel-blue eyes lifted at the entrance of a stranger, and she squealed, slapping the table.

Talon's breath caught in his chest, and he couldn't move.

Lorin crossed to Ahria, lifting her. She grabbed his nose as he returned to Talon. "Ahria, meet Talon." The baby leaned over to reach for Talon's hair and Lorin laughed. "She'll pull it pretty hard if you let her. Want to hold her?"

Talon managed a nod and opened his arms to receive the child. "She can pull all she wants." He stroked her rosy cheek as she grasped a handful of his hair and inspected it. Her dark eyelashes fluttered with interest, a smile forming with a bubbling giggle as she tugged. The curve of her nose reminded him of Amarie's, and he couldn't help but trace his finger over the bridge of it.

She's perfect.

"Are you staying long?" Lorin's tone was hesitant.

Talon shook himself from his reverie and blinked back the heat in his eyes. "Yes." His voice caught. "If that'll be all right with you? I'd like to stay indefinitely."

Lorin smiled warmly. "You are very welcome to stay. Amarie told us a lot about you. I have a spare room here, and Ahria... will be lucky to have you as her father, too."

Father.

Ahria ceased her pulling to yawn, her chubby hands rubbing her eyes. She flopped forward, resting her head on his shoulder as she cooed.

Talon embraced her, rubbing her warm back and feeling everything else in his world melt away.

As he kissed her head, Ahria heaved a slow breath.

Swaying back and forth, Talon whispered, "I'll never leave you."

Chapter 27

Autumn, 2612 R.T.

Sitting up, she winced. Her body ached, stiff muscles protesting each movement.

"Easy. Don't rush it." A hand touched her shoulder.

Looking to her left, she eyed the black-haired auer standing next to her. "Who are you?" Furrowing her brow, she tried to remember where she was, but her mind came up blank. She blinked at the open chamber around her, a roughhewn ceiling of vines dangling loose. Small green motes swirled around the tips, casting an eerie glow throughout.

The woman beside her smiled and brushed a strand of hair behind her ear like a mother might. "My name is Kalstacia. I'm here to help you with the waking process."

"Waking..." She scoured her mind for memories. "What's happening? Why don't I remember my name?"

"It's a side effect, but your name is Amarie." Kalstacia lifted Amarie's wrist from the stone surface she rested on and massaged the achy joint. "Can you rotate your wrist for me?"

Doing as told, she cringed. "Gods, I feel like I fell down the stairs outside the Great Library in Capul," she muttered and then paused. "Have I been there?"

Kalstacia continued to rub the joint, but then progressed further up her arm. "Yes, you have. Your memories of places and environments should still be maintained. It's only your identity and people you won't remember."

Amarie focused on her green eyes. "Did I know you?"

Kalstacia paused as she walked around the stone platform to the other side. "Yes. We knew each other. But it'll be different now."

Amarie's gaze followed and landed on a man lying on a similar stone platform, asleep. "Why?" She watched the still form of the dark-haired man, a thin, pale scar running from his temple to his jaw. "Was this a punishment?"

Kalstacia followed Amarie's gaze but returned and prodded at her ribs. "No. You chose this. Though Slumber is not generally voluntary, it was for you. But it's important to wake you now for several reasons."

Amarie looked at Kalstacia. "Does it have to do with how much my body hurts?"

Kalstacia smiled again, and it held a reassuring energy to it. "Yes. You're still recovering from extensive injuries, and it's important to rehabilitate you properly. I'll introduce you to your trainer as well." She touched Amarie's shoulder again. "Are you ready to stand?"

Nodding, she accepted Kalstacia's help in rising from the platform and turned to lower her boots to the ground. "My trainer? For what?"

She looked beyond the auer at her side into the dark shadows of the chamber. Side by side sat more identical stone platforms, each with a body resting on it. The roots from the ceiling draped down over the figures, light flickering like stars on their faces. She couldn't make out details of those beyond her direct neighbor, who looked slightly older than herself, with ruggedly handsome features.

"They will train you to properly manipulate your Art. It will take years. Then you will return to Slumber." Kalstacia encouraged her to her feet, watching her stagger.

Amarie could barely straighten her left leg, the muscles tight.

"Come." Kalstacia offered her a hand. "There is still much to explain."

Epilogue

Twenty years later...
Summer, 2632 R.T.

Amarie, wake up!

Her eyes shot open, and she gasped in a breath of musty air. Vivid streaks of violet washed through her sight before fading to a pale green. Motes of light buzzed above, following the curves of roots within the dirt ceiling.

Beside her, on a stone bed, a man coughed as he struggled upright. A lock of chestnut brown hair fell over his brow as he hunched over the edge of the altar.

Amarie touched the surface she laid on, finding similar roughness as she sat up. "Who are you?" Her own voice echoed with a foreign tone, not matching the voice that had woken her.

The man rubbed his face, a stubbled dark beard along his jaw. In the dim light, his steel-blue eyes still shone. "I..." His voice echoed like hers through the chamber. "I don't know." He reached towards the twist of roots that dangled over the stone bed he'd been laying on, his fingers hovering curiously beneath them.

A flash of the green light surged through the space, and he recoiled as she blinked the specks from her vision.

Furrowing her brow, Amarie slid off the stone to her feet, her boots quiet on the dirt floor.

"Where are we?" The man stood slowly, thick black fabric swaying around his ankles as his cloak settled into place.

"I don't know." Amarie shook her head, staring at her hands. *Why can't I remember anything?*

Circling the rectangular stone platform, she paused near the head and trailed a fingertip over an inscription in the stone, written in Aueric.

> *Amarie Xylata*
> *2612 R.T.*
> *Wake if necessary.*

Amarie frowned.

Necessary?

The man flinched as he touched his forehead, a low hiss escaping his mouth. "Gods, it feels like a dire wolf is digging into my head." His cloak drifted to the side as he rubbed, exposing the hilt of a dagger in his belt. Its black, glass-like surface reflected the green motes.

She glanced down at herself for a weapon but found none. Her veins heated, calming her nerves with a reassuring rise of power.

I have the Art.

"You don't have a headache?" He squinted at her, scratching his right forearm through his tunic.

Amarie shook her head. Her eyes wandered to the inscribed stone at the head of his altar. "Mine says my name. What does yours say?"

He hissed again, shuffling to the end of his stone bed. Blinking, he touched the plaque akin to hers. "I guess it's a name. Kinronsilis? Gods, who would name their kid that?" He crouched to get a closer look. "I don't think this is a language I can read."

Gritting her teeth, Amarie approached and waited for him to step aside so she could read it. "Kinronsilis Parnell. 2611 R.T. Wake upon direction from Damien Lanoret."

He glanced from the text to her, a sideways smile on his handsome face. "Any idea what that means?" He shifted back onto his heels, looking up at the dirt ceiling, roots woven into patterns to support the odd light.

"No." Amarie shivered. "But I want to get out of here. This place doesn't feel right."

Kinronsilis grunted in agreement, looking behind her towards the open doorway. "Maybe we'll find answers to why I remember things like dire wolves and you can read that language, but not our own names." Walking forward, he brushed past her, but paused and turned back, holding out a hand to her. "Shall we go together?"

Amarie looked at his hand, her heart quickening. She swallowed, ignoring the swell of pressure in her chest as she took his warm hand. "What if we're enemies but don't know it?" Her gaze lifted to meet his.

His fingers slid comfortably between hers, and he squeezed. "Maybe without our memories, this is our chance to start over, even if we once were." That oddly charming crooked smirk crossed his lips again. "What's your name?"

Stepping with him, she resisted the strange inclination to touch the scar on his temple. "Amarie. My name is Amarie Xylata."

To be continued...

Kin and Amarie will return in Part 4 of the Pantracia Chronicles.

The series continues with...

ASHES OF THE
RAHN'KA

www.Pantracia.com

Damien risked everything to forge a new path, but madness may find him before redemption does.

Damien deserted the Helgathian military with little hope for survival and hides under the guise of Bastian. When he meets Rae, a gorgeous thief, he naively fails to realize she plans to collect the prize on his head.

Although she'd abandoned her guild, Rae sends word to a trusted ally about Bastian and his potential bounty. But when an ancient power chooses him, and he saves her life, a war between her loyalties ensues.

As their fates entwine, Damien and Rae overcome trials of magic and haunted pasts. Rae's choice affecting Damien's fate could grant Pantracia's most tyrannical country the power of the Rahn'ka, if insanity doesn't claim him first.

Ashes of the Rahn'ka is Part 1 in A Rebel's Crucible, and Book 4 in the Pantracia Chronicles.

Manufactured by Amazon.ca
Bolton, ON